Praise for

THE VANISHING STAIR

The Vanishing
STAIR

MAUREEN JOHNSON

KATHERINE TEGEN BOOKS
An Imprint of HarperCollins Publishers

Katherine Tegen Books is an imprint of HarperCollins Publishers.

The Vanishing Stair
www.epicreads.com

Library of Congress Control Number: 2018959001
ISBN 978-0-06-233809-9

Typography by Carla Weise
    20 21 22 23   PC/LSCH   10 9 8 7 6
❖
First paperback edition, 2019

To all the Muderinos. SSDGM.

FOUNDED
EA
1935

ELLINGHAM ACADEMY

I.

8.

2.

9.

3.

4.

10.

5.

11.

6.

12.

7.

13.

14.

NORTH

CATS KNOW BEST

1. WORKSHOP
2. ASTERIA
3. GENIUS
4. ARTEMIS
5. APOLLO
6. DIONYSUS
7. DEMETER

8. GREAT HOUSE
9. MINERVA
10. EUNOMIA
11. CYBELE
12. JUPITER
13. VESTA
14. JUNO

Where do you look for someone who's never really there?
Always on a staircase but never on a stair.

—Riddle found on the desk of Albert Ellingham on the day of his death, October 30, 1938

April 13, 1936, 9:00 p.m.

"HAS ANYONE SEEN DOTTIE?" MISS NELSON ASKED.

Miss Nelson, the housemistress of Minerva, looked around for an answer to her question. Though it was spring, it was still cold up on the mountain, and the residents of Minerva House were gathered close to the common room fireplace.

"Maybe she's with the nurse," Gertie van Coevorden said. "Hopefully they'll do something about her *sniffing*. She's going to make us all sick. It's disgusting. I'm going to be seeing the Astors soon. I can't get sick."

Gertie van Coevorden was probably the richest student at Ellingham; she had two Astors and a Roosevelt in her family tree, a fact that she managed to work into conversation at every possible opportunity.

"Gertrude," Miss Nelson said admonishingly.

"No, but *really*," Gertie said. "Now that she's not here, we can say it. She does have the most awful sniff, and she runs her nose along her sleeve. I know we're not supposed to treat them any differently. . . ."

Them meant the poor students, the ten or eleven scrappy people who Albert Ellingham had collected as part of his little game. Mix the rich and the poor.

"Then do not do so," Miss Nelson said.

"Oh, I know she's *bright* . . ."

An understatement. Dottie Epstein could run rings around the average professor.

". . . but, it is awful. I'm merely *saying* . . ."

"Gertrude," Miss Nelson said, sounding tired, "that really is enough."

Gertie turned up her nose and shifted her attention to the issue of *Photoplay* magazine she was reading. From the opposite side of the fire, Francis Josephine Crane, the second-richest student at Ellingham Academy, looked up from where she sat. She had made a nest for herself with her chinchilla lap rug and was shifting between a chemistry book and the newest edition of *True Detective* magazine. And she was watching everything.

Francis, like Gertie, was from New York. She was the sixteen-year-old daughter of Louis and Albertine Crane, of Crane Flour. (America's favorite! Baking's never a pain when you're baking with Crane!) Her parents were fast friends with Albert Ellingham, and when Ellingham opened a school and needed some new pupils, Francis was sent off to Vermont in a chauffeured car, with a van of trunks following that contained every possible luxury. Up here in Vermont, with the snowstorms and the comfortable ratio of obscenely rich and deserving poor, Francis was a settled matter, as far as her parents were concerned. Francis, for her part, was not settled; her opinion on the matter was not required.

Francis, who made it a point to speak to the servants, knew that while Gertie may have been connected in *name* to Astors and Roosevelts, she was in fact the biological daughter of a handsome barman at the Central Park Casino. The casino was where many of New York's rich and bored society women liked to spend their afternoons sipping drinks . . . and apparently doing other things. Neither Gertie, nor Gertie's father, knew this. It was a nice little piece of information Francis kept tucked away in her pocket for the right time.

There was always a right time for these sorts of things. Francis was rich enough and smart enough to have grown bored of possessions. She liked secrets. Secrets had real value.

"No one has seen Dottie?" Miss Nelson asked again, twiddling with her diamond stud earrings. "I suppose I'll call and have someone check the library. She's most likely there and forgot the time."

Francis knew Dottie Epstein was not at the library. She had seen Dottie hurrying into the woods a few hours before. Dottie was a strange, elusive creature, always squirreling herself away somewhere to read. Francis said nothing, because she didn't particularly like answering questions, and because she respected Dottie's right to hide herself away if she felt like it.

The phone began ringing upstairs in Miss Nelson's rooms and she rose to answer it. Perhaps it was the moody fog, or the fact that this was later than Dottie would usually stay away—something pricked Francis's keen sense of potential. She closed her magazine inside of her book and got up from her chair.

"Ooh, give me your rug if you're going to your room," Gertie said. "I don't feel like getting mine."

Francis grabbed the chinchilla with one hand and dropped it on Gertie as she passed. She walked down the dark hall to the turreted bathroom. After locking the door, she pulled off her shoes and socks and carefully stepped on the toilet seat, using it as a step stool to get up onto the windowsill. This was a precarious position—the cold marble sill was only wide enough to accommodate half of her foot, and if she lost her balance she would fall and crack her head on the toilet or the floor. She had to coil her fingers around the frame of the window and cling. But by doing this, she could get close to a small vent up near the ceiling, and that vent provided a muffled way to listen to the telephone conversations upstairs.

Francis tilted her ear to the ceiling and caught bits of Miss Nelson's end. She immediately noted the pitch of Miss Nelson's voice—it was higher, urgent.

"My God," Miss Nelson said. "My God, when . . ."

Miss Nelson was not prone to drama. She was a controlled woman, well-groomed and attractive and of a certain type—a graduate of Smith who taught biology. She had glossy chestnut hair, always wore the same pair of expensive-looking diamond studs, but otherwise rotated through the same few outfits. Like everyone who taught and worked at Ellingham, she was talented and sharp.

And now, she sounded afraid.

"But the police . . . yes. I understand."

Police?

"I'll meet you there when the girls are in bed. I'll get them off now. I'll come soon."

The phone went down with a bang, and Francis slipped from her perch and returned to the common room as Miss Nelson came down. She was trying to look casual, but she couldn't help the bright, urgent look in her eye, the flush in her face. She walked to the door and slid the big iron bolt. There was the smallest hint of a shake in her hand.

"Time for bed, girls," she said.

"Where is Dottie?" Gertie said.

"You were right. She's spending the night in the infirmary with the nurse. Now, to bed, to bed."

"It's only five to ten," Agnes Renfelt said. "There's a program I want to listen to."

"In your room," Miss Nelson said. "You can listen to your radio there."

Francis went to her room, number two, at the end of the hall. Once inside, she pulled off her dress and changed into a pair of black wool pants and a gray ski sweater. From the top drawer of her bureau she removed a candle and a pack of matches, which she put in her pocket. Then she sat on the floor by her door, ear pressed against it, and waited.

About two hours later, Francis heard Miss Nelson moving past her door. Francis cracked her door slightly and saw Miss Nelson heading toward the stairs at the end of the hall. She looked at the glowing hands of her bedside clock. She would give Miss Nelson a ten-minute start. That would be safe.

When the ten minutes were up, Francis exited her room and went to the spiral stairs at the end of the hall. She worked her way around to the back of the circular stairs. These stairs were enclosed in the back, and this enclosure looked solid, but Francis had discovered the secret of the stairs one night after spying Miss Nelson in the hall. It had taken her weeks to work out the trick of the stairs, but she eventually found that if you pressed on the right spot, a tiny latch would pop out of the bottom. You could use this to pull open a small doorway. Inside the staircase was what appeared to be an empty, tiny bit of storage space. But if you looked carefully, there was a hatch in the floor. Tonight, this hatch was open. Miss Nelson was usually careful enough to close it behind her.

The hatch exposed a raw, dark hole in the ground with a ladder that seemed to descend into nowhere. The first time Francis had climbed down, it had taken all her nerve. She had the feel for the ladder now, knowing how to ease her way down into the dark, taking each rung with care, ball of the foot first, never fully rolling onto the heel until she reached the floor below.

At the base of the ladder, Francis found herself in a tight passage made of rough stone. It was only a few inches higher than her head and just about wide enough for one person, and reminded Francis, not unpleasantly, of a tomb. She managed to pull up her arm and light the candle, and the sulfuric stink of the match filled the space and gave her a small halo of light.

She began her walk.

SECOND ELLINGHAM STUDENT MISSING AND
AT LARGE; POSSIBLY INVOLVED IN DEATH OF
HAYES MAJOR
A BATT REPORT EXCLUSIVE
OCTOBER 15th

There has been a major development in the investigation of
the death of YouTube star Hayes Major. Most readers will
be aware that Major, famous for his hit show *The End of It
All*, died during the shooting of a video about the Ellingham
kidnapping and murders of 1936. While working in a tunnel,
he was exposed to a fatal concentration of carbon dioxide.

Though the police have declared Hayes Major's death
an accident—the result of using a large quantity of dry ice
in order to achieve a fog effect for a scene—is the matter
settled? An intrepid Ellingham student detective named
Stephanie (aka Stevie) Bell launched her own investigation.
Bell was admitted to Ellingham as an expert on the 1936
kidnapping case. She became convinced that Major had not
placed the dry ice in the tunnel and was in fact killed either
by accident or intentionally by another person. Furthermore,
she concluded that Major did not write his hit series, as he
claimed to have done.

Bell approached this reporter and asked to review images
taken during the day of Major's death. Using information
from these photographs, Bell accused fellow student Element
Walker of writing the series *The End of It All* and having
a role in the death. Following a confrontation at Minerva

House, where Major, Walker, and Bell were all residents, school officials became involved. All remaining students from Minerva House were taken to the Ellingham Great House.

What happened next was unexpected and baffling.

Sources present at the Great House that night confirm that school officials questioned Element Walker, and that the school opted to stop their questioning to consult with an attorney and to contact law enforcement. Walker was left alone in Albert Ellingham's former office, with the door closed and people right outside. When the door was reopened, Walker was gone and has not been seen since. There are reports that she used a hidden passage in the wall to make her escape.

This reporter has to ask: Where could Element Walker have gone at night, with no supplies, no phone, no car, and no preparation? Ellingham Academy is on a remote mountainside. How did she get away? Did someone on the campus help her? How did she know about the passageway? Was she even involved in Major's death, or did she leave out of alarm?

Her disappearance has raised even more questions in this ever-evolving case.

Stay with the Batt Report for more exclusive updates.

O<small>UT OF EVERYTHING IN HER</small> P<small>ITTSBURGH NEIGHBORHOOD, THE</small> Funky Munkee coffee shop was the thing that reminded Stevie Bell most of Ellingham Academy. It was a 1990s relic, with a sign written in a kooky festival font. It had walls painted in bright, primary colors, each wall a different shade. It played an obligatory coffeehouse soundtrack of mid-tempo guitar music. There were blown-up pictures of coffee beans, and plants and wobbly tables to sit at, and oversized mugs. None of these things were features of her previous school.

The part she liked, and the part that was like Ellingham, was that it wasn't her house, and when she was here, no one bothered her.

Every day this week she had come and ordered the smallest, cheapest coffee. She would take this to the back of the shop, to a stuffy, small alcove room with red walls. The room was dark and dingy, the tables unbalanced and always a bit sticky. Everyone else avoided it, which is why Stevie liked it. This was her office now, where she did her most important work. If she had tried to do this at home, her parents might walk in. Here, she was in public, but no one actually cared what she was doing or even noticed her.

She put her headphones on but played no music—she needed some muffled silence. She put her backpack on the table, zipper facing her, and opened it. First, she removed a pair of nitrile gloves. These she had purchased at CVS the day she returned. It was probably an unnecessary precaution at this stage, but still, it could not hurt. She snapped them on. It was a very satisfying feeling. Using both hands, she reached down to the bottom of her bag and removed a small, battered tea tin.

The tin was too valuable to leave at home. When you find something of historical importance, you keep it close. It stayed with Stevie wherever she went—locked in her locker during the day, tucked in her bag at home. Out of sight. She periodically reached around to touch the lump on her backpack where it rested inside to make sure it was secure.

The tin was square and red, dented in several places, with rust along the lip. It read OLD ENGLISH TEA BAGS. She opened the lid. It stuck a bit, so it required a gentle wiggle. From inside she produced: a bit of white feather, a bit of beaded cloth, a tarnished, gold-colored lipstick tube with the mummified remains of a red lipstick, a tiny enameled pillbox in the shape of a shoe, some pieces of notebook paper and black-and-white photographs, and the unfinished draft of a poem.

These humble objects were the first pieces of real evidence in the Ellingham case in over eighty years. And the moment Stevie uncovered them was the moment her Ellingham dreams fell apart.

Ellingham. Her former school. Ellingham, the place she had dreamed of going. The place she had made it to for a short time. And Ellingham, the place that was now behind her.

No one in Pittsburgh really understood what happened to Stevie at Ellingham. They only knew that she had left to go to some famous school, and then that YouTube guy died in an accident there, and Stevie came back a few weeks later.

It was true that the death of Hayes Major was the start of Stevie's departure. But the person who was responsible for Stevie Bell's parents hauling her out of Ellingham Academy was named Germaine Batt, and she did it entirely by accident.

Everyone at Ellingham Academy had a *thing*, and Germaine Batt's thing was reporting. Before Hayes's death, she had a modest site and a small following. But death is good business if you are in the news. "If it bleeds, it leads," as they say. (*They* being . . . Stevie wasn't sure. People said it. It meant that bloody, gray, horrible stories always go to the top, which is why the news is always bad. People don't care when things go well. News equals *bad*.)

The piece that did Stevie in came out the day after Stevie confronted Element Walker about creating the show *The End of It All*. She knew that Ellie had taken Hayes's computer and stashed it under the bathtub in Minerva. Stevie also knew that Hayes could not have been the person who used the pass to get the dry ice that would kill him. Also, Hayes did not write the show that made him famous, the one that was about to get him a movie deal. Ellie did that.

That was all Stevie was trying to tell everyone on the night in question. Ellie had been confronted, first in Minerva, and then in the Great House. And Ellie had vanished from a locked room. Just like that. *Poof.* She had gone into the walls of Albert Ellingham's office, through a hidden passage, and from there . . . out. Away. Somewhere.

The school did not release that information. Ellie wasn't officially guilty of anything. She was a student who ran away from her boarding school. Except Stevie's parents had a Google alert for all things Ellingham after Hayes's death, and that's how they saw the Batt Report blog post about how Stevie had been investigating Hayes's death, and now there was a potential killer on the loose. Two hours after Germaine's story appeared, Stevie's phone rang, and ten hours after that, her parents were roaring up the drive to Ellingham, despite the school rules about no outside vehicles. The night had been tearful; Stevie cried all the way back to Pittsburgh, silently and without pause, staring out the car window until she fell asleep. The next Monday, she was back in her old school, hastily inserted into some classes.

The trick was not to think about Ellingham too much— the buildings, the smell of the air, the freedom, the adventure, the people . . .

Especially not the people.

She could send messages to her friends Janelle and Nate.

Mostly Janelle. And mostly it was Janelle sending them to her, dozens a day, checking in on how she was. Stevie could only reply to every third or fourth one, because replying meant thinking about how she missed seeing Janelle in the hall, in the common room, across the table. How she missed knowing her friend was on the other side of the wall as she slept—Janelle, who smelled of lemons or orange blossom, who wrapped her hair in one of her dozens of colorful scarves to keep it safe while she worked with industrial equipment. Janelle was a maker, a builder of small robotics and other devices, who was currently preparing a Rube Goldberg machine for the Sendel Waxman competition. Her texts indicated she had been spending a lot more time in the maintenance shed building since Stevie had been gone, and that she was getting much more serious with Vi Harper-Tomo. Janelle's life was full, and she wanted Stevie to be in it, and Stevie felt far and cold and none of that made sense here, at the shopping center with the Subway and the beer and cigarette place, in the Funky Munkee.

But she had the tin, and as long as she had the tin, she had the Ellingham case.

She'd found the tin in Ellie's room shortly before she left. She had dated it using online images. It was from somewhere between 1925 and 1940, and the tea was popular and widely sold. The feather was about four inches long and looked like it may have been attached to a piece of clothing. The cloth was two inches square and was a luminous blue, with silver, blue, and black beads, and had torn edges. Another piece of detritus. The lipstick had the word KISSPROOF on the side. It had been used, but not entirely. The pillbox was the only thing that looked like it might have value. It was just over two inches in length. It was empty.

These four items Stevie thought of as a group. They were personal, they concerned jewelry or clothing. The feather and the torn cloth were junk, so the reason for saving them was mysterious. The lipstick and the pillbox could have had value. All of these items likely belonged to a woman. They were intimate. They *meant* something to whoever put them in this tin.

The other two items probably had a lot more significance. They were a set of photographs of two people pretending to be Bonnie and Clyde. Stevie stared at them until her sight went blurry. The girl had dark hair cut in a sharp bob. Stevie had Googled some pictures of Lord Byron, the poet, and found he did have a resemblance to the boy in the photos. They had written a poem about themselves. But who *were* they? The trouble was, there were no online records of all the names of the early Ellingham students. Their names had never mattered—they were never part of the case. So they weren't printed anywhere. Stevie had searched the internet, read down every thread on every message board she frequented on the case. At the time of the crimes or in the following years, a few students had come forward and given statements or spoken to the press. The one who appeared the most was a Gertrude van Coevorden,

a New York City debutante who claimed to have been Dottie Epstein's best friend. She gave tearful interviews for weeks
after the kidnappings. None of these were helpful in identify-
ing the persons in the photos.

Then, there was the poem. It wasn't a good poem. It
wasn't even a whole poem.

> *The Ballad of Frankie and Edward*
> *April 2, 1936*
>
> *Frankie and Edward had the silver*
> *Frankie and Edward had the gold*
> *But both saw the game for what it was*
> *And both wanted the truth to be told*
>
> *Frankie and Edward bowed to no king*
> *They lived for art and love*
> *They unseated the man who ruled over the land*
> *They took*
>
> *The king was a joker who lived on a hill*
> *And he wanted to rule the game*
> *So Frankie and Edward played a hand*
> *And things were never the same*

Stevie didn't know a lot about poetry, but she knew about
true crime. Bonnie Parker, the famous 1930s outlaw who

Frankie was modeling herself after in the pictures, wrote poems as well, including a famous one called "The Story of Suicide Sal," which was all about a woman in love with a gangster. This poem looked like it was modeled on hers.

And there were several things in the poem that seemed to be about Albert Ellingham—the mention of games, the king who was a joker who lived on a hill. And in the poem Frankie and Edward did *something*, but what, the poem never says.

There was only one thing she could find that might explain anything about Edward and Frankie. Stevie had read the police interviews with the various suspects many times; they were collected in an ebook she kept on her phone. She had flagged a section in which Leonard Holmes Nair, the famous painter who was staying with the Ellinghams at the time of the kidnapping, described some of the students:

LHN: You see them all, milling around. You know, Albert opened this place and said he was going to fill it with prodigies, but fully half of them are just his friends' children and not the sharpest ones at that. The other half are probably all right. If I'm being fair, there were one or two others that showed a bit of a spark. A boy and a girl, I forget their names. The two of them seemed to be a pair. The girl had hair like a raven and the boy looked a bit like Byron. They were interested in poetry. They had a little light behind the eyes. The girl asked me about Dorothy Parker, which I took as a hopeful sign. I'm a friend of Dorothy's.

There was no question in Stevie's mind that these two students described by Leonard Holmes Nair were the same two students in these photographs.

Anyway, the critical clue was actually contained in the photographs—or rather, between them.

Her phone buzzed. There was a text message from her mom: Where are you?

Stevie sighed.

Walking home.

Get a move on, she replied.

It was only four o'clock. At Ellingham, Stevie's time was her own. When she ate, what she ate, when and where she studied, what she did between classes . . . all of that was up to her. There was no one looking over her shoulder. Now she was back in her family's domain.

She drained her coffee and carefully returned the items to the tin. Headphones back on her head, she started the rest of the walk home. It was the lead-up to Halloween, and every business and home had a pumpkin or an autumnal banner. There was still a little late-summer lift in the air before the cold snapped down and killed everything right to ground level.

Winter would be unbearable here.

Her phone rang. The only calls Stevie got were from her parents and from Janelle. She was surprised to see Nate's number appear. Nate was not a caller.

"Let me guess," Stevie said, on answering. "You're writing."

Nate Fisher was a writer. At least, he was supposed to be.

When he was fourteen, he wrote a book called *The Moon-beam Chronicles*. It started out as a hobby. Then, as he published parts of it online, it grew more and more popular until it had a robust fandom and Nate wound up as a published author. He had even gone on a book tour and appeared on some morning shows. He had gotten into Ellingham on the back of this achievement. Stevie got the impression that he liked it there for some of the same reasons she did—it was remote and people left him alone. At home, he was that writer kid. He didn't like publicity. His social anxiety made every event a nightmare. Ellingham was a retreat in the mountains where he could be among people who also did weird things. The only problem was, he was supposed to be writing book two, and book two did not want to be written. Nate's entire existence was avoiding the writing of book two of the Moonbeam Chronicles.

Which is why, Stevie surmised, Nate was calling her.

"Not going well?" she asked.

"You don't know my life."

"It's that bad?"

"Do books have to have a middle?" he said.

"I think whatever happens in the middle is probably the middle," Stevie said.

"What if there's just a beginning where I tell you everything that happened in book one in a series of contrivances, like found scrolls and speeches and drunk bards at the tavern who tell the story to some traveler and then it's like two hundred pages of question marks and then I explain where the dragon is?"

"Is there kissing?" she asked.

"I hate you."

"You can't write *anything*?"

"Let's just say that I needed to have Moonbeam fight something and the only thing I could come up with was called the Pulsating Norb. It's like a wall that jiggles. The best thing I came up with this week is a wall that jiggles called the Pulsating Norb. I need you to come back here and kill me."

"Wish I could," Stevie said, hitting the button to cross the intersection. "I'd like to meet a Pulsating Norb."

"How is it there?" he said.

"The same. My parents are still my parents. School is still school. I didn't realize how much the place stinks like cafeteria and hot dishwater before. Ellingham is all . . . woody."

When she called up the sense memory, Stevie felt a pain run through her. Like a punch in the gut.

"So how's everyone else?" she said quickly.

"Uh . . . Janelle is all in love and power tools. And David, I guess . . ."

And David, he guessed. Nate paused long enough for Stevie to know that there was a *there* there. Only Janelle knew most of the facts—that Stevie and David Eastman were some kind of thing. David was an annoying rich boy, scruffy and difficult. Whatever ability he had—and apparently he had considerable ability in computer programming—he hid from the school and others. His likes were video games, not going to class, not talking about his past . . .

And Stevie.

Janelle knew that David and Stevie had made out several times. Nate likely guessed; he did not want to know details, but it would have been evident. There was something neither Janelle nor Nate knew about David. Something Stevie was holding on to. Something that could not be said.

"David what?" Stevie said, trying not to sound too interested.

"Nothing. I should go, I guess. . . ."

Stevie suspected that Nate wasn't going because he was going to write; he was going because this was probably the longest phone conversation he had ever had, at least voluntarily.

"My parents have a sign hanging in the bathroom that I think sums it up," Stevie said. "It says: 'Believe in yourself.' Have you *considered* believing in yourself? I can send you that quote on top of a pic of a sunset. Would that help?"

"Good-bye," he said. "You're the worst."

Stevie smiled and pocketed her phone. It always hurt, but now it hurt a tiny bit less. She picked up her chin and took firm, decisive steps. She'd read somewhere that the way you move could influence your inner state—take on the shape of the thing you wanted to be. FBI agents walked decisively. Detectives kept their heads up, their eyes moving around. She fastened her hands on her backpack straps to pull herself to a straighter stance. She would not be broken. She quickened her steps and almost bounded up the crumbling concrete path to her front door, turning away, as she always did, from the weathered KING FOR SENATE sign that was still on their lawn a year after the election was over.

"Hey," she said, knocking the headphones down to her neck and pulling off her coat. "I decided to walk. . . ."

It seemed they had a visitor.

2

SOMETIMES THE DEVIL COMES TO PEOPLE IN STORIES—THE UNEX-
pected visitor with the pleasing voice. The devil is not
supposed to show up in life. The devil is not supposed to be
in living rooms in Pittsburgh in the autumn twilight, sitting
on the green sofa from Martin's Big Discount Furniture, in a
room magnetically pointed at the television. And yet, there
he was.

Edward King was in his fifties, but still looked a bit
younger. His hair was dark with a waving curl, forced flat. He
wore an impeccable gray suit, one of those suits that stand
out because they do not shine or bag. His unlined face was
a mask of affability, his smile a gentle, *who me?* twist. He sat
back deep into the sofa, his legs widely crossed, as if this
was where he spent every evening. Stevie's parents sat in the
matching recliners on either side of the sofa, looking atten-
tive and wide-eyed, and frankly, confused.

"Hello, Stevie," he said.

Stevie was stranded in the doorway, feeling a cold paraly-
sis come over her limbs.

Edward King was the worst man in America.

Well, that point could be argued. But Edward King was a powerful man. He was a Pennsylvania senator, based here, out of Pittsburgh. This was the man who wanted to keep "outsiders" and "bad elements" out of America, which largely meant people who weren't white, weren't rich. For Edward King, wealth was goodness. There was no climate change in his world—the earth was there to produce more life-affirming dollars. This was a man who wanted to be president.

"Stevie," her father said, a slight warning tone in his voice. She knew what that tone meant. *We know how you feel about this, but this man is a senator and our personal hero, and if you think you are about to storm out or go into some political tirade, you are much mistaken.*

Stevie felt that old tyrant in her chest, the unsteady heartbeat that signaled the start of an anxiety attack. She grabbed the doorframe like it was a life preserver. Her parents didn't know that this was not the first time Stevie had come this close to Edward King.

"It's okay," he said. He was too clever to smile broadly; it was just a gentle hint of a smile. "I know that Stevie may not be my biggest fan. We can have different opinions. That's what makes America great. Honoring our differences."

Oh no. *No, no, no.* He'd lobbed the ball at her. He wanted to play.

Oh, she would play.

If she could breathe. Breathe, Stevie. Breathe. One intake of air and she could get the whole apparatus moving. But it was a no-go from her diaphragm.

"Stevie," her father said again, though the tone was less stern. "Come sit down."

The floor was coming up to meet Stevie a bit. *Hello,* said the floor. *Come see me. Plant your face in my bosom and be still.*

"That's all right," Edward King said. "Stevie, you do whatever makes you comfortable. I'm just here to talk to you all, see how you're doing after the events at Ellingham."

Another move in this chess game. Now that he was saying she could stand, maybe the move was to sit. Or she might be giving in to what he wanted. Too much input. The golden twilight was dimming fast and the shadows were falling across the carpet. Or was that just her vision? The floor really was inviting. . . .

STEVIE! she screamed to herself. *YOU. MUST. RE-INHABIT. YOUR. BODY.*

"I want to congratulate you on the remarkable work you did at Ellingham," Edward King went on. "Your investigative powers are really exceptional."

Her parents looked at her as if they were expecting her to dance or maybe pull out some puppets. Still, her body and voice refused to participate.

Okay, she said to herself. *Points for not being on the floor. But you've got to move. You can move. You can speak. DO SOME-THING.*

"We're sorry," her mother said.

"Don't be." Edward King spread out his hands in a generous gesture, as if this was his house. "Actually, Stevie, and you may not like to hear this, you remind me of a young me a bit. I stood by my principles. Even if others around me didn't always like it. You've got backbone. So what I've come to ask, come to talk about, is this . . . and I ask you all to hear me out. I've come to ask that Stevie return to Ellingham."

The floor could have completely fallen away and revealed a cloud city below.

"I'm . . . sorry?" Her mother was now off her footing.

"I know, I know," Edward King said apologetically. "I'm a parent of a student there as well. Please. Let me make my case. I have something to show you."

He reached into a sleek leather case leaning against his leg and pulled out several glossy folders.

"Have a look at these," he said, passing one to each of her parents. He held one toward Stevie as well, but immediately set it on his lap when it was clear that she would not make a move for it.

"Security?" her father said, examining the folder.

"The best firm in the country. Better than the secret service, because it's private. It's the firm I use. And it's the firm I've hired to wire Ellingham. I always thought there should be a better security system there, and after recent events, I managed to convince the board to allow me to install a network."

Her parents were looking through the folders, dumbfounded.

"I did this," he continued, "because Ellingham Academy is a very special place. They cultivate individual talent. What they've done for people like Stevie and my son . . . I truly believe in the mission. Albert Ellingham was a great man, a true American innovator. And new American innovators are being made at Ellingham right now. I'm asking you, please. I think Stevie should return. The campus is safer now."

"But that girl," her mother said. "Everything that's happened . . ."

"Element," Edward King said, shaking his head. "Do you want to know what I think?"

Her parents always did, and for the first time, so did Stevie.

"I believe what happened was an accident. I think those two students were out of their depth and Hayes died. I think your daughter worked it out. And I think the girl panicked and ran. She'll be found."

"The school should have been more careful," Stevie's father said.

"Now here's where I disagree with you," Edward King said, in his congenial debate voice. He leaned back into the sofa. "I don't blame the school. I'm a big believer in personal responsibility. The school locked up those materials. You know, those students are old enough to know better than to break into a locked storage area, to steal chemicals. Personal responsibility."

This was one of Edward King's big talking points: A RETURN TO RESPONSIBILITY. It meant nothing as far as he was concerned, but people liked the slogan. She saw her parents lulled by the familiar word.

"My own son—he's going to be eighteen in December, on the seventh. I can hardly believe that myself. But that's an adult. This wasn't the school being careless. If it had been him—and God forbid, of course—God forbid my son or Stevie, but . . . if it had been him? I'd say the same."

The words came out of him like poisoned honey—so sweet, so perfect, and all wrong. Everything was wrong and scrambled. Reality needed to be rebooted.

He let the matter settle on the room, and Stevie saw it working. She saw the possibility opening in front of her.

"I've come to offer Stevie a ride," Edward King went on after a moment. "That's how strongly I feel about this. I have my SUV outside that can handle lots of bags, and I have a plane at the airport. A private flight. It doesn't get better than that."

What do you do when the devil turns up in your living room and offers you everything you want?

"Why?" Stevie said, her voice dry. It was the first word she'd said.

"Because it's the right thing to do," Edward King replied.

That was the first direct lie he'd probably told in this room, and the most telling. It was also a lie that rang clear and bright with her parents, who believed, who really *believed* that Edward King was the standard-bearer for some kind of glorious, real American truth that you could buy and hold in your hands and own. Edward King had come here to do the Right Thing and was going to make it all happen in his God-given jet.

"And it's of course a thank-you to two people who do so much work for me," he said, indicating her parents. "You run an office for me here. I owe you. So . . ."

He turned to Stevie.

"What do you say?" he asked.

April 14, 1936, 2:00 a.m.

WHEN SHE WAS EIGHT, FRANCIS CRANE'S FATHER TOOK HER ON A tour of one of their flour mills that had been destroyed by an explosion. They walked around the remaining shell of the building, with the ceiling blown out and the sky revealed above. The walls were covered in scorch marks. Many of the machines were burned, partly melted, pieces hanging from cables. The words CRANE FLOUR were barely visible on the wall.

"All of this," her father said, "from flour, Francis. Simple flour."

This was when Frankie learned of flour's combustible properties. The most domestic, most harmless-looking substance could blow a hole through a wall. So much energy from something so benign.

For Francis, this experience was life-changing. It was the most wonderful thing she had ever seen. She fell in love with explosions, with fire, with the burn and the boom. There was the taste of danger on the tip of her tongue. This was when Francis began her journey to the other side of life—the broken remains, the smoldering scenes, the back doors, the servants' quarters. Down, down, down to wherever she needed to go to feel that spark. She had her harmless pleasures—little fires in the wastepaper basket, stealing Edie Anderson's hat and sending it to Valhalla with a match on the lake in Central Park, going perhaps a bit too far once with a box of firecrackers. She was known to leave a party or slip out of the house and take a taxi whenever she heard the fire engines going. She would sit outside all night, watching the flames lick the sky. And now she was creeping under the ground beneath Ellingham Academy and counting her steps.

One hundred, one hundred and one, one hundred and two ...

She kept her right hand in front of her, holding her candle. It was burning down fast, sending trails of hot wax over her fist and taking the flame closer and closer to her flesh. Her left hand trailed behind her like a rudder, running carefully along the wall to help orient herself in space. The tunnel was so tight that if she stepped only an inch or two in either direction her arms would scrape along the walls. That wasn't such an issue in the early part of the tunnel, which was made of smooth brick. As she went on into the depths, the builders had given up and used bits of stone to make the walls—rough, occasionally jagged bits that were likely the product of demolition of the rock.

A person could get stuck down here.

One hundred and fifty, one hundred and fifty-one ...

If anything went wrong down here—if she got stuck, if the tunnel came down, burying her in rock—this kind of risk thrilled her.

One hundred and sixty.

She stopped and pulled her left hand in front of her to reach around until she found the empty space she was looking for—this was where the tunnel bifurcated. She took the left tunnel and kept going, restarting her footstep count at one. This path went on farther than the last. Finally, she felt the space widen. She puffed out the candle and moved forward blindly in half steps until her hands felt the rungs of a ladder. A moment later, she pushed open a hatch and climbed out of the base of a statue, deep in a copse of trees on the far side of the campus. She took a deep breath of the cold, foggy air.

This was the best part—physically crawling out onto the grass in the dark, like some newly born creature of the night. Her eyesight had grown used to the void, and now the night seemed brilliant and alive. She didn't need a candle to find her way through the trees to the path to Apollo. She picked up a small stone from the ground and took careful aim at an upstairs window.

A moment later, she heard the slide of the window open. A knotted rope slithered down. She saw Eddie's feet first. He had tattooed stars on the soles of both his feet in black ink. He wore nothing but a pair of blue silk pajama bottoms; he made no concessions to the cold. He dropped the last few feet elegantly and shook back his blond hair. Apollo was a big building, intended for classrooms, but it currently housed four male students on the second floor. Eddie shared this side of the building with only one other person and could have walked right out the front door, but where was the fun in that?

He followed her into the grove of trees, and once there, he pressed her back into a tree. She took his face in both hands and kissed him roughly, running her hands down his bare back.

Edward Pierce Davenport was the first and only person Francis had any respect for. He came from the same kind of wealthy background as she did; he was from Boston and his family was in shipping. Eddie had made it his life's mission to disappoint his family, and he had been doing exceptionally well at this. There were tales of seducing maids, wandering naked through formal dinners, filling an entire bathtub with champagne. He had been expelled from four of the best schools in the country before his parents got on their knees and begged their friend Albert to take Eddie to the mountains where he might stay out of trouble for a few minutes. Or, at least, make trouble in a remote setting. That was enough.

Eddie and Francis met the first day, at the picnic on the lawn, making eyes over the cold fried chicken and lemonade. He saw the copy of *True Detective* she had in her bag. He quoted some obscene French poetry. And that was that. Eddie was suddenly tame, or so he seemed. Francis, it was said, had been a very good influence.

Eddie introduced Francis to poetry—the swirling, wild storms of the romantics, the jigsaw realities of the modernists and surrealists. He conveyed his dream—to live a life in which every impulse was to be followed. He showed Francis the various things he had learned in his romantic life, and Francis was an apt pupil.

Francis told Eddie about bomb-making and read him stories of Bonnie and Clyde and John Dillinger and Ma Barker. Eddie embraced them at once. They were poets—machine-gun poets who brooked no compromise, who rode any road they wished, who drove laughing into the sun. And so, on the lawns, in the library, in corners and basements, Francis and Eddie formed an inseparable bond.

Over that fall and that cold winter, they began their study into the art of crime. At the right time, they would take one of Ellingham's cars, fill it with dynamite, and leave. The time would be soon, when the ice melted off the mountain. On a clear day, when no one was looking, they would go drive west and rob banks. Francis would blow out the vaults. Eddie would write their story. They would make love on the floors of safe houses, on the road itself until the road ran out.

She pulled back from the embrace to tell him what was going on—Dottie missing, the police coming—but he eased down to the ground, taking her with him. Her desire to tell him this interesting news was overridden by a different sort of desire. There was nothing in this world as beautiful as Eddie lying there on the ground, his chest bare. He was not a nice boy; he was a dirty, wild boy, almost as dirty and wild as Francis herself. She had been with other boys before, but they fumbled. Eddie knew precisely what he was doing. He played with his speed. He could move slowly—achingly slowly. He drew her down now and ran his hand along her side inch by inch until she hardly felt like she could bear it.

"I have something to tell you," she said, breathless. "You'll like it."

"I like everything you tell me."

There was a sound nearby and the two of them froze in place. Albert Ellingham walked past, his pace quick. Francis pointed at him silently and indicated they should follow. They kept their distance, trailing along toward the still-under-construction gymnasium building.

The room Albert Ellingham had entered was for the new indoor swimming pool. It was a large, vaulted space, cold and open, with white and aqua-blue tiled walls. The pool had no water yet—it was just a smooth concrete opening. There was no heat, so the room felt like an icehouse. Francis was cold in her coat; she could only imagine what Eddie was feeling. But that was the thing about Eddie—he never registered pain.

Inside the doorway, there was a large cart full of building supplies. As the only light in the space came from a single lantern on the far side of the room, Eddie and Francis were able to secrete themselves behind this with no difficulty. The high ceiling, empty pool, and tiled walls provided perfect acoustics; they could hear every word even if they couldn't see much from where they were crouched.

"Albert!" Miss Nelson said. Francis heard quick steps and looked over the cart to see two figures embracing. Francis slapped herself mentally. Of course. This is why Miss Nelson's hair was so carefully done. This is why she wore small diamond earrings that were unobtrusive and yet far beyond her means.

"Marion," Albert Ellingham said, his voice husky. "Something has happened. Someone has kidnapped Alice and Iris."

Now the cold on the outside was matched by a cold within—but cold with a spark, like the light madness of the sky before one of the wild Vermont snowstorms.

Kidnapped.

"That letter," he said. "Truly Devious . . ."

Francis had the urge to vomit. Beside her, Eddie hissed excitedly through his teeth.

"You need to take this," Albert Ellingham said.

"My God, Albert, I don't know how to fire one of these things."

Had Miss Nelson been given a *gun*?

"Cock the hammer, pull the trigger. Now, listen to me. I have coaches coming at daybreak. The students must be on them, and so must you be. Wake them before sunrise. Have them take only what they need. I'll have everything else sent."

"Albert, one of the children is—"

"There's no time. Take the train to New York and go directly to the apartment. I'll contact you there as soon as I can. Go. You need to go now."

"Albert, I'm sorry. I'll—"

"Now, Marion." Albert Ellingham—America's king of newspapers, of radio—sounded on the verge of tears. Francis and Eddie hunkered down as Miss Nelson hurried back out the door. They heard Albert Ellingham convulsively sobbing for several minutes before he did the same.

3

ABOUT AN HOUR AFTER STEVIE FOUND EDWARD KING IN HER HOUSE, she was in the back of an SUV, making its way toward the airport. The sun had long set, but there was an extra darkness in this car from the tinted windows. There was an additional shadow in the form of the person sitting next to her, on the massive leather seats, sipping a bottle of sparkling water and consulting his phone. Edward King had said very little on this ride. His security agent sat in front of them, staring straight ahead. There was nothing but the muted lights outside and the various little controls within.

As promised, the back of the SUV had enough room for Stevie's boxes and bags. Some had never been unpacked and were simply ready to go. Her clothes had to be gathered up from hampers (some still dirty) and the dryer and the closet and drawers. All her little possessions, her banged-up books and overwashed black clothes, and sheets with bright stains on them where a laundry pod had exploded . . . a bag of hastily collected cords . . . all of these things were lifted and stuck into the back of the SUV with a clinical competence by the driver and the bodyguard, like law enforcement taking the evidence away from the scene. Bag it. Stick it in the car. No matter how shabby, no matter how small.

Stevie kept her backpack with her, clinging to it. This was all she really needed, should she decide to open the door at a light and spring out. Her computer. Her wallet. Her meds. Her notes. Her phone. The tin.

"So," Edward King said, tucking his phone into his pocket. "You excited to go back to school?"

Excited was not the right word. Stevie *needed* to go back and she *wanted* to go back, but the accompanying emotion was anxiety. Anxiety and excitement are cousins; they can be mistaken for each other at points. They have many features in common—the bubbling, carbonated feel of the emotion, the speed, the wide eyes and racing heart. But where excitement tends to take you up, into the higher, brighter levels of feeling, anxiety pulls you down, making you feel like you have to grip the earth to keep from sliding off as it turns.

This was the sympathetic nervous system at work, her therapist had told her. To work with anxiety, you had to let it complete its cycle. Stevie tapped her foot against the SUV floor, telling the cycle to get a move on. What was she anxious about? Going back to the case, going back to her friends, going back to her classes, going back . . .

To see Edward King's son. And he was a complicated person to go back to.

The last time she had really had contact with David was the morning after she had confronted Ellie, and Ellie had run. She and David had returned to Minerva together. They went into Ellie's room and sat on her bed. David had looked so beautiful that morning. The light came down on one side of his face and he seemed to glow. His dark hair fell in finger-length curls that flopped rakishly across his forehead. He had eyebrows that had natural peaks, raised in constant amusement. His nose was long and fine. His worn T-shirts pulled against his frame, revealing muscled arms. . . .

She wanted to kiss him, but there was a noise outside, something overhead. He got up to see what it was, and she leaned back and put her hand on the tin. It was tucked in Ellie's bed.

The noise was a helicopter landing on the lawn. David ran outside. Stevie assumed the helicopter was part of the search effort, but when she reached David and saw what he was looking at, everything changed. That was when she saw the word KING on the side. That was when she looked between Edward King and David and saw the resemblance for the first time. David said to her, "Meet my dead dad."

What happened next was very strange. Edward King stopped halfway when he saw David and Stevie. He nodded, then turned toward the Great House. The helicopter left. There was no one around at that moment who read the side or saw Edward King, at least that Stevie could tell.

David turned to Stevie and said, "And now you know."

He waited for her reaction, but none came. Her brain could not process this—that the only guy she had ever felt like this about, had so much contact with, that David was the son of . . .

With every passing second of her silence, David's smirk grew wider.

"Yeah," he said. "That's what I thought."

He turned and walked away. Those were the last words they exchanged. David avoided her for the rest of the day, and she avoided him the day after that. And then she was gone. They had not communicated since. She had thought about reaching out to him a few times, but too many emotions jumped in the way—revulsion, fear, sadness.

It made sense, sort of, that Edward King was bringing her back. The cycle was now complete.

The SUV drove around to some back area of the airport, to a chain-link fence with a glowing red gate and a security guard. The driver held up something, and the glowing red bar rose, admitting them to the space beyond to a small freestanding building. Inside the building there was no security line, no gate, no jetway. They walked into an empty room that sort of looked like the lobby of a bank, threw their things onto an X-ray machine that was waiting there for their use with an operator who seemed to have no interest in the contents that were revealed. They were waved on, past a few comfortable chairs and a display of glossy magazines and newspapers, all free to take. They went out a set of automatic doors and were right back outside, walking toward a plane.

Stevie had only been on a few planes in her life to see her

grandparents in Florida. This plane was not like those. It was *extremely* small. A man in a white shirt and a captain's hat waved to them and ushered them up four narrow steps that were part of an opened hatch. The door, if you could call it that, was a little hobbit opening. Stevie had to tuck her head in and pull her bag to her chest to squeeze through. Inside, the world of the plane was a calming creamy white. There were six seats—two facing forward and four in a little grouping, two and two facing each other. Edward King took one of these and waved Stevie to the one opposite. Stevie took the one on the other side of the small aisle.

"You'll like this," he said to her. "Once you fly private, you'll never want to go back. Enjoy this. It's fun."

The bodyguard came in and took one of the forward-facing seats, then pulled out a book and started reading. The captain and the copilot followed up, one of them pulling the door shut behind them. It was far too . . . simple, for Stevie's taste. Just a little hatch pulled closed by some guy. He turned a lever, and that was that. They ducked into the little cockpit, which was entirely open and exposed. The bank of lights and controls stood out in contrast to the dark sky in the windscreen. You weren't supposed to be able to see the cockpit, and you definitely weren't supposed to be able to go right up to it.

"Need anything, boss?" one of the pilots leaned back and asked.

"Anything, Stevie?" Edward King said. "We have sodas, snacks. Would you like a Coke? We have some really nice chips. I love these. I can't eat them—cholesterol, but . . ."

Stevie would have liked a Coke and also some of the fancy potato chips that were being passed back in a basket. They were the fancy, thick-cut, small-batch kind in all sorts of flavors—the ones that always cost a buck or more. But she wasn't taking one more thing from Edward King. Follow the Wonderland rule: Don't eat or drink anything.

Seeing that Stevie was going to resist his basket of fancy chips, Edward King shrugged and shoved it back behind him.

"I think we're ready to go," he said.

And that was that. No safety demonstration. No one telling her to put on her seat belt, even. The tiny plane moved forward, turned onto a runway, and then it started to speed. Pittsburgh was going by in a blur, and Edward King was sitting politely on his creamy white leather throne, using his phone. *Using his phone.* On a plane.

No rules mattered.

Stevie felt her stomach lurch as the plane lifted gently from the ground.

"We're going to bump a bit," one of the pilots leaned back and said. "Bit of cloud cover. Should pass after ten minutes or so. We might get a bit more once we get into Vermont. Weather's been rough there, and we may hit some pockets over the mountains. Nothing to worry about."

Little planes always crashed, didn't they? The tiny craft bobbed gently in the air, and Stevie at once realized how ridiculous life was. She was flitting in the wind, next to the worst person she could conjure. If this went down, Edward

King went down too. Was she prepared for that? If she had the choice, would she will this plane to go thundering down on some field if she could wipe out Edward King? Was she willing to fall from the sky to save America? Her brain was spitting out weird ideas.

"Why are you doing this?" she said. It was odd to hear her voice coming out in this quiet, polite plane.

"You speak! I'm glad. I thought you might be sick. Are you sure you wouldn't like a Coke?"

"Why are you doing this?" she asked again.

"You mean taking you back to Ellingham Academy on a private plane?"

Of course that's what I meant, you sanctimonious asshole.

"Well," Edward King said, putting his phone back into the inner pocket of his jacket, "I think that's where you belong."

"So this is a service you provide to everyone?" she said.

"No," he said, smiling a bit. "No, of course not. No, and you're very smart, Stevie, I know that. I appreciate that. You know what? I *am* going to have a bag of these chips. I only eat them on planes. I don't know why. But one bag . . ."

Stevie watched him pull the basket back up and carefully go through it. It was the practiced happy interest of a politician who had to look invested in whatever people brought his way—cakes and potluck dinners, presentations by children and senior citizens, ceremonies for people he never knew. It was a professional smile, a way of knowing when to pause and break someone else's conversational flow to put the focus back on himself, to make it oh so very casual that when the poison came out everyone would say, "But what a nice, ordinary guy. He likes chips like the rest of us."

So she would wait. She would say nothing. She pressed back farther into the seat, and the seat took her, because the seat was expensive and made to take whatever the sitter wanted to inflict on it.

"Sounds strange," Edward King said, yanking a green bag from the basket. "Dill-pickle flavor. It's really good."

He opened the bag and pulled out a chip with his long fingers. His hands were so like David's, it made Stevie's skin crawl. Long and elegant. Hands that would fit around a neck.

"The first reason," he said, popping the chip into his mouth and then talking through the chew, "that I am personally taking you back to Ellingham has to do with the exceptional work you did in finding out what happened to Hayes Major. I am a parent, Stevie. My son is at your school. And I was as concerned as anyone."

So concerned that your son said you were dead rather than claim you as a parent.

"So there's that," he said. "But, as you've worked out, there is something I would like from you. I need your help."

There was cool air coming from one of the discreet little vents in the wall. Stevie pulled in her breath, sucking in the flow.

"I know, I know. You don't want to help me. I heard about some of the stunts you pulled with the local volunteer office. You changed all those volunteer lists, had everyone calling

SeaWorld and the American Girl store with all the dolls. That was pretty funny, to tell you the truth. I don't mind things like that. Livens things up. But I know you wouldn't want to do anything that would further my political interests because our interests don't . . . *align*."

He was still polite, being casual and charming and studied in his delivery. But he looked up at her, and she saw in his face that same darkly playful look that David had. Stevie had done those things, but she never thought it would actually get back to him. This senator—this man who wanted to be president—knew Stevie had played with his campaign. It was not a comfortable thought.

"What I need from you," he said, "is something I think you'd be very agreeable to. It doesn't conflict with your views."

He put another chip in his mouth and the air dropped out from under the plane for a moment. Stevie clutched at her seat.

"You know David," he said, unaffected by the loss of altitude, "my son. He's a friend of yours. I know he thinks very highly of you. The way I know that is because he said nothing about you, even when I asked about you several times. I wanted to know about this housemate of his who had solved the case, the one he was standing with when I arrived at your school so early in the morning, before anyone should have been awake. And he said not a word. Which means he doesn't want *you* to have anything to do with *me*. Which means he likes you. It's not a sophisticated code."

Stevie felt herself relax a bit, and something warm came

over her in this cold, strange plane. David had put up a shield. David *liked* her.

"David," he said, putting the bag of chips down on the seat opposite, "is a bit hard to manage. Do you have any idea how many schools he's been to?"

He shook his head as if she had replied.

"I think six? Maybe seven? He has an uncanny way of expressing his dislike of a place. Once he doesn't like it there anymore, things go wrong. I'd like things to stop going wrong. He's almost out of high school. This is his last year. He just has to make it to June. And he's doing well at Ellingham. When you left, he started making trouble. Not going to class. Being disruptive. It won't be long now before the school will be forced to kick him out. I think if you return to Ellingham, he'll settle down. So I'm taking you back there. You get to go back to a place I think you very much want to be, and you have a very simple job—make sure David stays there too."

"How am I supposed to do that?" Stevie said.

"I think he likes having you there. You seem to be a reassuring presence. I am, in no way, suggesting you should do anything . . . personal. That is entirely none of my business and it would be completely inappropriate on all levels for me to suggest it. I just think he considers you a friend, and he may be more inclined to stay if you were at the school. That's all."

"What if I don't want to talk to him?"

"A little polite conversation isn't hard. As long as David is there, you're there. I'll see to it. And if you have any problems with that deal, I can turn the plane around and take you right back home. It's no trouble at all. Think it over."

I can turn the plane around. It was parent talk, but with real power, and Edward King knew it. Stevie fell silent and watched the lights appear on the ground below through the patchwork of clouds. She felt the outline of an object in her bag—the one truly precious, irreplaceable item. The tea tin. The clue. Solving the case had been such a dream before, but now it was a real possibility. She had something no one else had. This was her chance.

Stevie was quiet for some time, feeling the cold coming from the window of the plane, watching her own reflection, her short blond hair sticking up. Who was she? *Who could she be?*

"What do you say, Stevie?" Edward King asked. "Have we got a deal?"

"Yeah," Stevie said, turning away from her reflection. "We have a deal."

4

SOMETIMES, IN MOMENTS OF CONFUSION OR BOREDOM, STEVIE BELL ran through the scenes of famous murder novels or shows in her mind. As she sat in another SUV making its way along the rock-lined mountain roads of I-89, away from Burlington and toward Ellingham, her brain decided to run through the opening of *And Then There Were None*, arguably Agatha Christie's finest work, and maybe the most perfect mystery ever written. Ten strangers find themselves on their way to a remote private island, accessible only by a small boat. All have been invited there under different pretenses, by someone they can't quite remember meeting. All have been made good offers, so they all go. It's not long after they arrive that they realize none of the stories quite tally, and then . . . then the bodies start dropping.

Going to Ellingham was a little bit like that.

It was remote. You could only get to it by the official shuttle. The letters came and invited you and maybe you never fully understood why. Stevie was returning because of an offer—an offer she could not refuse.

Oh, and there had been a dead body.

Hayes Major could not be forgotten in all of this. Hayes—he of the blond hair and beefy calves and even tan, with his honeyed voice and good cheekbones. Stevie had soon discovered that Hayes's greatest talent was getting other people to do his work for him—his homework, his papers, his projects, his video series. Hayes had loads of people working for him. He was kind of a jerk.

He had not deserved to die, no matter how it happened. And Stevie wasn't really sure of that herself. All she knew for sure was that Hayes hadn't written his own show. She had figured out that Ellie had written it in exchange for five hundred dollars and she had hidden the fact. Stevie had also worked out that Hayes was on Skype with his girlfriend, Beth Brave, at the time he was supposed to have been across campus taking the dry ice that killed him. So, someone took that dry ice. And the most likely person to have done that would have been someone who held something against him, like, say, having written a show for him thinking it would go nowhere and then finding it was going to be made into a movie and maybe worth millions. . . .

But loads of people had things against Hayes. And Ellie grew up on a commune and wore garbage as clothes and didn't seem to care about money. . . .

Thump, thump. Her heart was going faster. There was no reason to go down this mental road, no reason to revisit the guilt. She had pointed out a fact and Ellie had run away and now the crisis was over and she was going back to Ellingham to finish the job she had started.

Edward King had not accompanied her on this leg of the journey. He'd gotten back in his plane and gone off who-knew-where. The last thing he said to her was "It's up to you, but it's probably easier if you don't mention you came back on my plane. All the school knows is that your parents gave you the green light to return. Your mode of transport might not be popular. Probably best to say you flew and leave it at that." The minivan that met her at the airport was from a local cab service, and the driver paid her no attention, leaving her alone with her thoughts in the dark. She put in her earbuds and tried to listen to music, then to a true crime show, but she couldn't concentrate on anything. So she let it go silent.

She knew she should call Janelle and Nate, or at least text them to say she was coming, but she found she was paralyzed. They would have questions and she had no answers yet. She barely understood it herself. So she ran mystery plots through her mind and looked at the rock walls that lined the highway.

The minivan pulled into the rest stop and the driver turned off the engine while they waited for someone from Ellingham to arrive. A blue Toyota soon pulled up beside them. Stevie saw the familiar head of steel-gray hair. Security Larry wasn't wearing his normal uniform—he was off duty, dressed in jeans and a very Vermonty red-and-black-checked jacket.

"Well," he said as Stevie stepped out of the minivan. "You made it back."

"Did you miss me?"

"You're all I could think about," he said. There was enough of a soft growl in his voice that told her it was in some part true. While she had caused Larry some headaches (going tunneling, interfering with the investigation into Hayes's death, doing her own independent investigation, little things like that, no need to dwell on them) she had also won him over with her serious study of the Ellingham case and the fact that she had . . .

Well, she'd led him to Hayes's dead body. And then led him to the person who may have been responsible.

Larry picked up one of the lumpy bags of Stevie's dirty clothes and put it in the trunk of the car. Her belongings had been transferred several times now, and they didn't look any less shabby going into the Toyota. This appeared to be Larry's personal car—her arrival was too late to send out the Ellingham shuttle.

"What's been going on since I left?" Stevie said once they were both inside the car. Larry lowered the already muted country music he had playing.

"Everything stopped. School shut down."

"I knew it," she said.

Larry pulled out onto the road. It was so much darker here. The suburbs of Pittsburgh had more shops and strip malls, more gas stations, more light in general. Out here, the dark settled over the land until it met the rock or the trees, and then the dark fell over everything. The sky above was dotted with stars. Stevie felt a warm familiarity for the signs along the road, the billboards for ski lodges and maple candy and glassblowing. And there were the road signs along I-89 that she loved the most, the ones that just read MOOSE. She had noticed these when she rode up to Ellingham for the first time, the constant moose, moose, moose signs and yet . . .

No moose.

"Ever see a moose?" she asked.

"Yup," he said.

"What was it like?"

"Big."

This was a satisfactory reply. At least the moose was not a lie.

"So now that you're back," Larry said, "I assume you're going to be following the rules a bit more."

"I always did," Stevie said. "Maybe just . . ."

"You went into sealed tunnels, where someone died. You cornered a possible murder suspect in your house. . . ."

Stevie blushed in pride, which was probably not the reaction Larry wanted.

"I'm saying, this time will be different, right?" he asked.

She nodded.

"I'd like to hear you say it," he said.

"Rules," she said. "Follow them. I will. Promise. All of them."

"Good. Because I like you, and it would pain me to bust your ass and send you packing. You want to solve crimes, Stevie? You can't act like you're smarter than everyone around you and do it all on your own. That's how people get hurt."

"I know," she said. "I'm sorry."

"It's not about being sorry," he said.

Stevie slunk down in her seat at this and stayed that way, folded in over her waist, letting the seat belt cut into her neck as punishment. The car made the geometrically questionable turn up the treacherous path to the school. She had first come up this path in the morning, in the oversized school coach. There were a smattering of lights along the path, providing enough illumination to show the deep, shadowy crowd of forest, the narrowness of the passage, the dramatic dip over the stream at the base, then the climb, the climb . . .

The car crested the hill and two sphinxes appeared in the glow of two focused spotlights. There was a dark curtain of trees, and then it all opened up. There was a bright circle of light around the green, lights on in almost every window, lights pointed at the Neptune fountain, and the Great House sitting above it all. Bright. Ready.

Act Two was about to begin.

Larry let Stevie off on the circular drive.

"Come by the Great House in the morning," he said. "Dr. Scott wants to talk with you to get you set up. Ten o'clock."

"Yeah," she said. "Ten. I'll be there."

"Right then. Good night. I'll see your stuff is delivered."

Stevie walked toward Minerva House. The air was biting and cold, her footsteps loud and crisp on the stone pathways. Overhead, the trees made an unbroken canopy that blocked out the moon. She tightened her arms around herself as her head swam a bit. Anxiety again, percolating. So much of anxiety was anxiety about having anxiety. Would it come tonight? Would it suddenly wrap its fingers around her neck and warp the world, now, at the moment when she should be happiest? Would the universe crunch itself into a ball and ping itself right between her eyes?

There was a pleasant smell of wood smoke. There was a fire somewhere. The smell should have warmed her and made her happy, but it reminded her how far this place was, and different, and how much had been loaded on her today. She stopped and took a long breath through the nose and held it. Long exhale through the mouth in a steady plume of frost. She had been doing her breathing exercises every night for half an hour, religiously. They helped her take back some control, helped her body complete the cycle and reset itself. After a minute or so of this, the wood smoke became pleasant again. Or, at least, not as scary. She was going home, to her friends, to the place she loved. There was nothing to be frightened of.

She continued down the path. The tree cover was breaking, and there was a building ahead of her. In the dark, the tower on the end loomed a bit, and the Virginia creeper looked a bit creepier than in the daytime. The blue door was just as welcoming, and there were lights on in the common room and Janelle's room. Upstairs, all the lights were off but one on the end. Nate's room. Stevie reached to her pocket for her pass to tap herself in before she remembered that she no longer had one. She stood there for a moment, unsure of what to do. She was about to go over to Janelle's window, when the door opened.

"Stevie!"

Pix—Dr. Nell Pixwell, the faculty resident of Minerva—was wrapped in a massive plaid flannel robe. She had allowed her shaved head to grow to the point where there was a faint brown fuzz showing—a winter cut, for warmth. She raised her arms in the air in a cheerful greeting.

"I only got the call an hour ago! I'm so glad, I'm so glad. We missed you so much. Get in here!"

The common room of Minerva was swelteringly warm. There was a fire crackling away in the fireplace, where two smiling pumpkins stood at attention at either end of the mantelpiece. The moose head over the fireplace had been decorated in orange and black winking lights. Enough time had passed since she left that they had started preparing for Halloween.

"Janelle probably has her headphones on or she would have already come out," Pix said. "She's going to faint from shock. Go on. Go say hello."

Stevie walked slowly to the hallway where the downstairs rooms were and knocked on Janelle's door. When there was no reply, she knocked louder. After a moment, Janelle appeared in blue flannel pajamas covered in pictures of cat heads, and her crafting tool belt at her waist—a handmade blue canvas wraparound with deep pockets full of wire cutters and a variety of tools Stevie could not identify. She had put her hair up in two bunches, and her headphones were around her neck, still playing music loudly. She stood in her doorway for a moment, unmoving. Then . . .

"Ohmygodwhatishappeningwhydidn'tyoutellmewhen-didthishappenohmygod."

Stevie was wrapped in a massive hug that smelled of orange blossom perfume, coconut oil, pumpkin, and a tiny bit of industrial solvent.

"How, how . . ." Janelle stepped back and felt Stevie by her shoulders to take a good look at her. "How . . ."

"It happened fast," Stevie said. "Like, today fast. They changed their minds."

"What? WHAT. Oh my God. . . ."

In the next moment, she had Stevie by the wrist and was pulling her along to the tight circular stairs at the end of the hall. Stevie had a moment of remembrance here—on the day she arrived at Ellingham Academy, the first person she met in Minerva was Hayes Major. He recruited her into carrying his stuff up these cramped, twisting steps. She had been profusely sweating, and he looked so cool and crisp. He kept talking about phone calls he was getting or making to people in LA. And Stevie had no idea why he was telling her about his phone calls because she had not asked and did not care. But that was Hayes all over. All talk about his movie deal and how popular he was, getting people to do his work.

These stairs would always make her think of Hayes.

When Janelle and Stevie knocked on Nate's upstairs door, all was quiet for a moment. Janelle knocked louder, and eventually the door creaked open.

Nate had pushed all the furniture and all of his belongings up against the walls. His desk chair was upside down on his desk, the bed tipped up to make floor space. On the wooden floor, there was some kind of pattern, a spidery form of blobs and lines made from carefully sliced black masking tape. Nate sat in the center of the web, dressed in faded blue flannel pajama bottoms and a saggy green T-shirt that said I'M HERE BECAUSE MY GRANDKIDS AREN'T GOING TO SPOIL THEMSELVES. His room smelled of a spicy clove supermarket air freshener and a general, light boy stink. It was a warm, strangely welcoming smell.

"Look," Janelle said, pointing to Stevie. "Look. *Look!* Look."

Nate blinked at Stevie, then slowly unfolded his long frame from the ground. His hair had not been cut since his arrival at school, so it was hanging low over his forehead and scraping his neck. He was a few hours behind on a shave, and he scratched at the shadow along his chin. Nate had the same expression Stevie had come to love—vaguely annoyed by everything, except maybe Stevie and Janelle. But for sure everything else.

"Is this a trick?" he asked, raising one eyebrow.

"Not a trick, not a trick," Janelle said. "She just showed up."

"Poof," Stevie added.

"And . . . you're back?"

"From outer space," Stevie said.

"What's it like out there?"

"You don't want to know," Stevie replied.

"Nate, she is back—*what are you doing?*" Janelle said. "She's back!"

Janelle bounced on the balls of her feet a bit.

"I'm hugging you with my mind," he replied.

"I'm awkwardly accepting your hug in my mind," Stevie said. "And what are *you* doing?"

She pointed to the tape creation on the floor.

"Writing," he replied.

"With tape? On the floor?"

"It's a map," he said, gazing around.

"Of Moonbright?"

"No."

It was best not to make further inquiries.

Stevie looked down the dark hall to David's room. There was no light coming from under the door, and no sound at all.

"He's not home," Nate said. "Or, I don't know. Maybe he is. I wouldn't bother."

"Come on," Janelle said. "Let's get her stuff in."

As Janelle headed for the stairs, Nate slipped Stevie one of his rare smiles.

"How did you do it?" he asked.

Stevie's mind flickered back to Edward King and her promise not to speak. It would not help her. It wouldn't help anyone.

"Magic happens," she said.

Stevie's sad pile of belongings had turned up in the common room. Pix gave Stevie the key to her room. As she unlocked the door, Stevie was at first shocked by the dark and the cold of this once-familiar space. When she switched on the light, she heard a moth start bumping confusedly against the shade. The walls were bare, the drawers still half-open from when she had dumped the contents so sadly and unceremoniously the other week. The closet door was half-open as well. It looked like exactly what it was—the scene of a person leaving in a hurry, tears in her eyes.

Between the three of them, they made short work of getting the boxes and bags inside. Stevie opened a garbage bag full of clothes and dumped them out, which made Janelle recoil and run for hangers and a fabric steamer. Nate unpacked her books—something Stevie would never have allowed anyone else to do. Tonight was special, though, and Nate was careful with them, putting them into sensible stacks by genre and type.

"So," Stevie said, testing the waters again. "Where's David? You made it seem like he's out, or something?"

Janelle paused, her hand in the pile of Stevie's crumpled sheets. She and Nate shared a look.

"Oh, he's *here*," Janelle said.

She let that remark hang in the air for a second.

"Okay?" Stevie said, looking at the two of them. "What does that mean?"

"She means," Nate said, turning away from the books, "that David has gone full weird."

"He was always that way," Janelle said in a low voice.

"Yeah, but now he's completed his journey. Our little caterpillar has turned into a freaky butterfly."

"Tell her about the screaming," Janelle said. "Because I can't."

"The screaming?" Stevie repeated.

"The other morning he started something called 'screaming meditation,'" Nate said. "Guess what happens in screaming meditation? Did you guess screaming? For fifteen minutes? Because that's what happens in screaming meditation. Fifteen. Minutes. Outside. At five in the morning. Do you know what happens when someone screams outside for fifteen minutes at five in the morning at a remote location in the mountains, especially after a . . ."

The implied *dot dot dot* was "student dies in a terrible accident or maybe murder and another one goes missing."

"When security got to him he claimed it was his new religion and that it is something he needs to do every morning now as a way to talk to the sun."

So this is what Edward King had been referring to.

"Sometimes," Nate went on, tapping the books into place so that the spines lined up perfectly, "he sleeps on the roof. Or somewhere else. Sometimes the green."

"Naked," Janelle added. "He sleeps on the green *naked*."

"Or in classrooms," Nate said. "Someone said they went into differential equations and he was asleep in the corner of the room under a Pokémon comforter."

"Your boy has not been well," Janelle said. "Nothing was right here without you. But now you're back! Everything will be okay again."

Nate left not long afterward so that Janelle and Stevie could talk. Stevie found she was exhausted, though. Earlier that evening, she had been at the Funky Munkee. Now she was back at Ellingham. Everything that happened in between made no sense. Sensing that Stevie needed to sleep, Janelle made up the bed to her personal satisfaction and watched as Stevie drank a full bottle of water to help her readjust to the altitude. Then she put a second bottle by Stevie's bedside.

"Vi's going to meet us at brunch tomorrow," she said. "Get some rest. I'm right next door if you need me."

Janelle knew that Stevie sometimes had panic attacks at night.

"Thanks," Stevie said, "for everything."

When Janelle was gone, Stevie stood at her window for a long time, looking out at the dark and her own reflection. Like the stairs, the window came with a memory. The night before Hayes died, she had a dream. At least, she was pretty sure it was a dream. She remembered light, and looking at her wall, and seeing words on her wall, like the Truly Devious lettering. She had not been able to make them all out and the message was scrambled in her mind. Stevie had awakened with a jolt and rolled out of bed, crawled along the floor to this very window. She had pushed a heavy textbook out of it, hoping to strike anyone who was lurking underneath, but no one was.

It never made any sense that anyone would project a message like that on her wall. It was too much work, making the image, getting something to project it, hiding in the dark. People did complicated things at Ellingham, but there was no one she could think of who would do something that elaborate to her. . . .

Except maybe David. David was probably capable of an elaborate joke. But he liked her, as it turned out, so why do it?

And this had happened right before Hayes died. What were the chances?

Janelle had spoken to her that night, talked her through it, about dreams that were so vivid they completely mimicked reality. It was why some people think they see ghosts in the night, or figures by their bed. The space between sleep and consciousness can be thin. And Stevie had been fully immersed in the Ellingham story on that day, and had actually gone into the tunnel where the kidnappers had been. Her brain was full of the crime and was projecting it back at her.

Stevie turned back and looked at the place on the wall where the message had been, even if only in her mind. What had it said? *Riddle, riddle on the wall* . . . something murder. Something about a body in a field . . . something Alice.

This was the wall that she had shared with Ellie. Minerva was so empty, so doomed. Dottie Epstein and Hayes Major were dead, and Element Walker was on the run.

Was it Ellie? Was the note some kind of art thing? Did it have something to do with the trick she played on Hayes with the dry ice? Did Ellie have a broken sense of humor, or did she secretly hate everyone?

Ellie didn't seem like the hating kind, but you never knew.

Stevie crossed the room and went to her bag, which was resting on the floor in the corner of the room, and removed the tin. When she reached inside this time, she wanted only one of the objects—the photographs. One in particular. It was thicker than the others, because it was actually stuck to another photo. What was between the photos was the key.

It was a word.

A single word, cut out of a magazine. The word US.

This word, these two letters stuck between some old photos, was the reason Stevie had to be here, because this word was the first clue in eighty years. The Ellingham case was often called the Truly Devious case, because the family had received a letter that week, informing of the crime to come. It was composed of cut-out letters from magazines and newspapers. Stevie, like any person devoted to the case, could recite it by heart:

LOOK! a RiddLE!
TiME FoR FUN!

ShoULd WE USE
a RoPE oR GUN?

KNiVEs aRE shaRP
ANd GLEAM so pREttY

Poison's slow,
Which is a pity

Fire is festive,
drowning's slow

Hanging's a
Ropy Way To Go

a broken head,
a nasty fall

a car colliding
With a Wall

Bombs make a
very jolly noise

Such ways to
punish naughty boys!

What shall WE use?
WE can't decide.

JUST LIKE YOU CANNOT RUN OR HIDE.

HA HA.

TRULY, DEVIOUS

What she had found in Ellie's room was proof that there were students on the campus who loved gangsters, who wrote poetry about taking down the king on the hill who liked to play games, and who were cutting words out of magazines and gluing them into things. In short, she had found that Truly Devious could have been a student here at Ellingham. And if Truly Devious could have been a student, then a student could take them down, even all these years later.

That is, if this student could deal with the person who was somewhere above her now . . . someone she longed to go up and see, someone whose presence thrummed through the floorboards. She felt her body growing warm just knowing David was so close. She recalled every sense, every touch. The soft curl of his hair, the curve of his neck, his kiss.

Edward King's voice was in her head, making a mockery of everything she had ever felt about David. She could not go upstairs. She could not look for him. Maybe she had to avoid him forever. Avoid the feeling. Avoid all contact. That was the only way.

She clutched her comforter and pulled it over her face, blotting out the scene and calling down the night.

You know the story of Ellingham Academy and the famous kidnapping/murder plot. But did you know these twists in the tale?

1. **ALICE IN THE ATTIC:** According to one story, Albert Ellingham engineered the kidnapping himself as part of a game. When the game went wrong and two people died, he had to cover up what he had done. He took his daughter, Alice, back to the house and raised her there in the attic. Servants were told not to go there, even when they heard her footsteps above them. Eventually, Alice became too old for the attic, and when she could not escape, took her own life. Her ghost walks the floors there, and some people say you can hear her playing with her toys.

2. **THE SECRET OF THE LAKE:** Another story claims that Iris and Alice Ellingham were not kidnapped at all. In this version, Iris had a breakdown and murdered Alice by drowning her in the lake on the property. This event was witnessed by a student named Dottie Epstein. In order to keep this secret, Dottie was killed and the kidnapping story was invented. Iris was kept hidden, but she eventually escaped and killed herself. In despair over what had transpired, Albert Ellingham later drained the lake. Naturally,

the ghosts of Iris, Alice, and Dottie still appear on the edge of where the lake once was. So. Many. Ghosts.

3. **THE SUNKEN TREASURE:** Pirates, rejoice! Is there a sunken treasure to be had? This story claims that after his wife's body was found, Albert Ellingham collected her jewels and dropped them into Lake Champlain in a weighted box. So if you have scuba gear and some time on your hands, you might want to have a look. No ghosts, but treasure is better anyway.

4. **THE HEIR TO THE THRONE:** If you thought that last one sounded good, this story will blow you away. This report claims that after the kidnapping and murders, Albert Ellingham rewrote his will, leaving his fortune to anyone who could find his daughter, dead or alive, provided they were not responsible for the crimes. The Ellingham estate and businesses are worth in excess of two billion dollars today. Get hunting!

5. **THE KIDNAPPING THAT NEVER WAS:** No ghosts or fortunes here, just a damn good game. This story claims that the kidnapping and murders at Ellingham Academy never happened at all. The entire affair—the search, the investigation, the bodies—all of it was part of Albert Ellingham's greatest game. The student who died, Dottie Epstein, was an actor. The game concluded when he faked his own death in

an explosion two years later. In this happy-ending version, all the players were alive and lived together in complete anonymity, leaving fortune and fame behind. Or at least fame. They probably took the fortune.

So which one do you like? The ghosts? The treasure? Or the happy ever after?

5

"I WANT TO JUMP IN THOSE," JANELLE SAID, HOPPING AHEAD ON THE way to breakfast. "But I don't want to mess up what they've done. It's so tempting."

The next morning, Janelle, Stevie, and Nate were heading toward the dining hall. On weekends, the school offered brunch. Stevie had usually slept through this before, but the excitement of being back had woken her early. Even Nate emerged and came downstairs. They were now making their way to the green on an aggressively beautiful fall morning. The sky was a vibrant royal blue, a *throbbing* blue. Some of the maintenance crew were blowing leaves into gigantic mounds.

Janelle was dressed for the occasion in a burnished orange sweater and jeans and a chunky black scarf, with a spicy autumnal perfume that smelled of bergamot and clove. Stevie was wearing the least wrinkled and most likely to be clean clothes from the trash bag—a black hoodie and some stretched out gray leggings. This was not surprising, as 90 percent of Stevie's clothes were black or gray or stretched out and her tops were more likely to be hooded than not. She marveled at Janelle, who moved through the patches of sun that came through the leaves, with her perfect style. It wasn't fancy, but it made every moment feel like an occasion. Many people existed; Janelle lived.

Stevie looked up at the thick canopy of leaves over her head as she wound her way down the paths that snaked toward the Great House. These were the early changing leaves, the prime ones, the burnished golds and the meaty reds. As she reached the green, the view widened. Up here, on the mountain, she had one of the best views of the bright halo of color that overtook the land. The view was hallucinatory, with oceans of gold and orange all around the horizon, marbled with red that looked like rivers of lava coming down from the mountaintops.

She had never been an autumn person; the shortening of the days gave her the jitters, possibly because she had been prone to anxiety attacks at night, and the more night, the more possible anxiety. But it didn't have to be that way, and she decided she was going to become an autumn person here. Flannel was okay. Apples were fine. Pumpkins were the watermelons of fall. Were these the thoughts autumn people had?

Was this even real? Last night, with Edward King in the living room and the plane ride and the bargain, and now this almost-psychedelic view? Had she lost her mind some time ago?

"This one," Janelle said, stepping up to one of the massive leaf piles. "I'm going in."

Nate turned and regarded one of the piles with a scientific air.

"Lot of animal feces in there," he said.

"Nate," Janelle said.

"I'm just saying. Leaves are like a big litter box. Lots of animals up here. Foxes. Deer. Raccoons. Moose."

"No moose," Stevie said.

"Birds," Nate went on. "So much bird shit. Bat shit. Lots of bats. Bat shit is very valuable, you know. It's called guano."

"I know what guano is," Janelle said in a warning tone. "But I don't want to hear about poop. I want *crispy leaf fun*."

"Squirrels still have to poop," Nate continued.

"Squirrels have to poop," Stevie repeated sagely.

"Why are you ruining my perfect fall morning?" Janelle asked.

"We all have a calling," Nate said. "This is mine."

Janelle made a low sound under her breath. Stevie got the feeling her friends were putting on a bit of a show for her—Janelle was extra perky, Nate a bit more dour. They were showing her it was all fine and normal and just like before. Except, as they walked, Stevie was noting little objects on the trees, on light poles, on corners of buildings—discreet little orbs.

The eyes of Edward King.

"There's a lot of new security," she said.

"Oh yeah," Janelle said. "They did that last week."

"I, for one, hail our new security overlords," Nate said, loudly, at the nearest orb.

"I think it's a good idea," Janelle added. "We're pretty remote here, and . . . things happened."

They were coming up on the cupola, where a makeshift memorial to Hayes was sitting in a state of minor decay. What shocked Stevie the most was the sheer quantity of . . . sad. There were flowers, not scattered here or there in single roses, but bunches. Bunches sitting on dried and desiccated bunches, filling the entire floor. There were drawings and notes and pictures. There were small electronic candles, because real candles would have made the whole thing go up in a giant blaze.

"They keep coming," Janelle said. "I guess they're slowing a little, but every day the deliveries come and maintenance puts them here."

The wind stirred some of the now-dying flowers on the memorial.

"This is cheerful," Nate said. "Can we eat? Let's be morbid over food."

The Ellingham dining hall was a large space that looked like a ski chalet. It had a high, peaked ceiling with exposed beams that crossed the space. These were now occupied by a line of jack-o'-lanterns, looking down judgmentally over the assembled. The cafeteria at Stevie's old school was a festival of linoleum, with hot metal trays full of tacos and tater tots and oversteamed broccoli. The Ellingham dining hall had been given more money to feed fewer people, and it did it with some style. It had automatic sensing dispensers that filled your bottle with still or sparkling water. The menus were written on blackboards in colored chalk. Brunch was a serious affair, with an omelet station (with tofu, if you didn't eat eggs). There were fresh pancakes and waffles, made with all kinds of berries, or bananas, or chocolate chips. Every breakfast meat was represented, along with their vegetarian counterparts. There was a make-your-own smoothie station, fresh bread, local honey, a whole shelf of teas, different coffee blends with every kind of milk. And, of course, there was maple syrup, the very lifeblood of Vermont. It was this warm syrup smell, along with the wood smoke on the breeze, that said Ellingham to Stevie.

Stevie got a custom waffle with chocolate chips, and a full ramekin of warm syrup. As she turned with her tray, she saw that she had been noticed. Assembled in front of her was all of Ellingham. Or, most of Ellingham. On the left, sitting with a few people from Juno, was Gretchen, Hayes's ex-girlfriend, the pianist. She had lent Hayes five hundred dollars and finally dumped him when she got tired of his user ways. Stevie had seen Gretchen and Hayes arguing on the day Hayes died. It was Gretchen who told Stevie how Hayes recruited other people to do his work. Gretchen was hard to miss, with her mighty crown of fiery red hair.

Two tables down were Maris and Dash, the other two people who had worked on Hayes's video. Maris was a singer. She had jet-black hair and tended to dress like she was always about to go perform a set at some smoky little cabaret. Today she wore a snug black sweater and a pair of jeans with high boots. She was fully made up, even though it was still pretty early on a Sunday. Maris always had a smoky eye. Dash was a stage manager who wore large, floppy clothes. He was the one who really ran the video production. They saw Stevie, and Maris waved. This drew more attention, and got Kazim Bazir, the head of the student union, up on his feet and hurrying over.

"Stevie!" he called. "Oh my God! When did you get back? This is amazing!"

"Last night," Stevie replied, suddenly feeling shy.

It was a nice greeting, even though Stevie and Kaz didn't really know each other very well. Kaz was always enthusiastic. His special interest was the environment, and he spent a lot of time getting Ellingham to convert over to composting toilets. Kaz cared a lot about composting toilets.

There was someone else watching closely—a small person with large, luminous eyes. She was wearing a brown sweater and peering at Stevie over the top of her tablet.

Germaine Batt.

Technically, Germaine had done nothing wrong. It wasn't her fault that her story was the thing that made Stevie's parents pull her out. But the feeling was still there.

David was not in the dining hall.

"How do you feel?" Nate asked as they walked to a table.

"Like the prettiest girl on syrup mountain," Stevie replied.

They took a table by the window. Janelle's head was on a swivel. She was watching for Vi, of course. The three of them settled in to have their brunch. Stevie sliced into the crisp chocolate-chip waffle and dipped it into the warm syrup.

Vi Harper-Tomo came bursting into the dining hall. Stevie

had never really seen anyone burst into anywhere before, but that's what they did—sending the door flying back, rushing in with arms flailing. Vi was dressed in their favorite outfit— wide white overalls and a gray sweatshirt, silver-blond hair spiked high.

Vi greeted Stevie much as Janelle had, with an incomprehensible string of affection.

"I can't believe it," they said.

They turned to Janelle. There were greeting kisses at breakfast now, like a couple from TV. Nate tore his waffle slowly as the pair leaned cozily into one another.

"You know we're cute," Janelle said to him.

"Cuteness is my favorite," he said.

"It's good for when you write romances in your book, right?" Stevie said.

"I don't write romance. I write about finding dragons and breaking magic rocks in half."

"The *real* magic rocks are the friends we make along the way," Stevie replied. "Right?"

"He's happy for us," Janelle said. "This is how he shows it."

Nate looked up at all of them, dark shadows under his eyes.

"This is why I prefer books to people."

"We love you too," Janelle said.

Even though Janelle had food, she accompanied Vi up to the food line. Nate centered his scrambled eggs on his plate.

"So," he said. "What changed your parents' minds?"

Stevie dunked her waffle nervously into the syrup pool.

"Who knows?"

"They just said, 'We're sending you back'?"

"I mean . . ." Stevie nervously rubbed under her eye. "We talked about it a little, but . . ."

She was dancing on the edge of the truth, telling a lie of omission. One step could send her into falsehood.

"I don't know what motivates my parents," she said.

There. She lied. So simple. It fell out of her mouth. *Plop.*

"You guys ever hear anything about Ellie?" Stevie said, changing the conversation. "What's going on with that?"

Nate was still studying Stevie's expression, but then he seemed to give up and returned to his eggs.

"Nothing," he said. "I mean, they looked. There were police around for a few days. Low-key, but they were around. I think they may have had dogs, even. She must have gone to Burlington. She knows a lot of people there."

Stevie sipped at her coffee and looked out the window. They were facing toward the back, to the thick line of trees that bordered the property. During the day, they were a bright, bold wall. At night, they loomed and contained multitudes. The area where the school was was flat, but it dipped down dramatically as it went toward the road, and there was a river that bordered it on two sides. The other way out was up, toward jagged rocks and higher peaks and thicker woods.

Getting out would not have been easy. Stevie wasn't even sure Ellie had a coat on when she vanished that night.

"It's not your fault," Nate said.

"What?"

"It's not your fault," he repeated. "Whatever Ellie has done—why she ran—that's not on you."

"I know that," she said, concentrating on the squares in her waffles. "Are people saying this is my fault?"

"No," he said quickly. "No. Just . . . no. Forget I said anything. I think Vi and Janelle are about to make out on top of those mugs."

Stevie turned and saw Vi and Janelle locked in an intense embrace by the coffee station.

"It's been a long week," Nate said. "Don't leave again. Don't leave me with these people."

"Which people?"

"Any people."

"I don't count as people?"

"Of course not," he said. "It's been all feelings and love. I want to go back to numbness and avoidance. You're great at that stuff."

She smiled and tapped her phone to check the time.

"I have to go," she said. "Meeting with Call Me Charles."

"Go forth and learn or whatever, I'll see you at home."

Home.

Yes. This was home. This home welcomed her as she was, which was unusual in her experience. It was also, and more familiarly, the place where she had to tell the biggest lies.

April 14, 1936, 3:00 a.m.

"WE HAVE TO READ THE SIGNS," EDDIE SAID. "THE DARK STARS MAY have aligned for us. It's time for us to go."

Eddie was squatting on the floor of the gymnasium, bobbing lightly on the balls of his feet like a broken jack-in-the-box. Francis did not believe in Eddie's astrological fascinations, but she usually entertained them. Not tonight. Everything was coming unspooled.

"Let's *run*. Let's start the plan."

"No," Francis heard herself say. Her voice was like stone. "No. Not now. We'll never make it now. Don't you know what this means?"

"It means the dark star . . ."

Edward was about to go on one of his poetic nonsense trips about the dark star and the silver princess and all these characters he had in his head. He took his poetry too far sometimes, got caught up in symbols. Francis cut this off.

"Whatever is going on," she said, "our letter is mixed up in it. There will be cops, Eddie. Lots of cops."

"So what? We're going to be outlaws!"

"If we go now," Francis said, "we'll get caught in the first hour. We need to wait. Be cool about it."

"Where's the fun in that?" Edward said, moving close to her, his breath on her lips.

"The fun," she said, pushing him back gently, "is making our escape and getting out. When we go, we go forever. We need to be *smart*."

This is where it always fell apart with Eddie. He was so wild, he had the imagination, the dreams. But he didn't think about practicalities, like G-men, police dogs, and roadblocks. He wanted to be an outlaw without the discipline or practice of being an outlaw. It was up to her to keep him in line. That's why she had done so much of her own preparations. She had to get back to Minerva, back to her room. The things she needed were there.

"They're making us leave anyway," he said.

"Maybe for a day or two. Maybe only for a few hours. You need to trust me. Keep your cool. Go home."

She pressed her lips hard against his and left the gymnasium. She couldn't risk using the tunnel. Miss Nelson might be in it, and the hatch on the other end would likely be bolted. She would have to go above ground.

There was one advantage tonight, a blue sulfuric fog. This would likely be her only protection against the men with the shotguns. The air was bitingly cold now and the fog went into her nose and mouth, tangling its way down into her lungs. She was up by the library, and in theory she only had to make a straight shot across the top of the green to get home.

But the door would obviously be guarded and the entire area exposed. She would have to take the long route around, all the way through the far end of the campus, through the half-finished sites down near the road.

She stayed low, moving from one tree to the next. She tripped over the roots and branches, and the leaves crunched under her feet. She saw the first gunmen in their overalls and coats, their shotguns slung over their shoulders. There were three of them, talking together, by the cupola. She got down, her heart beating fast. They would shoot tonight. They would not hesitate. For one second, she tried to imagine the hot bullet sinking into her chest, the impact. It made her heart race painfully and her hands grew slick. She considered calling out, asking them for help. They would take her home to Minerva. She would get in trouble, but she wouldn't get shot.

No. She pressed to the ground. She would be a cat. They loved cats here. "Cats know best," Albert Ellingham would say. She would slink and slide. It was a big campus. She had the courage. Tonight, she would prove herself.

The hardest part would be crossing the road. That was the most open area. She would have to climb down the decline into the woods and cross somewhere in the dark. Francis made her way down the steep slope. Her expensive coat caught on brambles and made her trip, so she tucked it up and crab-walked her way down several feet. If she tried to stand, she was likely to tumble and hit every tree and rock all the way to the river. The rock cut her hands as she grabbed at the ground. Everything smelled of dirt and decaying leaves.

"What's that?" one of the men said.

She froze.

A light shone through the trees.

"Probably an animal," another replied.

Francis was very close to being sick. She swallowed hard and waited, not moving an inch. She froze. It must have been fifteen or twenty minutes later before she moved again. Once she had made it a good distance from the statues and the men, she crept to the road's edge and, taking a deep breath, she ran across. It was a very slender road, so it was just a few steps. She fell into the culvert on the other side and bashed her face. But she did not cry out. She crawled on her belly into the dark.

Then, she went back up the hill. This was much harder. Her breath was labored now. Cops and robbers. G-men and guns, sneaking in the dark. And she was doing it. Francis Josephine Crane, the flour princess of Fifth Avenue, was crawling through the dirt and the night. She dug her nails into the ground with determination, not caring about breaking them. She didn't care about her clothes or her shoes. *This* was life.

She crested the top of the incline and emerged on the other side of the road. Now she had to wind her way back up to Minerva. She moved slowly, working her way from building to tree to statue. The fog wrapped around her like a fur coat. It was *easy*.

By the time she reached Minerva, she no longer worried about how she would get back inside. She would simply find a way. The door would be locked, but the window of her room was not. She went around the back of the building, then peered around the corner. No one was outside. She crept along and made her way to room two. She tested the window first, trying to push it open. It did not give.

Dottie's room? Dottie was a sneak too. Did Dottie leave her window propped? She sometimes talked about liking to have it open a bit, how it reminded her of home, with the open window by the fire escape.

She crept over to room three and looked at the window of the dark room. There was a tiny, tiny gap, only as wide as Francis's finger, but it was enough. She got a stick and levered it up, ever so carefully, then pushed it, working slow and silent. Then she hoisted herself inside and closed it, inch by precious inch. She was inside Dottie's room, which, while technically like her own, was so much shabbier. There were no fur throws, no special furniture, no skis, no trunks of extra clothes, no radio or phonograph. Just what the school provided, and books. Piles of books. Neat, and all over.

Francis went to the door, and seeing no one, stepped out into the hallway and . . .

"Francis Crane!"

The overhead light came on, and Miss Nelson stood there, looking flushed and furious.

Francis Crane, the flour princess of Fifth Avenue and future outlaw, was busted cold just footsteps from her door. She opened her mouth to speak, though she was not sure what she would say. Something would come out. Miss Nelson, though she was in charge, was generally passive. She would say she was sorry and . . .

Miss Nelson was not passive tonight. Her rounded features looked sharper, and there was something in her face that suggested she knew exactly where Francis had been.

"In here," Miss Nelson said coldly, pointing to the common room. Behind her, a figure appeared. A man in overalls and a flat cap, holding a shotgun.

Francis forgot to look surprised at this, and Miss Nelson's eyes grew narrow. Francis had given it all away. She did as she was told, going into the common room, where one lamp was lit. The man with the shotgun went to the front window to look out.

"You will sit there," Miss Nelson said, pointing to the couch. "And you will not move. At all. You will sleep there."

She turned to the man by the door.

"She doesn't move from that spot," Miss Nelson said.

6

THE GREAT HOUSE WOULD NEVER FAIL TO IMPRESS STEVIE. THIS WAS exactly the effect it was intended to have. It was Albert Ellingham's palace, designed by several of the most famous architects and designers of the era, to be a showstopper. The wood was rosewood, imported from India. The pink marble, the Austrian crystal, the Scottish stained glass ... everything in sight had been brought from some corner of the world for the express purpose of being part of this room, just to be seen, to be admired by Albert Ellingham and all he chose to invite.

Right next to the front door, there was a head of steel-colored closely cropped hair, and under it was Larry, as dependable as a grandfather clock, sitting at his large wooden desk. He was staring grimly into an Ellingham mug.

"Hey, Larry," Stevie said. "What's wrong with your coffee?"

"Some jackass bought pumpkin-flavored K-Cups for the machine. If I wanted to ruin my day like that I'd go ahead and eat a candle."

"Not a PSL fan?"

"A what?"

The door to the small security room behind him was tipped open. This had originally been one of the Ellingham receiving parlors. When Stevie had last seen it, it had some desks and a few monitors. Now the furniture had been removed on two walls and replaced by narrow control desks that faced walls of large mounted screens, stacked two high, showing every angle of Ellingham Academy, with the views switching every ten seconds or so.

"That looks . . . complete," she said.

"Let me give you the tour," he replied, standing up. "Come in."

Stevie followed cautiously. If Larry was showing her the security system, it was for a reason. He took a seat and typed something on a keyboard. Stevie's name came up on one of the screens, then he began to see her morning's journey told in reverse. There she was at the Great House door. There she was approaching the Great House. There she was walking down a pathway, alone. She stopped to stare at one of the cameras. She was scowling at it. There she was leaving breakfast. There was a close-up of Nate, Janelle, and Stevie going in to breakfast. . . .

"How is it doing this?" she said. "Facial recognition?"

"Sometimes it gets it wrong, and it's not very useful at night, but overall, it's not bad. There are also sensors in different locations that can read your ID at six feet. They call them 'listening posts.' There are over eight hundred of them."

He hit return and her images were cleared.

"Here's the thing," Larry said. "People don't tend to change their behavior without reason. But make people see why they should . . ."

"Point made," Stevie said. "I get it. You see it all."

Larry did the thing where he pointed two fingers toward his own eyes and then to her.

"And you leave any further inquiries to the appropriate authorities. Not that there will be any further inquiries."

"Appropriate," Stevie said. "Authorities. Yes."

"Good. They're waiting for you upstairs. You know the office."

Stevie backed into the main hall, then headed up the grand, sweeping staircase. On the landing, there was the painting of the Ellingham family, done by their friend Leonard Holmes Nair. You couldn't just walk by the painting. It demanded to be seen. It wasn't overly large, maybe four feet high, which was nothing in proportion to the space. It was the color that gripped you first—the blue and yellow that swirled through the sky and slipped into the figures of the family. The bodies were almost an afterthought; the faces were the focus, and they blended in with the moon and the trees. It was like the landscape and the skyline were absorbing them, pulling them apart from each other and away from the world.

It was a frightening painting.

"Yes," a voice said. "But we have that. We don't *need* it. We'll get it in a year or two."

The voice belonged to Dr. Jenny Quinn, the assistant

head of the school, the one who looked like she drank student tears and ate lesser academics.

"He wants to have a say, Jenny."

That was Dr. Charles Scott. They were having a discussion directly above her, on the third-floor landing. They were not speaking loudly, but the acoustics in the hall were better than most theaters, and Stevie was directly under them.

"He *shouldn't* have a say. Do you really want to be part of his narrative? Do you want him to be able to say he made Ellingham 'safe'?"

That had to be a reference to Edward King. Stevie backed up a bit, to make sure she was not visible. But there was no hiding from Larry, who saw her lingering.

"No," Dr. Scott said. "I don't like him any more than you do. But wouldn't you rather have him do this? At least it's useful. He feels like he's done something and then he'll go away, hopefully."

"He's not going to go away. The man is a disease and his son isn't much better."

"I think that's unfair," Dr. Scott said. "Isn't it worth trying to make him into someone who could do some good, rather than become a copy of his father at some prep school somewhere?"

"I think you're fooling yourself. I want to have a board meeting."

"And I'm fine with that."

"*Right upstairs, Stevie,*" Larry said, his voice booming up the steps.

The conversation above her stopped abruptly, and a few seconds later, Dr. Scott appeared next to her, having come down the back steps, the ones the servants used.

Dr. Charles Scott, aka Call Me Charles, was the head of the school and Stevie's adviser. Out of all the Ellingham faculty, he had the most bouncy personality, the one that said "Learning is Fun!" in giant Comic Sans. He tended to dress in expensive geek chic—superhero T-shirts with designer jeans. His hair was somewhere between blond and the earliest hints of gray. Today he wore a fitted black cashmere V-neck and gray wool pants, looking every inch the aged version of the perfect New England preppy guy. He sproinged up to her like a cartoon tiger.

"Hey!" he said. "Look who it is! I'm so glad your parents changed their minds."

"Me too," she said.

"Come on. Let's talk."

Charles's office was along the right-hand corridor. All of the upper floors of the Great House were open to the main foyer, except for the attic. The dark wooden doors were all very serious and handsome, but for Dr. Scott's, which had a message board full of stickers and signs that said things like CHALLENGE ME and STAND BACK, I'M GOING TO TRY SCIENCE. His office had been Iris Ellingham's dressing room, the famous dressing room that Flora Robinson disappeared into the night of the kidnappings. Many of the original features were still there. The pale silver wallpaper glowed bright in the autumn morning light. That was the real thing; Stevie recognized it from the photos. Some of the shelves and wall fittings were still there. Now, of course, the room was also full of bookshelves, a desk, chairs, file cabinets, a printer. Any open space on the wall was covered in Dr. Scott's diplomas and certificates. He had a lot.

He waved Stevie into a chair and sat behind his desk, where he clasped his hands together.

"How *are* you, Stevie?" he asked.

"Fine?"

He nodded and examined her for a moment, taking in her expression and body language. She straightened up.

"I can't tell you how happy I was to hear you were coming back," he said. "It's very brave what you're doing, after all that's happened."

"It's fine," Stevie said.

He made a noise of satisfaction.

"You may have noticed we have some new security around here," he said.

"I saw."

"It may provide you with an additional layer of reassurance. Nothing is going to happen here. We had some tragic events this semester, but that's behind us."

Both Larry and Call Me Charles had now brought up the security system. Both had their reasons, but were they also telling her they knew Edward King brought her back? If so, why not just *say* it? Maybe no one knew. It was possible.

Whatever the case, it was making her paranoid.

"Do you feel ready to get back to work?" he asked.

Stevie felt very ready to get back to her work, which was dealing with the fact that she had made the first major breakthrough in the Ellingham case in eighty years. But he probably meant schoolwork, and the answer to that was no, she was not ready for that.

"Definitely," she lied.

"I've messaged all your teachers, so we'll get you back up to speed. There may be some bumps along the way, but we'll work it out."

There was a clock ticking somewhere in the room, loud, like a bomb. She glanced around for where the noise was coming from and saw a heavy green marble clock on the mantel, surrounded by books and framed photographs.

"Was that clock there before?" she asked.

"No," Charles said. "We were rearranging some things from Albert Ellingham's office and I brought it up here. Isn't that a beauty? The story is that it belonged to Marie Antoinette. I don't know if that was ever proven. I heard there was a piece of Marie Antoinette's porcelain here at some point. . . ."

"A shepherdess," Stevie said.

Charles blinked behind his Warby Parkers.

"Iris collected antique French porcelain," Stevie said.

"Of course you would know about that," he said. "Anyway, it seemed so sad to have something so beautiful in a room no one really goes in. It should be looked at. But, let's keep to the subject at hand. Do you know this book?"

He pulled a copy of *Truly Devious: The Ellingham Murders* by Dr. Irene Fenton from a stack of books on his desk. Stevie had worn this book through. It was the first read many people did on the subject.

Stevie nodded.

"I assumed so. I got a call from the author. Dr. Fenton teaches at the University of Vermont, in Burlington. She's working on an updated version and she's looking for a research assistant. We've placed several students at the university as research assistants. In your case, I don't think we've ever had such a good fit for a project. How would you feel about doing that?"

Stevie tried not to actually bounce in the seat, but this was unsuccessful. Her spine became a spring, and she bolted up. Life had handed her a gift, a beautiful, unexpected gift.

"What would I have to do?" she asked.

"Organize research, check facts." Charles said it all casually, as if this wasn't the greatest thing in the world. "I can give you some credit for English and history for the work, as well as credit toward your individual project. And because of all the work you've done on this subject already, I can advance you a little time and credit to make up for anything you've lost."

She was already nodding.

"Thanks," she said.

"You never have to thank me for work you've done yourself. And I figured you would say yes, so I've set up your first meeting for tomorrow. Take the Burlington coach in the morning. She'll meet you at the Skinny Pancake at noon. It's a coffee and crepe place on the waterfront. You'll like it.

Very popular. Sound all right?"

It sounded better than all right.

"Now . . ." He opened his laptop. "Let's get you updated on all your units for your classes as well. I don't know if you happened to continue any work on your reading or your language learning modules . . ."

Hahahahahahahahahahahahahahahahahahahahahaha.

A half hour later, with a new schedule and an alarming set of "personal academic benchmarks" to meet, Stevie was released back into the wild, feeling a confusing blend of joy and terror, which was often a ticket to a ride on the anxiety roller coaster. There were people around, and she could have spoken to any of them. She could find Janelle and Nate and Vi. They would be happy to talk to her.

Stevie was not going to do any of those things. She often found that when everything felt a little too much, she could not talk to anyone, even if she actually wanted to. She had a tendency to go where other people were not, to step into shadows when people walked toward her. She had a fondness for headphones and screens and ducking away, even as part of her wanted to be with friends. Which meant she was going to the library to find some people who were probably dead. Namely, she was going to find Frankie and Edward, and Frankie and Edward were most likely to be found in the materials she had been hoping to get from Kyoko Obi, the school librarian.

The library, called Asteria, was one of the campus's most magnificent buildings. Albert Ellingham thought libraries were holy spaces of learning, so he designed it to look like a small Gothic church, with a turret. On the inside, it had a wild quality—because of some architectural peculiarity, when you opened the door, it sent in a channel of air that swirled up through the open space, up and up around the balconies with their intricate spun-steel metalwork that was like petrified lace. Colored light poured in from the stained-glass windows that portrayed Greek titans: Helios, Selene, Metis, Eos, Leto, Pallas, and Perseus.

Kyoko sat at a stool at a monumental desk, looking like a judge on high. Except, in this case, the judge wore a fleece and still had the marks from a bike helmet in her hair. Kyoko also ran the school's biking club and actually went up and down the entrance path on her bike every day, a feat that should easily have qualified her for the Olympics. The library was sparsely populated—a few people sat at the massive working tables, and they all had headphones on, so it seemed okay to speak.

"You don't waste time," Kyoko said, greeting her. "I only just got the message that you were back."

Stevie meant to smile and nod, but she ended up enacting the shrug emoticon.

"I need some research material," Stevie said. "On here, on the school. I need to see anything about the first class. Lists of students for sure. Do you have those?"

Kyoko nodded and took a swig from her Ellingham water bottle. She put a little sign out that said: THE LIBRARIAN WILL BE BACK and waved Stevie through the dark wooden door with the words *Library Office* written in gold.

The front part of the Ellingham library was a grand place, with its iron and glass and dark, carved wood, and the glorious selection of books. Many of the books had been around since the school opened in 1935—fine, handpicked volumes, many bound in leather, silent witnesses to the events that unfolded there. But it was the back office of the library that got Stevie excited. The back office contained the large metal shelving units of document boxes.

If you loved crime, a document box was a beautiful thing. Anything could be in it. Files. Clues. Evidence. The document box was the thing to pick through, to find the lead, to find the single sentence on the single piece of paper that made you stand so suddenly that your head spun and then you'd know that you cracked the case.

That's how it happened in Stevie's head, anyway.

"The early archive is back here," Kyoko said, indicating one of the shelving units. "You want . . ."

"The first year. 1935–36."

"Right," Kyoko said, heading to the end of the first row of shelves. "The 1935–1936 school year at Ellingham Academy was incomplete because of the kidnappings. The school's first full academic year started in the fall of 1938. You know all that."

Stevie nodded.

"It was also a very small class. It was the experiment year. So the records aren't as extensive. There was no full yearbook. However, the school had produced a guide for the first class."

She opened a folio box and removed a small clothbound book. On the front it read: ELLINGHAM ACADEMY. The paper was thick and brownish, and the ink was a brownish red. The lettering looked hand-drawn.

"There is a box of photographs as well," Kyoko said, handing Stevie a flat storage box. From the rattle of the contents and the weight, it didn't sound like it contained a tremendous amount. "You can take those out into the main study room."

Stevie lifted the box and followed Kyoko back out, then settled herself at one of the big wooden tables and switched on a work lamp. She tried to contain herself as she opened the book. The first page contained an elaborate map of the campus, indicating buildings that were complete and buildings to come. There was a letter from Albert Ellingham welcoming everyone, a list of teachers and faculty . . . Stevie kept flipping until she got to the students. Each one got a third of a page. Frankie was staring up at her from the bottom of the very first page of entries. There was the girl who had dressed as Bonnie Parker. Stevie read the entry underneath.

Francis Josephine Crane, New York City
Birthday: February 15, 1919
Interests: Chemistry, films, ballet

"Got you," Stevie said under her breath.

A few pages later, she found the next person she was searching for.

Edward Pierce Davenport, Boston
Birthday: November 12, 1918
Interests: Literature, opera, art

In his school photo, Edward had a rakish grin, like he knew something the others did not.

A bit like David.

Stevie dug through the box of photographs. Many were of the buildings or the construction sites. Some were shots of the mountain view. There were pictures of the students sitting at desks and worktables in stilted poses. One pose was a dead ringer for an ad for an ambulance-chasing legal firm with about ten people gathered around, smiling at one open book. Many of the furnishings were exactly the same as they were now, including pictures in this very library. She easily found Francis and Edward in a few of these photos. One thing jumped out at her: Francis and Edward looked rich. Francis was wearing two different fur coats in the photos—one short white jacket and a longer, dark one. Edward also had a long fur coat, and he stood with the casual ease of a rich guy—the lean, the half smile.

Could these two students have kidnapped Iris and Alice Ellingham and Dottie Epstein? That would have been impossible, surely? Someone would have noticed that two students were missing on the day of the kidnapping, right? How would they have gotten off campus? They probably didn't have cars. *Why* would two students kidnap Iris and Alice Ellingham? And they wouldn't have been able to also beat up George

Marsh, Albert Ellingham's FBI agent friend, in the middle of the night, or make the ransom calls, or have a boat on Lake Champlain two days later to collect the additional ransom money. Not alone. Could they have been working with other people?

Did any of this make sense?

Dottie Epstein turned up in the photos as well, and she did not look rich. Her clothes were plain, and she wore the same ones in most of the photos. But she looked much happier than Edward or Francis. Her smile was always wide, and she usually had a book in her hands or under her arm.

"Can I scan these?" she asked Kyoko.

"Sure."

She allowed Stevie into the back again and pointed her to the scanner.

"When I first got here," she said to Kyoko, "you showed me some old library records, things the students requested."

"Yeah?"

"Could I see it again?"

"You really are jumping back in," Kyoko said with a smile. "I'll go and get it."

When Stevie had first looked at this list, it was to see the many materials Dottie Epstein had requested. Her initials, *DE*, were next to her items. But someone else had requested pulp magazines: *Gun Molls Magazine, Vice Squad Detective, Dime Detective, All True Facts Detective Stories*. The initials next to most of these were *FC*. Francis Crane.

"Do you have any of these?" Stevie said.

"I've looked for them," Kyoko said. "I'd love to find them. But they must have disappeared a long time ago. The students who asked for them probably took them and never gave them back."

The students who took them, Stevie thought, probably took them and cut them apart. If she could find these magazines online, she could look at the letters. She could compare the typeface of those magazines to the photographs of the Truly Devious letter. Or someone could. The FBI. Someone.

She didn't have all the answers, but she had something. Now she had to do some of the drudge work and scan all of this to add to her files. She put on her headphones, turned on *My Favorite Murder*, and started with the student guide. Page by page, photo by photo, she got each image.

After an hour or so of this, she returned to the main study room and opened her computer. Time for a basic search. Very little turned up about Francis Josephine Crane. It looked like there were a few references to her in social registers, some notes about her debutante ball, but nothing that seemed to go past around 1940, and not in much detail.

Edward Pierce Davenport, however, did turn up several things. Wikipedia had a brief entry:

Edward Pierce Davenport (1918–1940) was an American poet. His only published work was the 1939 collection *Milk Moon*. Davenport was best known for his relationships with other American expatriate writers and poets in France in the late 1930s, and for his reckless lifestyle. He committed suicide in Paris on June 15, 1940, the day the Nazis entered the city.

There was a little footnote there, so Stevie clicked it. It led her to a small excerpt from a longer book.

On June 15, 1940, the day after the Nazis entered Paris, Edward Pierce Davenport spent the day consuming opium and violet champagne. At sunset, as loudspeakers in the street announced the night's curfew, he donned a gold dressing gown and climbed to the rooftop of his Parisian apartment on the Rue de Rennes in Saint Germain. After toasting the city and the setting sun, he downed a last glass of champagne and swan-dived from the building into the street below. His body landed on a Nazi vehicle, denting the roof.

"A fourth-rate poet," said a friend, "but a first-rate death."

"Your friends are real dicks," Stevie said.

"I know," replied a voice, "but they're the only ones I have."

This is when the screaming started.

7

Squirrels, in Stevie's experience, were not obedient creatures, prone to forming themselves into well-regulated groups that moved as one. These squirrels were far too coordinated to her liking. They were streaming through the library, perhaps a hundred of them. They were coming down the wrought-iron steps, skittering along the edges of railings, all in an unbroken flow.

This was only slightly more distracting than the sight in front of her. Spread out on the table was a pair of familiar hands—long, elegant hands. There was the worn-out T-shirt; strong, wiry arms. She followed these up to find brown eyes flecked with gold looking at her.

Stevie yanked her legs up as squirrels began running under the tables.

"That's weird," David said, observing the chaos. "So, when did you get back?"

Stevie fought the urge to hit him with her laptop, largely because she did not want to damage it.

"What did you do?" she hissed.

"*Me?*"

"Don't be a dick," she said.

"That ship has sailed. Hang on. We can't fight yet. Where's my hug?"

"Out!" Kyoko said, pointing at David. "Everyone *out*."

"Well, that's not conducive to learning," David said under his breath.

Stevie grabbed her stuff, sweeping one or two photos from the collection into her bag, and hurried out as Kyoko started running around the library, checking windows and closing doors.

The light outside seemed overly bright after the thoughtful shade of the library. David grabbed at his neck and rubbed the stubble that had accumulated there.

David Eastman, or David Eastman King, was a shade under six feet, his build wiry, like he had been made of bundles of snapping electrical cables that had wound themselves together into a person, sparks still coming from the ends. His clothes were always tattered, and not fashionably tattered. His jeans had not been ripped by professionals. The holes and marks on his surfer T-shirt—he had made those himself through wear and carelessness. He wore a Rolex with a shattered face on his freckled arm, along with several string bracelets. Everything on his face was too narrow, too fine. The lines sharp. His eyes always looked half closed, but they had more life behind them than most. It's the creature that pretends to be asleep that you need to watch out for.

Even in his roughest state, he was beautiful to look at. In

fact, if she was being honest, he was more beautiful in this state. Except in his jaw she saw Edward King. And his smile. And everything that had made him and supported him. It was a taste she would never be able to get out of her mouth.

"What the hell did you do?" she said.

"I'm excited you think I'm so powerful, but I don't control the local wildlife. God. So *jumpy*."

I am your mandatory friend, she thought.

For a second, she considered giving up, right then and there. No way. No way could she carry on with whatever weird pretense.

The case. The tin. The evidence. Her one chance.

Pix was hurrying across the green with some kind of box or carrier in her hand. She cast a look at David as she went, but did not come over to them or stop moving.

"Did you know," he said as Pix hurried on, "that Dr. Nell Pixwell is a trained wildlife conservator? One of her many skills."

"What are you doing?" Stevie said. "Why did you send Pix to pick squirrels out of the library?"

"I need your help," he said. "Now. We've got maybe an hour?"

"For what?"

"Ellie's room," he said. "I need you to do the thing you do. Look through it."

Stevie rubbed her face in disbelief.

"It's what you do," he said.

She was about to snap back that it wasn't *what she did*,

except it was what she did. She had gone through David's room once, when left alone in there, just to try to find out what he was hiding from her. It turned out he was hiding a lot, so that was fair enough. And she went through Hayes's room after his death when she'd had the idea that something wasn't right, and it turned out something *wasn't* right, and Hayes was gone, so no harm, no foul.

"No," he said. "It's a good thing." He was being serious, and his entire expression and bearing changed. "Let me ask you a question. Does Ellie seem *outdoorsy* to you?"

"Outdoorsy?"

"She's the only smoker I know who can't light a match, Stevie. I saw her try. It was amazing. She uses a lighter because matches *are too complicated*. Last winter, I seriously thought she would kill herself trying to deal with the snow. She doesn't own boots. She has zero sense of self-preservation. She can't drive. She's made to live in cities and make art stuff. Now, think about what it would take to get down off this mountain by yourself. The answer is: a lot. I've tried it."

"I thought she snuck off all the time to go to Burlington," she said.

"With me. She had friends down there with the cars. I helped get them on campus by messing with the camera at the entry gate. Ellie has a lot of talents, but she's not handy. So you're telling me that she ran away from here on no notice, carrying nothing, with no phone, no one waiting on the back drive . . . that she got herself *across the river*. She didn't use the bridge. As soon as she took off, Larry had someone on the road. That river is about ten feet deep, rapid, and cold. So she runs, alone, for miles, through the woods in the dark, downhill, over a mountain river, to the road, which is now being watched. . . ."

"Okay," Stevie said. "Okay. So what are you saying?"

"I'm saying something doesn't make sense and I want you to do the thing you do and look through her stuff before it's gone, because you are really good at that and I can't think of anything else. She's my friend. And I don't know where she is. If anyone could figure out where she's gone or if she's okay, maybe it's you."

Was this a trap? Because it seemed like a trap.

Yet he said it plainly enough that Stevie felt it was probably the truth. David and Ellie had always been close friends. When Stevie had first arrived at Ellingham, she had watched the way they fell all over each other. Stevie thought they were dating. They weren't. They really were just friends.

Also, David was not stupid. He knew that once this idea was introduced to Stevie's brain, it could only take root and grow. The vines would twist around her every waking thought until all other brain activity would be squeezed out and all that would be left would be the leafy jungle of desire to *search*.

And the tin *had* come from Ellie's room.

"You know you want to," he said. "Janelle is over in the maintenance shed working on her project, and Nate won't notice."

They had been reunited for all of ten minutes, and already

the library was infested with squirrels and he was calling on her to break into a room.

This was home. It all checked out.

Minerva was quieter than normal when David and Stevie walked into the common room. The moose head on the wall was the only witness, and for a moment, Stevie wondered if it had been mounted with cameras. Moose eye cameras. Did Edward King want to watch and see when his son got back to his dorm?

A stupid thought. A nervous thought. Her palms were sweating. David was just behind her, and she could feel his shadow on her back like it was made of fingers.

"Janelle?" she called.

Nothing.

"Nate. You here?"

The moose just stared ahead.

"Told you," David said. "All ours. Nice and cozy."

Just her and David alone in the house—the whole house. Alone.

"Is the door locked . . . ?"

David produced a key from his pocket.

"Where did you get that?"

"Don't worry about it," he said.

Even in the bright midday sun, the hallway in Minerva was very dark, lit only by a very tiny stained-glass window by the stairs at the end of the hall. There was a wall sconce, but no one ever turned it on during the day. Stevie walked gently past Janelle's room and her own, down to the end, where room three lay waiting.

Ellie's room was just a little bit different from Janelle's and Stevie's. It was a touch larger, with a little alcove nook. There were three small boxes piled there, so some of her stuff was still here, but by no means all. When Stevie had last been in this room, the bed was piled in colorful blankets and spreads. There was stuff everywhere—art supplies, paints and pastels and pencils, boas, piles of dirty but colorful clothes, books, prints and drawings and melted-down candles and wine bottles with peacock feathers coming out of them. Those things were all gone. The bed now looked like what it was—a small, wooden, institutional frame with a plastic-covered mattress. The poems and drawings Ellie had put on the wall were still there, like ancient graffiti. Quotes, song lyrics, snatches of poetry in French and English, slashes of color, crude and bright drawings, splatters . . . Ellie's mind was an active and colorful place and she decorated her world with its contents.

The way to handle a scene was to start wide and work your way in, so that's what Stevie did. She walked around the edge of the room first, looking at the writings and drawings, checking in the drawers and closets to see if anything had been left behind. The bureau top still had a thick covering of makeup dust and wax, as did the bedside stand.

Stevie opened the closet door. There was nothing but a crumpled plastic shopping bag. When she had satisfied herself that the room itself had nothing to tell her, she went to the boxes and had a careful look-through. The top one contained clothes, as David said—Ellie's thrift-store finds and Parisian punk. Balled-up vintage T-shirts, flowing hippie pants covered in paint, objects that defied definition. The next box contained what appeared to be the used bedding stripped off the bed, and the box below that, towels and bath supplies. Stevie looked through Ellie's mix of store-brand shower gels and shampoos and her French body oils before putting everything back in the boxes.

"Anything?" David said from the window. "How are the little gray cells?"

She waved him off.

This room had contained everything of Ellie's here at Ellingham. She'd had the magic tin in this room. Stevie had to try harder. What did this space tell her about Element Walker?

Stevie got down on the floor on her stomach and rested her chin in her hands. Old glitter still sparkled from the floorboards, and bits of feather were snagged on splintered pieces of the wood. Down here, she could smell Ellie's incense, the endless incense she burned against the school rules.

"No fires, Ellie," Stevie said out loud.

"What?" David said from the window.

"The first thing I heard about Ellie on the first day, before you got here. You were late and we were having the orientation talk thing . . ."

Stevie scanned the room from her vantage point—a vista of dust bunnies.

"Pix said to her, 'No fires, Ellie.' Ellie must have caused a fire?"

"Oh, yeah. Last year. She knocked a candle over."

"In here?"

"Yeah. In here."

"And yet she can't light a match," Stevie said, mostly to herself. She pushed herself back up to her knees. Where do you look for Ellie, the smoker who can't light a match? Albert Ellingham was trying to find people too—he was always looking for his lost daughter. All of this was about his lost daughter. And now there was another lost daughter on the mountain.

Against a box by the door, Stevie saw Roota, Ellie's beloved saxophone. Ellie could not play the saxophone, but that never stopped her. She had purchased Roota with the money Hayes gave her to write *The End of It All*, and that money came from Hayes's ex-girlfriend Gretchen. The day Stevie met Ellie, she was playing Roota in the tub at the end of the hall while dying her dress, and herself, pink. It was there that Stevie discovered the bits of metal under the tub, the ones that had marked Hayes's computer when Ellie stashed it there.

So much of this came down to Roota.

Stevie went over and picked up the saxophone. That's when she saw it—a scorch mark leading up to the wall. The mark had been scrubbed over, painted away. And, something else. Something wasn't right in that little patch of the room.

"Don't you think it's weird about the matches?" Stevie

said, getting down to look at the wall.

"That's why I said it."

"No," Stevie said. "You said it to explain to me why you didn't think she would do well alone in the woods. Don't you think that's *odd*? Ellie's an artist. She's good with her hands."

It looked like something had fallen—there was one dark mark that stretched out. But the weird thing was that something about the wall was . . . uneven? She got right up to it and ran her hand along it to the molding between the wall and the floor. There was a gap. A tiny, tiny gap, a few millimeters.

"Pass me my bag," she said to David.

He pushed her bag in her direction. She yanked it over and shuffled through it until she found a pen. She pulled off the cap and used it to pry into the space. David made his way over to her and perched next to her, sitting on his heels.

"Turn on your phone flashlight," she said.

"What is it?"

"I don't know yet," she said impatiently. "Flashlight."

He turned on the flashlight function. By now, Stevie had wiggled the board free. It gave rather easily. It had been pulled loose before, clearly. Behind it was a hole in the base of the wall, about the size of a fist.

David had no snark now. He silently handed her the flashlight. Before she took it, she reached into the front pocket of her bag and pulled out a pair of blue nitrile gloves and snapped them on.

"Really?" he said. "You carry crime-scene gloves?"

"You can get them in any drugstore," she said, taking the

phone from him. "Treat yourself."

She flattened herself on the floor as best she could and turned her head to the side to get a view into the space. It appeared to be a shallow space, dark, webby. She positioned the phone's light to get the best illumination she could and reached in, slowly, in case there were wires or sharp edges. She poked finger by finger until she hit the back of the space. It was about as long as her hand. Almost big enough for the tin but not quite.

She lifted her neck and stretched it, then reached her fingers up.

There was space there. The hollow went all the way up. Plenty of space for the tin.

"So there's a hole?" David said. "That's pretty good. I mean, you never disappoint with your . . ."

"Shut up for a second."

She craned her hand around to get a full sense of what might be there.

"Maybe Janelle has one of those laparoscopic little cameras," she said. "Or . . ."

Her finger hit something. Something fabric.

"I've got something," she said. She wormed her fingers into the space, looking for something she could hook on to. Was it more of the beaded fabric, or the thing the feather had come from? Was it more of the photos, a bag . . .

The thing pulled free and landed on the floor inside the hole. She wrapped her hand around it and was pulling it out when her brain sent her the alert that something was amiss with this object, but sometimes when you start a movement, you can't stop. She pulled the thing out of the hole.

Whether it was a large mouse or a small rat, she did not know. It was dead, and had been for some time. It still had fur in places, but in others it was exposed to the bone. Overall, it was hard, possibly mummified by being in the wall.

"Oh," she said, jerking away her hand. It was not an adequate expression of horror, but it was all she had. When you find yourself holding a mummified mouse-rat, words may fail.

"That's not Ellie," David said, looking over and grimacing.

Stevie got up and scooted away from the thing, ripping off her gloves. She shoved them in her hoodie pocket.

"Are you *keeping* those?" he said.

"I can't put them in the trash in here," she replied.

"You think they're checking her trash?"

"I don't know. *You* asked me to come in here."

"Okay." He held up his hands. "What do you think?"

Stevie surveyed the room again.

"What was she wearing that night?" Stevie asked.

"She had ballet shoes on," he said. "I remember looking at them."

"And a little dress. Ballet shoes and a little dress."

He had a good point. It would be hard to get down the mountain in that.

The room told her about Ellie—that she was a freewheeling artist, an impractical dresser, a French speaker, messy. She liked wine and cabaret. She had a lot of colored pens and drawing books. Her medium was everything. She was color and glitter and chaos.

David was looking at her expectantly, waiting for her to make some kind of proclamation, but she had nothing. The room had no secrets to share. The only thing it had given her was a dead rodent, and now she had to get rid of it.

"Let me think," she said. "I . . ."

David's phone buzzed. He looked at it.

"Looks like I have a date. Gotta go up to the Great House. Someone thinks I put a bunch of squirrels in the library." He tucked his phone in his pocket. "Thanks for looking. Maybe it was stupid. I . . ." He shrugged. "Better go," he said.

When he was gone, Stevie found herself quaking internally, and it wasn't just because she had to scoop up the rat with some cardboard and take it out to the woods.

8

DETECTION HAS MANY METHODS, MANY PATHWAYS, NARROW AND subtle. Fingerprints. The lost piece of thread. The dog barking in the night.

But there is also Google.

After dumping the rat, Stevie sat down and looked up the names she had uncovered.

Francis Josephine Crane had lived long before the existence of social media, long before every moment and movement could be tracked, but she still lived in a time where the life events of a prominent young woman could be traced. That she was a prominent young woman was the first thing Stevie found out when she sat down in her own room.

Francis Crane was the daughter of Louis Crane, the founder and owner of a company called Crane Flour. The internet had plenty to say about Crane Flour, one of America's most popular brands between 1910 and 1945. Many people collected Crane Flour tins. The most important fact about Crane Flour seemed to be that one of their factories exploded in 1927, killing eight people and wounding thirty.

Crane was roundly denounced for insufficient safety precautions, and Crane Flour winked out of existence about twenty years later, purchased by some larger company that folded it into another company, and into another.

Francis hid among these stories, concealing herself in the depths of available information. Stevie caught a glimpse of her in a list of attendees at a ball held in New York on September 19, 1936. Then her name appeared in a list of the 1937 incoming class at Vassar. There was no mention of her in any list of graduates.

Finally, Stevie found herself reading selections from a book called *Better Than Homemade! The Story of Baking in America*, which was published in 1992 and patchily uploaded in the form of a bunch of bad scans. This was the longest piece of information she could find on Francis:

> *Louis's daughter, Francis, was well known for her literally*
> *hell-raising ways. In despair, her parents sent her away*
> *to join the first class of their friend Albert Ellingham's*
> *new academy in the hills of Vermont. Unfortunately, her*
> *stay there was concurrent with the infamous Ellingham*
> *kidnapping, and she returned home. The Crane family, it*
> *seemed, attracted disaster.*

"What do you mean, 'literally' hell-raising ways?" Stevie said aloud. "She literally raised hell? What, is she summoning demons?"

There were other annoying things, like the fact that the

author said "hills of Vermont" and not "mountains." So it made the claim that Francis and her family attracted disaster seem a little dubious. But still, this was an intriguing paragraph. It was also the only one that mentioned Francis.

Stevie found the author's name, Ann Abbott, and read down the list of her other works (*Jell-O! The Wobble that America Loves, Salad Days: How Salad Became Popular*). Another few minutes of poking around produced an email address. Stevie wrote her an email and asked her if she had any information about what became of Francis. She had just sent it when there was a knock at her door, and Janelle poked her head in.

"What are you up to?" she asked.

Stevie glanced up at the corner of her screen and realized that she had been scouring the internet for Francis Crane for over three hours. It was almost six thirty.

"Work," she said, shutting her computer. "Lots to catch up on."

Janelle stepped into the room. The light smell of lemons trailed in with her.

"You're wearing your lemons," Stevie said. "For luck?"

"I'm just happy you're back," Janelle said, sitting on the edge of Stevie's bed. "When I'm happy, for luck. I just love lemons. Here. I made you something."

She handed Stevie a small plastic object, about the size of a deck of cards, with two wheels.

"It's a self-balancing robot," she said. "You can attach your phone to it. I was playing around with some spare parts, and working on inertial measurement units, and I just wanted to make you something, so . . ."

She shrugged happily as Stevie accepted her friendship robot.

"How's your project going?" Stevie asked.

"I'm glad you asked. Do you want to see specs?"

Janelle bounced off the bed and returned a minute later with her laptop open. She showed Stevie several videos of machines rolling around and swinging things. She had the same intensity that Stevie had when she was talking about murders, except this was pipes and motors and things that spun and moved. All of this was interspersed with a detailed analysis of Janelle's favorite K-drama, *Love Lessons with Tofu*. Janelle's mind was a busy but perfectly organized place, running like one of her impossible machines. TV show plots ran alongside mathematical formulas, which blended seamlessly into smoky-eye tutorials, which catapulted her into romance before dropping her gently back into a bed of physics. And also, she answered every single one of her texts within a minute.

She did not, however, know about crime, and she would probably not be interested in what Stevie had just discovered (or not discovered, really) about someone who was related to someone else who made flour.

Janelle's phone buzzed, and she glanced down at it.

"Everyone's going over to the yurt," she said. "Vi is on their way over."

"You and Vi seem so happy."

Janelle did a tiny squee. It was an actual squee, a real one. A pip of joy.

"I'm trying to learn a little Korean," Janelle said, "but languages aren't really my thing. Vi's fluent in Korean and Japanese, and they thought I'd like to learn Korean the most. Do you want to go over? Let's get Nate and go over."

Before Ellingham, yurts had not been a part of Stevie's life. She had never even heard of them. When she first saw the massive, circular tent structure, it reminded her of a circus, both inside and out. Outside, all big top. Inside, it was a mass of colorful rugs, beanbags, futons, and cushions. It was the place where people gathered to hang out, play games, read, do work. It was a strange structure—it had no windows, and the inside was a skeleton of sunburst beams that supported the ceiling and a lattice that held up the walls. There was a woodburning stove in the middle that kept it all toasty, and lights and colorful decorations hung from the ceiling.

Janelle and Vi sat propped up back-to-back on the floor. Nate was sitting with them, though his attention was on a game on his tablet. The school was abuzz with the story of the squirrels. It seemed common knowledge that it was David's doing, and he had not yet returned from his trip to the Great House. Back in Pittsburgh, if someone had infiltrated the library with fifty squirrels, that person would have been hailed as a hero. But Ellingham was full of library lovers, and there was the feeling in the air that this was, perhaps, a bridge too far. You could be naked, you could scream and hang out on the roof, but you do *not* mess with the place with the books.

"Nothing else got him kicked out," Nate mumbled as the topic floated up in their group.

"If they can prove it," Vi said. "I guess they have footage. They have footage of everything, because now we live in a surveillance state."

Janelle rolled her eyes just a tiny, tiny bit.

"Seriously," Vi said. "People are saying those cameras we got? They're from someone on the outside. The school didn't want them."

"Then who bought them?" Janelle said.

"I don't know. It's private, though. I know you think I'm a paranoid protestor, but it's true."

Stevie bit her lower lip. It appeared that no one knew about Edward King's connection to the school. This meant that the helicopter had not been seen up close. Stevie felt like she was sitting on a secret—palpably. Like it was an egg. If she moved, it would crack open.

"I don't know," Janelle said. "I get the problem, but I don't *hate* the cameras. There are . . . things around. Bears and moose . . ."

"No moose," Stevie said. "The moose is a lie."

"I'm just saying that considering everything that happened, cameras aren't completely the worst idea."

"All I'm saying," Vi said, steering the topic back to even ground, "is they must have seen him do it."

A new person came up to where they were sitting. He was tall. Actually, he was by far the tallest student at Ellingham, and maybe the tallest Stevie had ever seen. She practiced measuring people by height, as that was a useful observational skill. Witnesses routinely got heights wrong. The best way to note a height was to measure it against something that didn't move. In this case, this person was up to a large knot in the wood of the latticework that held up the yurt wall. Based on her other observations, this probably put the guy at six foot four, maybe five. He had a full build, like a football player, or like how Stevie guessed football players were built. (They existed at her old school, but they were not present for Stevie. She didn't care enough to make note of them. Stevie hated football, and she specifically hated the car commercials that were in football, with the meaningless slogans and aggressively masculine messages about how important it was for Americans to drive up rocks and treat every trip to the store or a soccer game like a single-person invasion. Maybe she was overthinking this.)

This person probably did not play football. He was fiercely pale—not like Nate, who had a gentle, bookish gray tone. This was a kind of paper-white, contrasted sharply by jet-black, obviously dyed hair. He had purple cat-eye contacts in, wore a Slipknot T-shirt, and had spiked black leather cuffs on both wrists.

"Hi," he said softly to Stevie. "I'm Mudge. I don't think we met before, but Pix asked me to get you up to speed on anatomy stuff. Do you want a Pringle?"

His voice was so soothing, he sounded like someone who might be on a recording or one of the meditation apps Stevie used when she had anxiety.

"I'm okay," Stevie said.

Nate peered up from his tablet and he seemed to regard Mudge as some kind of fellow traveler.

"Yeah, I want a Pringle," Nate said.

The can of Pringles was extended, and Mudge entered the group. To Stevie's surprise, he and Nate immediately started talking about a board game. Stevie was adrift in her small group, alone. Then she felt them. The eyes of Germaine Batt. They were watching her from across the room.

"I'll be right back," she told the others.

Germaine Batt was petite, just touching five feet. She had long, straight hair that today she pulled back in a bun. Like Stevie, she dressed for the job she wanted to have—she wore a black blazer with a white T-shirt under it, as if she might be called to be a talking head on the news at any time. She was sitting by herself on a pouf—not in the corner, as yurts have no corners—but tucked off into a nook with some screens and a coffee table. She sat alone, bent over her laptop. She was typing away when Stevie approached, but there was no pretense. They both knew they had been staring each other down.

"Welcome back," Germaine said. Her voice had a high register, and her words a hard, fast clip. She spoke like she typed.

"Thanks."

Stevie tried not to overload the word. It wasn't Germaine's *fault* that her article caused her parents to remove her from Ellingham. She didn't mean for it to happen. Still, it was hard not to feel the connection between Germaine and being ripped from the mountain and thrown back to the earth below.

"Something wrong?" Germaine asked.

"No."

"Seems like something's wrong. By the way, you still owe me a favor. From that night."

Stevie had forgotten about this. At the silent party, when Stevie was trying to figure out who had taken Hayes's computer, she had asked Germaine to show her some photos on her phone. She had promised a favor in return, but she didn't really think that she would be hit up for it.

"You figured it out because of my picture," Germaine reminded her.

"I know. So what do you want?"

"Nothing yet," Germaine said. "When it's time, I'll ask."

Stevie found she was clenching her jaw. She consciously released it, but it snapped right back into position.

"So," Germaine said, half closing her computer, "what do you think happened?"

"With?"

"Ellie," Germaine said, as if this was obvious.

"I think she got out through a passageway," Stevie said.

"Yeah . . ." Germaine rolled her eyes. "But where did she *go*?"

Stevie didn't like being treated like she was stupid, but since she had just had this conversation with David, she decided to take the indignity to find out why Germaine was also asking this question.

"Burlington?" Stevie said innocently.

"How did she get there?" Germaine said. "You can't walk there. She didn't call anyone—they have her cell phone records."

"She could have used another phone."

"Whose?" Germaine asked, raising an eyebrow.

"Maybe a friend's?"

As if on cue, the door to the yurt flapped open, and David entered. David had a way of walking—a way that suggested that he belonged anywhere he went. In this, he had his father's manner, which was gross and horrific. But there was something else, something of the rake in a casino movie, who has come in to knock the place over, or an entertainer who might at any point somersault into the center of the room.

Or maybe he was just walking in and her brain chemistry was telling her stories.

He had changed his clothes and was now wearing jeans and a formfitting black sweater, which complemented his dark curls and made the musculature of his arms and chest clear. He smiled at her and Germaine, then went over to Janelle and Vi. Mudge and Nate had gone to examine some of the board games on the shelves.

"A friend's phone?" Germaine said again.

"Yeah," Stevie said, getting up. "I don't think so."

"Maybe worth finding out?" Germaine called to her as she rejoined her housemates.

David was leaning on the back of the futon, talking to Janelle and Vi. Janelle had her face tipped up toward him, an expression of dull patience on her face. Vi's arms were crossed. They did not look impressed.

"I'm on house arrest," he said. "No trips to Burlington for me."

"Seriously?" Janelle replied.

"I know," he said. "I don't think they can do that."

"No," she said, "that's *it*?"

"Isn't that enough?" he said. "I didn't even do anything."

"Yes, you did," Vi said. "Everyone knows you did."

"Am I the squirrel whisperer?"

"It's not cool," Vi said. "You've been waking people up, you're damaging stuff we like, that we use. We all have issues, dude. Get over yourself."

"I thought learning was a game," David said. "Why is no one having fun but me?"

Vi shook their head and took Janelle's hand. The two of them stood up.

"I'll see you at home," Janelle said, and it was pointedly to Stevie only.

"Sometimes I don't think people like me," David said, watching them go.

"You know why," she said.

"A return to responsibility," he said, lifting his eyebrows rakishly. "You know who loves that?"

"A lot of people," Stevie said. "Just because . . ."

It seemed too dangerous to say *your dad* out loud. Stevie could feel Germaine's eyes on them, boring into the back of her head.

"I think I might go too," she said. "Want to come?"

"Sure," he said. "Why not?"

Germaine kept her head down as they passed, but Stevie saw her stealing a sideways glance at them.

"It was only, like, forty squirrels," David said when they were outside.

"How did you even get forty squirrels?"

"No magician reveals his secrets," he said. "You didn't find anything else, did you?"

His change of conversation was so sudden that Stevie lost the thread for a second.

"Look," Stevie said. "What are you suggesting happened to Ellie? You're saying you don't think she could have made it out? So you think she's here?"

"I'm saying . . ." He lowered his voice. "I don't see how she made it away from here that night, or the next few days. I don't know how she got out."

"But let's say she did, because that's probably what happened," Stevie said. "Do you know where she'd go?"

"She could have gone anywhere," he said. "Ellie grew up on a commune, she lived in France. I guess she's in a . . . I don't know, in a café basement in Berlin or something."

"Kind of hard for her to get out of the country."

"Okay. So . . . in an Airstream trailer in Austin selling designer tacos or a tree house in Oregon . . ."

"I get the idea," Stevie said. "She's not from anywhere, so if she's nowhere, it's like she's home."

David regarded her for a moment.

"Right," he said. "If she's nowhere, she's home. Yeah."

"Or she can just be in someone's apartment in Burlington," Stevie said.

"I think she would want to get out. If she could get to Burlington she could get in someone's car and go. I don't think she'd stick around."

"But why *run*?" Stevie said. "Why run if you did nothing?"

"Fear," David said.

"Of what?"

"Of being accused of murder."

"I never said she did it," Stevie shot back. "I said she wrote the script for *The End of It All* and took Hayes's computer, which she did."

"I know," he said. "I know. Calm down."

"Do *not* tell me to calm down," Stevie replied. "I'm the one who started this. I know what I'm saying. It's just . . . if not her . . ."

"Look," David said. "Maybe . . . maybe he did take the dry ice? Maybe Beth Brave was wrong about when she thought they were talking?"

"There's a call record."

"I know, but . . . what if it was wrong somehow?"

"Or what if Ellie did do it?" Stevie said. "She had motive. She had the ability. She could have done it as a goof, to mess with the video. She doesn't seem like someone who would know all the science. Why would she think that would hurt him?"

"Because that's not how she was," David said. "She wouldn't move hundreds of pounds of dry ice to mess up someone else's art."

For the first time, she heard his voice take on a raw edge.

"I'm just saying . . ."

"Look, I get what you did and it makes sense. I'm just telling you. She wouldn't do that. The one thing Ellie would never do is mess up someone else's art. That was like her religion. I know things ended kind of weird with us and maybe you don't trust me, but you have to trust me."

It was a sudden twist.

"You mean how your dad isn't dead and is Edward King?" she asked.

"I mean, if you want to get super specific about it. Just so you know, I wanted to tell you. I wanted to tell you right away. But there were two reasons I didn't. One, because my dad is Edward King, which means you would hate me. And two, my dad is Edward King, which means everyone would hate me."

"I didn't even know he had kids," Stevie said. "I didn't know he could mate with humans."

"Yeah," David said. "Nature finds a way."

Had he moved closer? It seemed like he might have. Stevie's mouth had gone dry. The thing about David was that he was very beautiful—long and lean and damaged and twisted, smiling at her. She saw Edward King's silhouette in David's features again. In his smile.

Good job, Stevie. That's right. Kiss him. That will make him happy.

Stevie stepped back a few feet, repelled by the thought. Her brain could not handle this conflict of input. There was something there, something that pulsed between her and David. And now there was Edward King hanging overhead, almost literally. He even had cameras on them. The thought made her queasy.

"I should have told Nate I was going," she said. "I'm going to go back . . . tell him."

David lifted his chin an inch.

"Sure," he said, with the slightest trace of a smile. "Nate. Yeah. I'll see you at home."

He turned and started walking back toward Minerva, his hands in his pockets.

Stevie stood on the path, trying to take in all the new information that shaped her life. She had always wondered how people got to lead interesting lives. Maybe this was how—you set up the conditions, and then you get the events. And maybe those events took you by surprise even if you wanted them to happen, even if you prepared. She had wished so much to work on this case, and now here she was, doing deals with the devil.

Maybe, she wondered, that was what it was like to plan a murder. Maybe you make successive bad deals with yourself that you can't back out of, until you make one that can never be reversed.

April 14, 1936, 6:00 a.m.

AT THE START, THERE WAS MUCH FRANCIS CRANE ADMIRED ABOUT Albert Ellingham. She was inclined to like a man who built tunnels for no apparent reason. He encouraged her love of chemistry. He instructed the librarian to order whatever crime magazines she wanted to read. Boys and girls took exercise together, took class together, shared meals. He told the staff to turn the other way when students were caught drinking. He liked to play games, and he and Francis had gone toe-to-toe in Monopoly several times.

Her appreciation for the man peaked when he took her on a walk of the property and showed her where they had blasted away the mountain with dynamite. He even took Francis to where the explosives were stored and let her hold a stick in her hands. She tried not to show her excitement, but it must have come through.

"You seem interested," he said with a laugh. "Go on. Tell me about dynamite."

"It's simply nitroglycerine, stabilized and absorbed by diatomaceous earth and sodium carbonate," Francis said.

"Unless you're using TNT, which is . . ."

"Well!" he said, laughing. "I wasn't expecting an answer that quickly!"

He reached out to take the stick back, and Francis's fingers reflexively coiled around it before she told them to release.

"It's a good thing you'll never need this," he said. "You could be dangerous!"

"I might be," she said.

Albert Ellingham roared with laughter.

"I have to be careful what we're teaching you," he said, laughing again. "Your father would murder me if I made you too dangerous to marry."

That was the moment it all broke for Francis. He had given her dynamite and he had laughed in her face. It was a joke to him, something he would never think of again. But it would be all Francis would think of.

She decided that if he liked games so much, she would play one of her own. It would be a good game too. Edward liked her idea of fun, so they made their great plan together.

The letter hadn't even been important to the plan. It had been, in Eddie's words, "a bit of art." She'd gotten the idea from the true-crime magazines that she loved so much. People in those magazines were always getting kidnapped, and the kidnappers always sent the messages with the cut-out letters.

She assumed this was a made-up thing, but one day she was sitting on the lawn reading *Real Detective* when she saw the man who was always hanging around, the one everyone knew was a cop. His name was George Marsh. He'd been all over the papers when he stopped a bomb from going off in Albert Ellingham's car—Frankie always read stories about bombs. Now he seemed to be Ellingham's private bodyguard. He was walking toward the Great House when she called out to him, making sure to use the purest form of her tony New York voice.

"Aren't you a policeman?" she asked.

Mr. Marsh had come over to her, looking bemused.

"I am," he said. "Or, I used to be. I work for the FBI."

"Oh, that must be so exciting! You must have seen all sorts of things. Tell me, do real criminals send notes like this?"

She held up her magazine, open to a page that showed such a note. He smiled.

"I'm surprised you read this kind of thing. Doesn't seem very *Ellingham Academy*."

"Oh," she said. "I love it. This story is about a kidnapping. Have you ever worked on a kidnapping?"

"Once," he said. "They're not all that common."

"What was it?"

"A banker's wife," he said. "Kidnapped while leaving her bridge club."

"Was there a ransom letter?"

"A call," he said. "Not a letter. They wanted fifty thousand dollars."

"What happened?" Frankie said, making sure to widen her eyes and look as innocent as possible.

"The banker paid. She never came home. Turns out she'd run off with her tennis instructor and the fifty grand was for them. We tracked them down in Miami."

He stubbed out his cigarette on the ground.

"Crank letters are often pretty dull," he said. "Once in a while you get a live one. One like that, with all those cut-out letters? You'd remember one like that. But I'll get in trouble with the management if I stand here talking about crime when you're supposed to be studying. Looks like you've got a serious book under that magazine."

He was correct. Francis had a textbook under the magazine. She was doing both.

"Organic chemistry," she replied.

"Better you than me, kid. I never had the brains for that."

He grinned and tipped his hat to her and continued on to the house. Frankie chewed the end of her pencil.

You'd remember one like that.

The idea came into her head at that moment. What if they sent him a letter? It was a joke at first. They'd never really send Albert Ellingham a note like this. But the longer she turned the idea over, the more it gained mass and form. The thing could be done—it just had to be done carefully and with style. Why not rattle the old boy's chain? Why not give him a little taste of her spark?

When she told Edward the idea that night, he loved it at once. He called it Dadaesque. And being Edward, he elaborated on it. Made it a poem.

"Poetic justice," he said, before kissing her.

Edward showed her a poem by Dorothy Parker that they modeled their work on. There were so many lovely ways to describe fiendish things. Edward added a *ha ha* at the end. It had to be signed, and this was the final flourish.

"It has to be truly devious," Frankie said.

"Perfect!" Edward added this to the draft. *Truly, Devious*.

For the actual construction of the letter, they lay together on the floor of the empty, newly constructed swimming pool, smoking and picking out letters. The paper was from a notepad Frankie brought from New York—basic, household stuff. They wore gloves and used tweezers, applying each letter carefully, tilting some, spacing them irregularly.

When the letter was complete, Frankie finished off the plan. She paid one of the day laborers to dump a pile of her mail into a Burlington postbox, saying they were personal letters and that the staff at the school went through their mail. For a dollar, her mail got the right postmark on the right date, placing them nowhere near the scene.

A beautiful piece of criminal art.

But now that letter had been swept into something else, something that had taken Iris and Alice Ellingham. And what about Dottie Epstein? These were the things Francis wondered about as she spent a sleepless night on the sofa. Would it be seen as a joke? Would it be traced?

The man with the shotgun sat by the door all night. He did not sleep. Neither did Miss Nelson, who spent the night moving around silently, bringing things down from her room in bags, going through paperwork. She cast only the occasional look at Francis, who gave up and nodded off.

At daybreak the other girls were awoken and told to dress.

"What's happening?" said Gertie, scuffing out in her heeled slippers.

"Nothing to worry about," Miss Nelson said stiffly. "A bomb threat was made. Nothing will happen, but for safety's sake you're all being sent away from campus."

There were cries and shouts and excitement about this change in routine. There was a rush for the bathroom and dresses and coats. What would they bring? Would there be breakfast? In the melee, Francis stole down to her room and slipped inside. There were things she would need, things that were concealed in her room, things she could not leave behind. She got next to her bureau and began to push. When she had moved it about a foot, she got down on the floor with a nail file and was about to start working the skirting loose, when Miss Nelson was in the doorway.

"What are you doing?" Miss Nelson said.

"I dropped an earring," Francis replied coolly.

"Come back into the common room."

"I need to change."

Miss Nelson went to Francis's closet, grabbed a dress, and handed it to her, then pointed to Francis's decorative screen.

"Change, then."

Francis took the dress and stepped behind the screen.

"I'll just say this," Miss Nelson said. "What is happening here is very serious. Talking too much could get people hurt. Do you understand me?"

Francis stopped with her dress halfway over her head.

"I don't care what you think you know," Miss Nelson went on. "There are lives at stake. I know you like your games, Francis, but this is real. People could die. And one of your own housemates could be in danger."

Francis gulped in some air, pulled the dress down, and stepped out from behind the screen. Miss Nelson was no longer the gentle and meek head of Minerva. She was a woman standing like a wall in her doorway. And for the first time that whole night and morning, Francis was afraid. She looked down at the spot in the skirting board. What was behind that board could cause more trouble than she wanted. Her secrets were sealed in that wall.

"Could I just . . . have a moment?" she asked as meekly as she could.

"No," Miss Nelson said. "I will pack your things. You will go."

Francis Josephine Crane walked out of her room, having no idea it was for the last time.

THERE WAS THE MOOSE SIGN AGAIN.

There would never be a moose.

The Ellingham coach was going on its Sunday run to Burlington. Only a few people were on today—not people Stevie knew well. Everyone had headphones on or was reading or playing something. Stevie was reading her tablet, where she had a copy of *Truly Devious: The Ellingham Murders* by Dr. Irene Fenton open. It was one of the first books she had ever gotten on the subject. She had flipped to the part about the discovery of Dottie Epstein:

May 16, 1936, was a soft day with hints of an early summer. It was five thirty in the morning, and Joseph Vance had started his milk run from Archer's Dairy Farm. He had thirty-five deliveries of milk, cream, and butter in the back of his truck and a vacuum flask of coffee for his journey. He had just made the first ten deliveries to houses outside of Jericho, Vermont, and it was a good time to pull off to the side of the road and have a mug of coffee and his breakfast roll. He parked on a bit of rough grass across from Babbett's Farm, drank and ate, and when he was finished, he went to relieve himself by a tree some twenty feet back from the road.

Joseph would later say he had no idea what moved him to go so far from the truck; this was a quiet area; no one was around for miles. Still, he moved back to the privacy of the tree, and while he was going about his business, he saw what appeared to be a sack on the ground. He moved closer. This is when he realized there were two legs coming from the sack—or, at least, parts of legs. They were discolored, ravaged by weather and wildlife. The rest of the body was still under a bit of dirt and some loose bits of wood. When Joseph moved these away, he saw the girl's curly hair, the remains of her face, and even a pair of glasses.

He ran several feet away and was violently ill. Then he got in his truck and drove directly to the police station. Little Dolores Epstein, the brilliant young student from the Ellingham Academy, had finally been found. When the body was removed and examined, a massive fracture would be found on the right side of her skull.

At that point, the Ellingham kidnapping became the Ellingham murder. In all of the publicity around the missing mogul's wife and his daughter, many would forget that the first known victim was a student, a poor little girl from New York City—a girl who taught herself five languages and showed a prodigious gift for translating ancient texts, a girl who did college-level chemistry and physics, who had a near-photographic memory of everything she ever read.

Later, Dolores's movements on that fatal day would be retraced. It is likely that she was in the dome in the sunken lake when the kidnappers came there to receive the ransom money. Dolores liked to hide herself away and read, and she had a well-known penchant for getting into out-of-the-way spaces. That day, she had taken a volume of Sherlock Holmes stories with her into the dome. It would be found on the floor.

It is possible, even likely, that Dolores Epstein saw the face of the Ellingham kidnapper, and that is why she had to die.

The coach rolled into Burlington. Burlington was a pleasant town—very college, touch of hippie, small-town America but with good coffee and snowshoes and yoga and crude profiles of Bernie Sanders spray-painted on walls. There were darker things too—signs of homelessness, some scenes around the courthouse that looked grim.

The coach let everyone off on Church Street, which was the main shopping street. Stevie walked down toward the waterfront, taking in the houses and shops and the general scenery. Ellie could have snuck off to any one of these houses or lofts. She could be hiding away, looking down at Stevie now from a window.

But was it so easy to stay concealed in a place like this?

Ellie would have to go out eventually, and Burlington wasn't so large. If she had come here, she'd probably gone on, maybe taken someone's car. Maybe she had headed west, to the desert, or California. Maybe she went up into Canada. That would be a quick and easy way of getting away from the American police. Maybe she had gone to New York or Boston, where it would be easy to hide.

But staying hidden forever was hard. Running was hard. You needed money. You needed ID and a phone. And it was hard to hide from cameras. They were everywhere. At traffic lights, at ATMs, on streets.

So maybe she was still here somewhere, tucked up in one of these hippie studios.

Stevie shook off her deliberations and continued down to the waterfront to the Skinny Pancake. There was a cold wind whipping off Lake Champlain that morning. It snapped in Stevie's face, making her eyes tear up. The view was stunning, what she could see of it through the tears—a smeared expanse of beautiful water, glorious fall trees bordering the other side. This was where Albert Ellingham sailed away on his final day, from the local yacht club. His boat had blown up upriver a bit—a victim, it was thought, of anarchists who wanted to get revenge for the death of Anton Vorachek, the man arrested for the murder of his wife and the kidnapping of his daughter. The anarchists had come for Ellingham before; this time, they seemed to have gotten him. And it was just up the shoreline a bit, in a place called Rock Point, where Albert Ellingham and George Marsh had lowered the marked bills down to a boat.

The Skinny Pancake was a large, very low-key place with a hippie vibe, a giant menu of coffees and crepes. Stevie was still in a big mood, money-wise, and ordered a large turmeric cappuccino. Might as well look fancy when you're meeting a professor for the first time.

"Hey, Fenton," the guy behind the counter said. "Usual?"

A woman of indeterminate age had entered the restaurant. She had a head of corkscrew curls, an equal mix of black and gray, which came to her shoulders. She wore glasses with thick, red frames. She was wearing a bulky purple sweater and a waterproof coat, brown corduroy, and clogs that made a clear, heavy thump on the wooden floor. She had a beat-as-all-hell leather satchel slung across her body.

Stevie recognized her a bit from the author photo, although she had been maybe twenty years younger in it. There was something more . . . haphazard about the person in front of her.

They looked at each other in a moment of mutual recognition.

"Are you Stevie?" she called.

Stevie nodded.

"Put our coffees together," she said to the person behind the counter. "She's with me." Then, to Stevie, "You mind if we sit outside?"

Stevie wanted to point out that it was October. In Vermont. On a lake. Dr. Fenton plucked a pack of cigarettes from her pocket and waggled them.

"Can't smoke in here," she said, pointing at the door.

Stevie wound her scarf once more around her neck and followed. Dr. Fenton sat down at one of the tables by the door, seemingly unaffected by the wind chopping at them. She pulled a cigarette from the pack of Camels and cupped her hands over her mouth to light it. Stevie didn't know anyone who smoked. Dr. Fenton seemed to pick up on this.

"Used to be you could smoke anywhere," she said. "You're probably not used to it. They treat us like pariahs."

She took a long drag, followed by a longer exhale.

"So. I understand that your interest at Ellingham is the Ellingham case. And that you had something to do with figuring out what happened to that kid, Mayes."

"Hayes," Stevie said, tucking her arms inside her red coat to conserve warmth.

"Hayes." Dr. Fenton let out a long plume of smoke, most of which was blown back in her face. "Sorry. You've read my book?"

"Of course," Stevie said.

"Of course!" Dr. Fenton laughed and coughed at the same time. "I like that. Of course. Also, call me Fenton. No 'Doctor.' Just Fenton. It's how I like it. Let's talk about the Ellingham case. Tell me what else you've read."

"What?" Stevie said. "All of it?"

"All the books, what articles, give me a sense of what you know."

"I know . . . all of it?" Stevie said.

"We're here to talk," she said. "Talk. Tell me about this case."

Asking someone to just talk about the Ellingham case was like asking someone to "just talk" about the past or "just talk" about science.

"Starting when?" Stevie said. "Night of, or days leading up to, or . . ."

"Night of," Dr. Fenton said, the cigarette gripped between her lips.

The guy from the counter came out with two coffees and set them down on the table, and Stevie went back to April 13, 1936, to Albert Ellingham pulling up the driveway. She went through all the known facts about the night—where everyone in the house was, the phone calls, George Marsh's trip, the marked bills, the drop. Occasionally, Dr. Fenton would quiz her. Stevie rattled back the necessary information.

"All right," Dr. Fenton said, after about a half hour and three cigarettes. "That's good groundwork. Tell me who you think kidnapped Iris and Alice Ellingham. Who is Truly Devious?"

"I don't know," Stevie said.

"Not Anton Vorachek?"

"Of course not."

Dr. Fenton looked at Stevie for a long moment and sucked on her cigarette. Stevie could hear the paper burning.

"This case is about money," Dr. Fenton said. "It was always about the money. Anton Vorachek didn't care about money. To solve the case, follow the money. Whoever kidnapped Iris and Alice knew how much money was in the safe in Ellingham's office. How the hell would Anton Vorachek know that?"

"Because the bank made regular deliveries," Stevie said. "The work crew was paid in cash. Lots of people knew that money was there. At least, that's what people said."

"Right. So everyone says. Except that those deliveries were done very carefully, and the amount of cash on hand varied. You would have to know when it went in and when it was going to go out."

Stevie said nothing, because she agreed. So did most people who looked at the case.

"So," Dr. Fenton went on, "then you have to look at who was in the house, and plenty of people were in the house. Full-time staff of twenty, plus, over a hundred people on the property every day of the week. The work crew, the staff of the school, and the students. Plus, guests. Leonard Holmes Nair and Flora Robinson were upstairs, and obviously by the time George Marsh arrived on the scene to help, Flora Robinson could not be found. Loads of people to choose from. But not Anton Vorachek. He was an anarchist, unpopular, the perfect patsy when someone had to go down for the crime. I mean, if you're going to believe that, then you probably believe Oswald assassinated Kennedy all by himself."

Stevie blinked a little at this. It seemed early to be getting into conspiracy theories.

"But this is 'The Ellingham Affair 101.' And I think you're a little beyond that."

She stubbed out her cigarette on the table, which was

kind of gross. The gray ash blew all around.

"Okay," she said. "You're hired. You have access to the attic in the big house, I hear."

Stevie nodded.

"Good." Fenton reached into her bag and pulled out a dog-eared legal pad. "There are some things I want cross-checked. Little details I need to get right. Some of them are architectural. I need to confirm where some things are, what they look like. Some other things you'll probably find up in the attic. I think there are household records up there. I need checks on things like guest lists, schedules, stuff like that. That should be in the household books."

She slid the notepad over to Stevie.

"All those things," she said. "Check them out for me. Write down any details. This is your job. Go forth and prosper."

She shoved the pad at Stevie, who glanced through it. Fenton had questions about things like menus, china patterns, who was at the house on certain dates, the color of the walls. Mundane stuff.

"My book will change everything," Fenton said. "I have information that will knock everything sideways."

Stevie looked up in interest.

"Like what?"

"That is for me to know, and maybe you to find out if you do your job."

This seemed like a big claim. But then again, Stevie had something in her bag at this very moment that could reframe the entire case. She brought it along because she refused to leave it behind when she was not on campus, and also because she'd had a fantasy of showing it to the professor, so they could immediately team up to bust the Ellingham Affair wide open. Dr. Fenton, or Fenton, had not inspired Stevie to open up. She was somehow . . . sadder than Stevie expected. Maybe it was the cigarettes. Maybe, though, it was something more. Something in her eyes and the way she sat. Something was not right with Fenton.

A guy was walking up to them, about Stevie's age. He was fair, with a spray of light gold freckles splashed out along his nose and cheekbones. He wore a well-fitted black hoodie with a blue wool jacket on top, and a ski hat. He used a single arm crutch on his left arm to walk, and had a canvas backpack covered in patches thrown over the other shoulder.

"I got a parking space," he said. "Hey."

That was to Stevie.

"This is my nephew," Fenton said. "Hunter. This is Stevie. Stevie is my new assistant on the book. You two talk. I gotta hit the restroom. Back in a second."

Fenton got up, grabbed the table as if unsteady, and then clomped her way inside.

Hunter leaned his crutch against the wall of the café and sat down where his aunt had been. They had only a slight resemblance—they had the same large blue eyes. His were bordered by thick blond brows that were permanently set on "furrowed."

"You're from Ellingham?" he said.

"Yeah. How can you tell?"

"Your name is Stevie. You're working on this book. You were in the news about the death on campus."

"Oh," Stevie said, feeling embarrassed by the obviousness of this. "Right."

"Have you been interested in the case long?"

"A few years," she said.

He bit his lip and nodded.

"I live with my aunt while I go to school here," he said.

Hunter was looking at his aunt's coffee cup. He picked it up, as if in an idle gesture, but it was too casual to be really casual. Something flitted across his expression and he set it down.

"What do you study?" she asked.

"Ecology," he replied. "Environmental studies. Going to try to save the world from global warming."

"Is that going to work?" she said.

"We have to try."

She nodded. She got that. You have to try. Trying is the first step to whatever comes next.

"I read about what you did," he said. "It was cool. You actually solved a crime."

"I didn't solve it," she said. "I . . . figured some stuff out."

"That girl, she's still missing, right?"

"Ellie. Yeah."

"I don't know where you go if you run from Ellingham," he said. "It's brutal up here. I'm from Florida. I never know how to cope with this place. . . ."

He trailed off, as if embarrassed by speaking. Then he nodded at the legal pad.

"What's my aunt got you doing?"

"Fact-checking some stuff," she said. "I think."

"Looks like a lot."

Stevie could hear the clomp of Fenton's clogs on the floor and she was back.

"All right," she said. "Get started on this. I'll see you midweek."

"There's no coach midweek," Stevie said.

"Then I'll see you when?"

"Saturday?" Stevie said.

"I'll see you Saturday. Come to my house. That's where my office is. I live on campus. Here."

She scrawled down an address and passed it over.

"Can I email you updates, or . . ."

"Nothing electronic, ever," she said. "*Ever.*"

"Okay," Stevie said. "Nothing electronic. Okay."

"Let's get moving. Where's the car?"

"This way," Hunter said. He reached over for his crutch. "I'll see you around?"

Did she imagine a lilt of hope in his voice? Stevie was not the kind of person who imagined that people wanted to flock to her side. She felt she looked good in her red vinyl coat, her short blond hair squashed under a black knit hat, plain black jeans. She was wearing lip balm, so that was something, and an eyebrow goo that Janelle had lent her and said would work well. Janelle knew makeup and was always trying to get

Stevie interested in a color palette or a highlighter. Mostly, Stevie forgot she had a body, and when someone else noticed her body, it made her look down and go, huh. Would you look at that. How long has that been there?

There had only been David for her, like that.

She had probably imagined it anyway. Hunter got his crutch and watched as his aunt gathered her things. As they said their good-byes and went off, she noticed two things. One, Fenton was not so old as to need assistance, and yet it certainly looked like Hunter had come to pick her up and escort her.

The second was that he turned and looked over his shoulder at Stevie, and he smiled.

10

Who becomes a murderer?

Stevie considered this word as the coach headed back to Ellingham that afternoon. Her reading and viewing and studying had taught her several things.

There's the horror-movie version: a shadow with a knife, the one who escaped from the hospital on the hill during that storm. It's the person living in the walls.

In mystery novels, it might be the smiling stranger, the one with the passing knowledge of poisons. It's the relative left out of the will, or the one recently added to it. It's the jealous colleague at the museum who wants to be the first to announce the new archeological discovery. It's the overly helpful person who follows the detective around.

On the all-murder, true-crime channel, it's the new neighbor with the boat, the one in his midforties to midfifties with the tan who has no past and who recently purchased a human-sized cooler. It's the person who lives in the shack in the woods. It's the unseen figure on the corner of the street.

On all crime shows, it's usually the third person the cops

interview. It's the one you sort of think it is.

In life, the murderer is anyone. The reasons, the methods, the circumstances—the paths to becoming a murderer are as numerous as the stars. Understanding this is the first step to finding a murderer. You have to shut down the voices in your mind that say, "It has to be this person." Murderers aren't a type. They're anyone.

Stevie put her head against the cool of the window and watched the moose sign go by.

"No moose," she whispered.

Element Walker. Stevie could see her now, almost physically. Artist. Try-too-hard. Friendly. The girl with the bruises on her shins from climbing, with the holes in the toes of her cheap satin slipper shoes. The girl with the baby socks tied in her hair and the old cheerleader skirt. Ellie, who had a saxophone as a best friend even though she couldn't play. The girl with the bottle of warm champagne she brought from France that she shared with two people she had just met.

Ellie, did you kill someone?

Did you mean to do it?

Stevie tried to propel her thoughts into the mountain air, as if texting Ellie with her mind. Tell me. I can help you. I'm sorry.

Why was she sorry? She had made the right conclusion. She hadn't actually called security—Nate did that. All she did was ask a question.

The day had gone gray and the rock walls of the road menaced on either side. This was a hard, beautiful place. It had many nooks, but it was cold and high. Ellie was a creature of color, of people. Stevie saw her as she was on the first day of school, dressing as a messy punk cheerleader with her matted hair bound up in little socks. And then, later that day, dying her clothes pink in the bath as she drank champagne with Stevie and Janelle and held court. Ellie liked to *perform*, not hide out away from society.

No. The facts were the facts. She lined them up, measured them. Ellie had written the script and stolen the computer. That was all she said, and it was true. It was true. She could not be blamed for what was *true*.

A couple of days before Hayes's death, *someone* took Janelle's pass when they were at yoga in the art barn. It could have been anyone. The bag was just sitting out in the hall. But it was someone who knew Janelle had access to the maintenance shed. *Someone* went into the maintenance shed using Janelle's pass and unloaded a massive amount of dry ice from the storage container. It weighed hundreds of pounds. It would have had to have been moved using a hand truck, or a golf cart, something large. From there, it was probably taken down the hatch entrance to the tunnel in the woods. Those blocks would have had to have been carried down the steps, down the tunnel, one by one. Then the room was closed up. To do what? Presumably create fog. But that's not what dry ice does when you leave that much of it in a space for that long.

She could see Hayes or Ellie getting the science of it wrong. Neither one of them were big on science, as far as she knew. She could see Ellie messing around to create something for effect, but . . .

It never really made sense. Unless Hayes thought he could do some big fog scene or Ellie thought she would mess up his filming. . . .

But why make a big special effect when you don't have anyone down there to film it? And there were easier ways to mess up his filming that would actually work.

If not Ellie, who?

She leaned her head against the cold of the window and the word thrummed in time with the moving coach: *murder, murder, murder, murder* . . .

Why did Hayes have to die? He was annoying. He cheated and used people. But in the end, he wasn't worth killing.

But neither was Dottie, until she saw something she shouldn't have.

Could Hayes have *seen* something? What was there even to see?

Her business was working on the Ellingham case, and the world had dropped the biggest, best opportunity right in her lap. Working with an author on a book about the case. This was her dream.

But Ellie was dancing in her peripheral vision.

They were turning onto the school grounds now, taking the treacherous path, the one with the trees so thick and low that they scraped the sides of the coach, and the steep slope that caused the gears to grind. There was the rushing river with the tiny wooden bridge. David had a point—getting through here was tough. It would be possible, she supposed, to go through the woods. But it would not be easy. And it would be terrifying in the dark. There was no way you could get through them without falling down the slope, tripping over the roots and fallen branches, falling into holes, knocking into rocks. And the only way over the river was the bridge. This was all as Albert Ellingham intended. The place was like a fortress. So if the bridge was watched and the back road was watched . . . how did Ellie magic her way out? Getting out of the locked room was almost nothing compared to this.

They were cresting now, passing between the dual sphinx statues. The coach stopped under the Great House portico and she stepped out into a slap of mountain breeze. Would it hurt just to have a look? Just a little look around, to satisfy whatever it was that was eating at her thoughts?

Stevie walked around the perimeter of the Great House. The back of the building was walled off, enclosing the sunken garden. She wasn't sure which basement window Ellie was supposed to have escaped from, but there were only a few possibilities. The basement-leading windows had deep window wells, and these were covered over by grates. Stevie squatted down and pulled on one. It was firmly closed.

Forget where Ellie went—how did she even get out of the basement? Stevie couldn't answer the first question until she answered the second. And there was someone who would know that answer. She found him in his usual place, at the big wooden desk right by the entrance door to the Great House.

"Just saying hi," she said as she stepped into the massive vestibule.

Larry looked up from something he was writing on a clipboard.

"Hi," he said. "Also, no."

"I didn't ask anything."

"You didn't have to. Whatever it is, no."

She pulled over a folding chair that was by the door and sat across from him.

"I went to Burlington today," she said.

"I'm glad to hear it."

"To meet with Dr. Fenton, who wrote *Truly Devious*. Did you read that one?"

"I can't remember," he said, still reading down whatever it was on the clipboard.

There was a smell in the Great Hall that was unlike anything else at Ellingham. Ellingham was all outdoorsy and wood smoke. The Great Hall smelled of polish, of leather, of cigarettes last smoked in 1938 whose molecules had infested the wood and crystal and marble and produced some new, ancient smell. It smelled of wealth. Not money—*wealth*. It was not like the pong of Fenton's cigarettes, which was stuck in Stevie's hair and her hat. Her vinyl coat was impervious. All hail the vinyl.

"Okay," she said when Larry refused to look up. "I was going to ask something."

Larry clicked his pen in warning.

"I wanted to know if you would show me where Ellie got out."

"I think I've answered that," he said.

"Isn't it better that I come to you and ask?"

"Yes. The answer is still no."

"Oh, come on," she said, lowering her voice and leaning down over the desk a bit. "Don't I deserve to see?"

Larry's face suggested that she did not.

"Come on," Stevie tried again, this time with a hint of sadness. "I feel . . . responsible. I mean, I brought her here, and if a bear ate her . . ."

Nothing. Larry was like the mountain rock they stood upon. She tried to look distraught, but didn't know how to make that happen. She ended up sticking out her lower lip a bit. Larry rolled his eyes and cast a look around the empty Great Hall.

"I'll get you plain coffee K-Cups."

"Go, Stevie," he said.

"All I'm asking is to *see* where it happened. That's all. It . . . freaks me out. I brought her here. Or, what I said did. I just want to see it."

Larry clicked his pen a few more times.

"If I show you, will you stop?" he asked.

"Definitely," she said.

Larry tipped his chair back a few inches, lowered his chin, and looked back into the half-open security office door next to him.

"Jill," he said, "take over for a few minutes. I have to go down to the basement."

"Yup," came a voice from within.

He reached into the desk drawer and pulled out a set of keys.

"Come on," he said, getting up. Stevie fell in step behind him.

"My uncle used to say to me, 'You're a pain, but I can't see through you,'" Stevie said.

"Your uncle had a point," he replied.

"It's my persistence that made me an Ellingham student."

"Uh-huh."

The Great House basement was accessed through a door in the kitchen, and the way to the kitchen was a wooden door under the grand staircase, which led to a half-set of steps to a partly subterranean space. The kitchen was a cavernous room with a white-and-black tile floor and white walls. Though the old appliances had long been removed and replaced with modern ones, there was still an air of the 1930s here—the wide wooden counters, a much-marked marble-topped table where pastries would have been rolled. There were massive cabinets and pantries, all with whitewashed wooden doors, slightly warped and cracking with age. The windows started only halfway up the wall, making the room slightly darker. Massive globe lights hung from the ceiling. Though it smelled slightly of the faculty's microwaved lunches and dirty coffee mugs, there was still a feeling of authenticity here. Stevie could imagine the house cook and her assistant working away.

"This way," Larry said, taking Stevie to an unmarked white door toward the far side of the room. "Watch the steps. They're warped."

Here, the Great House got a bit more real. The basement had a strong basement funk even from the entrance—a pungent, acrid smell that Stevie could feel on the back of her throat. The steps were saggy and made a noise like a scream when she stepped on them.

"You were always going to show me," Stevie said as they went down. "Weren't you?"

"If I didn't, you'd find your way down here some other way."

Stevie glowed with pride.

"It's a warren down here, so stay with me," he said.

Larry turned to the right, where they were immediately confronted with a wall. There was a small opening to the right side of that, which led to a space just a few feet square. This led to another chamber that was maybe ten feet square, that opened on either side to more little chambers. Each one was dark and had to be lit by a small pull-bulb.

Stevie had been in the recently excavated tunnel with Hayes the fateful week before he died. She had already been in some claustrophobic spaces. Though this basement was much larger, it had been cut into random little spaces with walls of old brown brick. It was a labyrinth.

"What is this?" Stevie asked as they twisted and turned through many tiny hovel-spaces.

"Albert Ellingham was a weird man," Larry said. "People

always forget that. He was weird. He and his friends used to play games down here. Some of these doors . . ."

They had, in fact, reached a door. He opened it to reveal a bit of brick wall.

"Are jokes. And just so people would never learn the layout, he'd regularly have the inner walls knocked down and moved."

"That's awesome," Stevie said. "Why is this not in any books?"

"Because no one is allowed down here," Larry said. "And all these pointless walls aren't on any plans. They're entirely cosmetic. I'd knock them down, myself, and make this space more useful."

Some of the middle areas were more full of objects— bigger, heavier ones. Large boxes, old appliances, piles of chairs and bits of old furniture. They had to squeeze through some of these. There were some heavy metal hatches in the floor as well. Stevie shone her phone light down on them.

"What are these?" she asked.

"Old storage areas. They used to keep supplies down here—apples, potatoes, preserved food. Those down there were some of the icehouse storage. They'd cut ice in the winter and pack it in with straw. Before there were freezers, there were icehouses. Now . . ."

They had reached one of the larger parts of the basement— a space maybe twenty feet long and half as wide across. It went all the way to the window. Larry pulled his phone from his pocket and turned on the flashlight function.

"Right now," he said, "we're just under Ellingham's office. This wall"—he tapped his hand on the wall to their right—"is permanent and load-bearing. And right here . . ."

He shone his light along the wall for a moment, then felt along with his hand until he located what he was after. He pressed hard into one of the bricks, and there was a dull *sprong*. He pushed against a bit of wall, and it gave way, revealing a narrow doorway on a hinge. Stevie instantly made a move for the opening, but he blocked her with his arm. "You can look in, not that there is much to see."

Stevie craned her head into the pitch-black opening. Here, the stench of dust and mold was truly terrible and she immediately sneezed. She got out her phone and shone it into the darkness. She could faintly make out a passageway, barely two feet wide, with a set of stairs at the end.

"That's how Ellie got out?" Stevie asked. "She took a hidden door from the office?"

"That's how she got out. She came down the steps, out through this doorway. Over here . . ."

He indicated the window. There were a few boxes shoved up against the wall.

"There were boxes just under the window. It was partially propped open."

Stevie stood for a moment, looking at the tiny window, caked in old dirt and cobwebs. It was covered by a grate on the outside.

"*How?*" she said. "How did she know?"

"I don't know," Larry said. "We've had people get into the

basement, but no one, to my knowledge, ever found this passage before."

"So she got out the window," Stevie said, looking up. "How did she get through that grate?"

"They're hooked closed down here," he said, pointing to a latch. "You undo the latch, push up. That's how we found it."

"So she gets through the passage, comes downstairs, stacks some stuff, opens the window and the grate, and climbs out. She did this all in, what, five minutes?"

"Something like that."

"So she had a five-minute lead on you. And all of this must have taken a few minutes, so she only had a minute or two to run from the building before you went after her."

"Give or take," Larry said. "We went to the basement first, we had to scramble people. So yes, she had about a five-minute head start."

"Where do you think she went?" Stevie said. "She didn't have anything with her. I mean, she had her coat. But she had no money. I guess she had her phone?"

"No calls were made, and there's no trace of the phone. She turned it off or ditched it somewhere."

"What do you think she did?" Stevie asked.

"Best guess, she made her way down to the road. We went down there right away, but she must have cut through the woods. The police looked at the rest stops on the highway, had eyes on the buses. Somehow, she got past. I think she knows people in Burlington. Maybe one of them came and got her. That's my guess."

"Not eaten by a bear?" Stevie asked.

"It's not impossible that she ran into a bear, but bear fatalities are rare, and we would have found some remains, most likely."

He said that a little too nonchalantly for Stevie's comfort.

"I think she'll turn up," he said. "Element's family had a history of living in communes. I think there are ways she could have gotten to one of those places and she's lying low. Loads of places like that up and around here. But eventually, people come out. No one wants to stay hidden forever. It's not human nature."

No one wants to stay hidden forever.

"Can I ask you something?" she said.

Larry indicated that she had been doing this all along and might as well just keep going.

"How do guilty people act?" Stevie asked.

"They lie, generally," Larry said. "Some fall apart right away, but some can keep lying to your face, cold as ice, and never stop."

"But is there something they do? Is there some kind of *tell*?"

"Yes and no," Larry said. "It's not them. It's you. Once you're around it enough, you learn how to spot it. But you can't rely on that. You have to go on the evidence. Even if you have the best instinct in the world, it's the facts that matter."

"You can't rely on your gut," she said.

"Not in determining guilt. But your gut can help you in other ways. It can keep you from getting hurt."

There was something just a little bit pointed in how he said it.

"Did Ellie seem *guilty* to you?" she asked.

"She seemed . . . scared," he said. "But she would have been."

A silence fell between them for a moment, filled with the remains of Ellie's fear.

"Look," Larry said. "We don't know what happened. But I tend to believe it was an accident, a prank gone wrong, or something like that. For all I know, they worked on it together, got the dry ice together. I think Element and Hayes were both kids who got into things they shouldn't. Whatever she did, whatever happened, I don't think she meant to do it. *If* she did it. She doesn't strike me as a dangerous person. You don't have to be afraid. And this place is wired now. There are perimeter lights, cameras. All the stuff I've been wanting for years. She's not going to come near you. I won't let her."

Stevie looked at Larry now and felt the sudden urge to cry. Something in her melted a bit. Was it gratitude? Pent-up fear? She balled her hands and turned back toward the dark side of the room, back at the dank basement labyrinth she was in. There were so many places to get lost in here, up here. In life. So many dark corners.

Stevie turned back to the small window once more. It was just wide enough to wiggle through. The whole escape would have required such . . . bravado. Ellie had kept her shit together.

Larry indicated that she should return the way they had come, down the little path of lights. He pulled the cord, and the chamber went dark. Only a bit of light came in through that window, like a dim, heavily lidded eye.

As Stevie stepped out of the Great House, she noticed there was something in the Neptune fountain that had not been there when she went in. David sat in it, the streams of water pouring from the open mouths of Neptune's mighty fish friends dumping onto his head, flattening his hair.

"This is what they call attention-seeking behavior," she said, approaching him.

"They're going to turn it off for the winter soon," David replied, opening his mouth for a gulp of fountain water.

"Is that clean?" she said. "Should you be drinking it?"

He shrugged. Then he stood, his clothes dripping, and climbed out of the fountain. He stuck his hands in the pockets of his shorts and walked along beside her as if there was nothing unusual about what he had just done.

"Therapy," she said. "It works."

"I've tried it. They always end up crying. I think I've helped them have some real breakthrough moments. You were in there a while. What were you up to?"

"Were you following me?"

"Not following," he said. "I just take an interest. What were you doing?"

"Just looking," she said.

"At what?"

"The basement."

"What did you see?"

"A maze," she replied. "The basement is weird. But it's clear how Ellie got out. She went through the passage, and then out the basement window."

"We know that," he said. "My question is, what happened then?"

"I don't know the answer," she said. "I'm trying. You asked me to look. I'm looking."

David shivered a bit in his wet hoodie. It wasn't proper fall weather yet, but it was definitely not the kind of day to be walking around in sopping wet clothes. Stevie couldn't help but take note of the fact that he was keeping track of her, and the fountain was done to impress her. And it was making an impression. It was bizarre—and he looked good wet.

"Well, look faster," he said.

Polite conversation isn't hard, Edward King had said.

Even David's voice was a little like his father's. The words were different, but the timbre was the same. The King poison touched everything.

"This isn't on me," she snapped.

"I didn't say it was," he replied. "It's just that time is passing."

"It's not my fault."

"I didn't say it—"

"Well, you're acting like it," she said, walking off.

It was amazingly easy to work herself into a state of indignation. She had to repel herself—not see David, not feel what she always felt around him. She had to drive the desire out of her. An argument was as good a way as any of distracting herself. But it only worked to a point.

Also, she had to wonder: Did David blame her for what happened? Did everyone?

"'ANATOMY,'" PIX SAID, WRITING THE WORD ON THE WHITEBOARD, "comes from the Greek. The prefix, *ana*, means apart. The root word, *tome*, is 'cutting.' 'Dissection' is Latin in origin. *Dis* means apart as well, and *secare* is the root word for cutting. So anatomy and dissection are linked in language and in practice. To understand how bodies work, you need to get in there and have a look."

Monday morning brought Stevie back to her first class, which was anatomy and physiology, taught by Pix. Anatomy was one of the things Stevie had looked most forward to studying at Ellingham—it was the kind of thing she would need to know. They had reached the dissection part of the program, which meant that they had moved into a lab. She had a new partner as well—Mudge, he of the colored contact lenses.

"On that note," Pix said, "come down here and get a dissection kit for each of your stations, along with a sheep heart."

Stevie reluctantly went down and got one of the trays, which was preset with scalpels, scissors, and probes. She reached into the cooler and removed one vacuum-packed sheep heart, which was a deep red, almost black.

"You want to cut or diagram?" Mudge asked.

Stevie looked at the heart. It looked like shrink-wrapped cooked beets. As much as she liked wearing the gloves, she was not enthused about this.

"Draw," she said.

"Cool."

They both put on lab gloves, and Mudge picked up the heart and cut the package open.

"You like anatomy?" she asked.

"I love it," Mudge said quietly.

"You want to be a doctor?"

"I want to work at Disney World," Mudge said.

Stevie looked up at her lab partner, all six and a half feet of him, with the dyed jet-black hair, the purple snake-eye contact lenses, and the spiked rings and bracelets.

"What?" he said.

"Disney World?" she asked.

"I love Disney World. Look."

He leaned down and pulled on the collar of his Slipknot T-shirt with his gloved fingers. There was a small object pinned to it. It was a Mickey Mouse enamel pin.

"This is a retired one-year-service pin," he said. "I collect them. I have about a hundred."

He stood back up.

"It's why I don't have any tattoos," he said. "Cast members can't have visible tattoos."

"You want to be a cast member?" Stevie said. "Like, play Mickey?"

"All staff are called cast members," he said. "I mean, eventually I want to be an Imagineer, but I'd like to start by working the park at the visitor level. What's the first incision?"

As Stevie stepped out of the building, still smelling of dissection, she found David sitting, waiting for her, wearing a pair of sunglasses and looking smug.

"Hello, Scooby," he said. "Have you had any brain waves?"

Stevie had conferred with him the night before, saying that she had looked in the basement. The basement hadn't really advanced her knowledge.

"I told you," she said. "It seems clear she went down through the passage, grabbed some stuff to get up to the window, and then climbed out."

"Which we know," he said. "I guess I'm just surprised she didn't tell me there was an escape panel in the wall over at the Great House. We shared that kind of thing."

"Do you know other places?" Stevie asked.

"I know all kinds of things," he said with a smile. "Maybe, if you're good, I'll share. But the point is, how does she go out the window and then vanish into thin air? For all the reasons I said?"

"So what do you think?" Stevie said. "If you were her?"

"Maybe she hid that night," he said. "That's been my feeling all along. I think she hid until she could figure out what to do. Lots of places she could have hid. But they locked shit down after that, that's what keeps getting me. No coat, no phone. I don't know. She used a phone somewhere. I just don't get it and can't get it. But . . . I guess I should go to calc."

"You're going to calc?" Stevie said.

"I make the occasional appearance," he replied. "Keeps Shorty on his toes. Dr. Short loves me. Everyone loves me. I'm lovable."

He lifted his sunglasses and winked at her, then spun to head to class.

What the hell did that mean? Clearly, they were friends again. Or David felt they were.

She shook off her confusion and headed to the Great House. She had work to do.

The Ellingham attic was a place of true magic. It was perhaps the most private location on campus, this cavern above it all, its expanse as large as the footprint of the Great House. It was shrouded in half-light through the blinds. This is where the detritus of Ellingham life had ended up, here on all of these metal shelving racks. Stevie walked among them again, letting the quiet seep over her. It smelled faintly of dust, but this was a fine, storied dust, gently trapped in velvets, resting like new snow on mirrors. Everything here was trapped in time.

A lot of it, Stevie remembered as she walked around to reacclimatize herself, was junk, really. Good junk, but junk. There were boxes of doorknobs. Stacks of plates. Boxes of old uniforms. Some things she had been wanting to revisit, like the aisle that contained the old items from Albert Ellingham's office—the things that hadn't really mattered enough to send on to any museum or archive. There were some telephones and cords, unused papers and slips. She dug into one of the boxes, where she had found the Western Union slip with the riddle that Albert Ellingham had written on the day he died:

Where do you look for someone who's never really there?
Always on a staircase but never on a stair

She dug around in this box again, eying her notepad to see if anything Fenton wanted might be in here. The box contained things like paperweights, staples, old letterhead, some little boxes marked in Smith Corona typewriter ribbon, F. B. Bridges finest-quality pen tips, Webster-Chicago Recording Wire, paper rolls for a Borough's Adding Machine . . . all these products that must have been something once, something you'd find everywhere, that meant nothing now. They were obsolete.

She sat down on the floor and read through the notepad that Fenton had given her. There were 307 items she wanted Stevie to check. Some would be relatively easy and quick—checking which rooms had connecting doors, confirming colors and materials and patterns. Some would require reading through the many volumes of household records. What struck Stevie was how mundane, even stupid, these details were. Or, at least, that's how they seemed. But detection, and maybe book writing, required research, and details mattered.

She opened a document on her laptop and worked out a rough plan of attack, bundling the items into groups that she could search for at the same time. With a little effort, she got them into seven lists, grouped by type. This kind of work soothed her and got her out of her head. Break it down, put it in order, make a list. Soon, Fenton's sloppy notes were in a clean format. She decided to start on the first list right then and there, and pulled down several volumes of household records.

The records contained all the daily workings of the Ellingham house: groceries and supplies ordered, meals served, tasks accomplished. Meat came on Mondays and Thursdays, fish four times a week, and the dairy made massive deliveries every day. Oranges and lemons were special ordered from Florida in the winter. Groceries, vegetables, and household goods came in sometimes three times a day. Cleaning was a massive, ongoing process. Aside from the regular house staff, local people came in by the truckload to scrub windows and patios, to polish the miles of rosewood, to dust the mountains of marble, to clean out fireplaces and cut and stack wood, to pack the icehouses, to repair anything that needed mending. There was the outdoor staff as well—a small army of gardeners to plant and weed and water and coax life out of the side of the mountain. All of this, plus the hundreds more who were working to finish the school. It became crystal clear just how much Ellingham Academy must have meant to the local people. *Everyone* must have worked there at one time or another. Everyone sold them things. Businesses depended on this strange man and his school in the middle of nowhere. It was so much effort for so few people, and at the same time, Albert Ellingham became the source of so much. An attack on him would have been an attack on everyone.

It certainly made a kind of sense that someone would have wanted Anton Vorachek dead. People would have known the family, depended on them. And so many people would have had a look at at least part of the grounds. They would not have known the tunnels, but the ice man would have known the basement, the deliveryman the kitchen, the cleaners would have seen the interior of the house. People talked.

Stevie shut her computer and closed her eyes. A feather. A bit of beaded cloth. A lipstick. A pair of would-be gangsters. What did it all *mean*? Did Francis and Edward talk to someone? Did they work with someone from the outside?

The answers were not available yet.

She dusted herself off and glanced around again. There were old friends to visit. Somewhere around here was a box of newspapers that Albert Ellingham had buried in the tunnel— it had just been excavated. They might contain something useful. She could not find it. She went on to the end of the room, to the attic's greatest treasure. It was a massive mound, about eight feet across, covered in a sheet. She pulled this off gingerly.

Underneath was another Great House, an exact copy. This had been made for Alice Ellingham after her disappearance.

It sat here, gathering dust, waiting for her return. She reached around to find the latch and swung it open, examining the rooms inside as they had existed in the 1930s. There were cooks in the kitchen, working with tiny pots. Iris's bedroom was there, her bed made in small satin bed linens, her dresser set with little brushes and perfume bottles. Stevie looked down on the scene like a goddess, examining the old bedrooms, the rustic bathrooms with their tiny tiles. And there was Albert Ellingham's office, with copies of his chairs, his desks, his rugs, and even some of the very things she had just been looking at.

There was even a doll of him. Stevie picked him up. The jointed china bent to her will. His face was painted with a benevolent smile. There was something profoundly disturbing about the dollhouse. Perhaps that was why it had never been displayed.

It was getting darker now. The attic had fallen into shadow. It was probably time to go to dinner. She replaced the doll. On her way out, she looked out the west-facing window toward the maintenance shed and the small faculty parking lot. There were just two very expensive cars down there. Doctor Quinn was walking toward one of them, a red sports car of some kind, switching out her glasses. It seemed fitting that she would drive something that looked like it should be zipping along some European mountain road, or perhaps the coastline of Nice. But the parking lot was not the real view. From here, she could see into the far distance, the mountains. What had it taken to build this place? To take an unbroken mountaintop that no one could live on and build a tiny empire? Albert Ellingham was obsessed with gods and goddesses. Was he trying to make his own Olympus, to own a piece of earth and sky?

Her phone buzzed in her pocket, and she pulled it out. It was a text from an unknown number.

Hope things are going well. —EK

Edward King, just letting her know that he was here. That he was keeping tabs. The text felt as palpable as a hand on the shoulder. She had not given him her number, but that was the whole point—he was telling her he did not need to ask for this information. It was his to take.

"You want to play?" she asked the phone.

But she had no move to make against him. The only thing she could do was work down this list, keep working her leads. He didn't own her—he had simply borrowed a part of her.

That was what she was going to keep telling herself.

12

HALLOWEEN, THE SEASON AND THEN THE DATE, CREPT SLOWLY UP ON the Ellingham campus. The scenery was repainted each evening, the leaves more gold than green. Some of the vines that snaked up the buildings turned a shocking red. Pumpkins began to appear in windows and doorways and nooks. The nights reached into the days with long fingers, dragging back time. Stevie fell back into the ways of Ellingham, and Ellingham fell back into her. Her room felt more snug. It smelled more familiar, of her comforter and Ellingham laundry detergent (they had a service—your laundry went out dirty in a bag and came back clean and folded), like the old smoke from the fire in the common room.

She tried to catch up with her classes, and for maybe a week she believed that she might even be able to do it. This confidence largely came from a one-night sprint doing Spanish modules until three in the morning. The burst left her feeling academic, maybe brilliant, maybe an unsung genius of her time. The euphoria came crashing down when she realized she was missing entire systems in anatomy, was four novels behind in English, and her history paper on the Harding presidency was something that would never really be written. Its existence was a little concept joke.

She had, however, made progress with Fenton's requests. She had been doing long hours in the attic, going over the tedium of the list. Stevie did not know she could be bored by details about the Ellingham case, but Fenton had accomplished it.

Now, on Halloween morning, she was on the coach again, returning with the first properly completed piece of work she had done at her entire time at Ellingham. It was good to do *something* right.

Before going to Burlington, Stevie had to assure Janelle that she would be back in time for that night's Halloween party. Stevie had always been Halloween ambivalent. There were many positive things about Halloween—true-crime shows always got an extra bump, other shows pulled out their murder-mystery episodes, and slinking around in the dark was generally more acceptable. But she could never get on board with the costumes. There was the first problem: being "cute." That had been the message her whole life. As a child, Halloween was that day Stevie was stuffed into a Disney princess outfit against her will. "You look so cute," her mom would say, as she safety-pinned the thin polyester Belle dress to the layer of warm clothes she had on underneath. "Don't you want to be a princess?"

Stevie did not want to be a princess. She was not sure what princesses were, or what they did. She asked to be a different princess, like Princess Leia, but this was rejected. The reason was never given. Stevie pointed to every costume in the store—a ghost, a pirate, a banana. It was no use. It was the Disney princess every time, the same costumes pulled out over and over.

It was an understood thing that Janelle Franklin took Halloween very seriously. She had organized and planned for it with the same precision and attention to detail that she applied to everything in her life. Stevie had watched her construct a Wonder Woman costume piece by piece for a week, sewing, applying, cutting foam, spray painting, and hot-gluing. More than once she had called Stevie in for help, and during these times she had grilled Stevie on what she was going to be. She did not accept Stevie's answer of someone who stays at home and does not wear a costume.

"Halloween is a chance to be whatever you want to be," Janelle said as Stevie hot-glued a foam piece in the form of a gold *W* to a corset that Janelle was wearing. "It doesn't have to be all sexy, sexy. That's patriarchal bullshit. I'm Wonder Woman because I love Wonder Woman. Who do you love?"

"The people who work at DNA databases?" Stevie said, checking to make sure the *W* was secure.

"Okay. How about detectives? What about Sherlock Holmes?"

Stevie rolled her eyes.

"What's wrong with Sherlock Holmes?" Janelle asked.

"Nothing is wrong with Sherlock Holmes," Stevie said. "But he's not a *costume*. He's . . ."

Stevie waved her hands in the air to try to convey that you didn't just dress up like the world's greatest fictional detective, the one upon whom real-world detection techniques were based, and no, it wasn't about the hat or the coat. Janelle guided her hand back carefully, because Stevie was still holding a hot-glue gun.

"Name another one," Janelle said.

"I don't know . . . Hercule Poirot."

"Good!" Janelle said. "Fine. Do that."

Stevie's costume budget was basically ten dollars, and less if she could manage it. The school permitted students to use the costumes at the theater. There, Stevie had found a suit that—if not entirely up to the exacting standards of Belgium's neatest detective—was good enough. She would slick back her hair and wear a hat. Vi had a can of dark spray that they would let Stevie use. She had bought the mustache online. She set all these things out on her bed on Saturday morning before getting on the coach to go to her meeting. Tonight, she had to play the part of detective. Now, she had to go to try to be one.

Fenton lived in the middle of Burlington, in the university area. The street she lived on was full of big Victorian houses that were likely once the homes of rich families. They had big wraparound porches that faced toward Lake Champlain. The university had taken over some of the fine brick buildings and made them into university property. The others—the big, rambling ones painted all kinds of colors— had been divided up into apartments for students, who put coolers and rocking chairs and hammocks on the porches and hung banners and tapestries in the windows.

Her house was a tiny sage-green one between a fraternity and a deli. It had a big screened-in front porch. This was filled with piles of newspapers, milk crates, and a lot of recycling. There was a theme in the recycling, Stevie noted. There were a lot of bottles in it. Many wine bottles, two whiskey bottles, a vodka bottle. She remembered Hunter picking up Fenton's mug and examining it.

This gesture suddenly made a lot more sense.

There was music blasting inside, so Stevie had to knock for almost a full minute on the peeling green door before it opened. Fenton answered, an unlit cigarette in her mouth. Today she wore an old pair of mom jeans and a baggy black sweater.

"Hey," she said, shooing a big orange cat back inside with her bare foot. "Come in."

Somehow, Fenton's house was everything Stevie knew it would be, and yet it still surprised her. The house smelled like cigarette smoke and cat and trash and a single scented candle that was probably supposed to cover all that but only made it worse. They had entered a living room that was mostly composed of books. Books on shelves. Books in stacks along the wall. Books all over a round table in the middle of the room. Books scattered on seats. There was a large television, and a cabinet full of DVDs. There were glasses and mugs everywhere, things in tinfoil that she could not identify. There were also some things that were likely Hunter's—a coat, some sneakers, some books on the environment. As she scanned the room, she spotted two more cats hiding out in the scenery. The smell hung over it all. Stevie tried not to show it, but she couldn't help but shield her nose.

"Something wrong?" Fenton said over the music.

"No, it's . . ."

Fenton turned off the music and the silence was abrupt.

"You like the Rolling Stones?" she asked.

"I . . ."

"Best band in the world. *Exile on Main Street*. Best album in the world. No arguments. Does something stink? Hunter tells me that all the time. I lost my sense of smell years ago. Open a window if something smells off. Come into my office."

Fenton put the unlit cigarette behind her ear and waved Stevie through a set of French doors covered in bamboo blinds. This room took things to a new level. The majority of the room was taken up by a massive walnut desk with a shaded green lamp. There was a much-used leather chair in the corner. There were books in here as well, kept in low, orderly stacks. These were interspersed with large cardboard file boxes and metal file cabinets. But it was the walls that really captured her attention. One wall was full of black-and-white photographs of people known to be in the house on the day of the kidnapping. There was a whole section of photos of Vorachek. Then photos of the house and grounds. Then maps, new and old. The one closest to Stevie was made of thin, frail paper but was in very good condition, showing the highways of Vermont in blocky blue ink. Several pushpins were in this map.

"Original road map printed in 1935," Fenton said.

It was a conspiracy wall. A true, real conspiracy wall. The only things missing were the bits of string that connected the various points.

"So," Fenton said, "how did we do?"

Stevie pushed over the notepad.

"I have two hundred and ninety out of three hundred and seven," Stevie said. "A few things were missing. I couldn't find the one china pattern you wanted."

Fenton *hmm*ed and flipped through the pad, rolling one of her gray spiral curls around her finger.

"Let me read through this," she said. "Go and get yourself a Coke or something in the kitchen."

Fenton waved Stevie off. Stevie went back through the living room, stopping to pet a big ginger cat on one of the sofas. The sofa was thick with cat hair, almost to the point where the color of the sofa was obscured. There were traces of cat litter around the floor, along with ash and specks of paper. Every exposed surface had water rings on it. She had a feeling that the kitchen would not be a pleasant experience, but some effort had been made. There were many dirty glasses, but they were clustered together by the sink. There were some empty wine bottles and a pizza box on the floor by the trash. Nothing good would come of opening the refrigerator. Stevie came from an uptight family, where the slightest smell or stain or smudge in the kitchen was unacceptable, and she just knew that there would be a smell in this fridge from something incorrectly sealed and outdated.

There were, however, some warm Cokes in a box on the

floor. Stevie took one, opened it, and wiped the top of the can with her sleeve before sipping. She glanced through the pile of books on the table, and had just opened one about the Yorkshire Ripper when she heard the door open.

"Hey!" called a voice.

She leaned over to look and saw Hunter coming in the door, leaning his crutch against the wall and dropping his backpack to remove his puffer coat. Stevie leaned back in, feeling weird about being in his house, drinking his warm Coke, even though she was allowed to be here.

"I couldn't get any limes," he said. "But I bought some lunch meat . . ."

He came into the kitchen and blinked in surprise.

"Hey!" he said. "Oh. Hey. Sorry. Hi."

"Hunter?" Fenton yelled.

"Yeah!"

"Get Stevie a Coke!"

Hunter smirked in gentle embarrassment and nodded at the Coke Stevie was holding.

"Sorry," he said. "It's kind of a mess in here. Are you . . . working?"

"Your aunt is going through some stuff I did."

"Oh. Cool." Hunter looked around, as if he was sorry for intruding in his own house. There was something sunny about Hunter. He had light hair. The cut was a little too short, probably a cheap and fast one, or maybe a home job. His smattering of freckles made him look younger than he was.

"So," he said, sitting down. "What's Ellingham like?"

"Intense," she said. "Really good. A lot."

"So how did you get in?"

"I just wrote about how I was obsessed with the case," she said. "I didn't think they'd take me. Someone liked me, though."

"I guess you have the something," he said. "Actually, I applied. I didn't get my letter from Hogwarts."

She realized for the first time that she was an insider to others who might have wanted to go there, wanted to have this magic. She was to be envied. It was weird, and not entirely comfortable, and she wanted to say something to make Hunter feel better, but she knew that if someone had said something to her in that position, she would have taken it as being patronizing.

"It's okay," he said. "I wasn't hanging on it or anything. I just knew about it because of my aunt and I took a shot."

He smirked and glanced around, as if embarrassed by everything he was saying.

"I still think I was a mistake," Stevie said.

"Everyone must say that."

"No one says that," Stevie said. "But me. It may be true. My friend Janelle is a genius. My friend Nate is an author. Everyone's *something* there."

"And you're something," he said.

"I like crime," she said.

"Who doesn't?" he said, smiling.

"Lots of people."

"Stupid people," he said.

This made her smile.

"Good work." Fenton was standing in the doorway. "You did this a lot faster than I expected. My lazy-ass grad students would have taken all semester. Come on."

Hunter grimaced just a bit, and Stevie got up to follow Fenton back to her office. Once inside, Fenton shut the double doors and then sat and looked Stevie over.

"You're serious," she said. "I like that. I thought we were going to be screwing around, but all right. Maybe we can do some real work together."

Stevie wondered what she had just spent a week doing if it was not real work.

"First rule," Fenton said, pointing at the wall of document boxes. "Don't put your stuff on the internet. Once you put it online, it's worthless. It's not yours."

She took the cigarette from behind her ear and lit it with a lighter from her desk.

"I assume you've read the Vorachek court transcript?"

"Of course," Stevie said. That was one of the first things anyone interested in the case did. Fenton pulled out a bound copy with what looked like a hundred Post-it notes flagging from the side. She licked her thumb and opened it to a blue-noted page.

"Here," she said. "Read from the highlighted lines."

It was the testimony of Marion Nelson, the housemistress of Minerva. These were the lines Fenton had highlighted:

PROSECUTION: *Miss Nelson, can you tell us when you first realized Dolores Epstein was missing?*

MARION NELSON: *It was right after nine that night.*

PROSECUTION: *Nine at night? Isn't that late for a young girl to be out?*

MN: *Well, no, not at Ellingham. One of the precepts of the school is that the children have freedom to learn and explore. The school is—the school seemed—and generally is very safe. So they can read, play, experiment, study. Dottie was a voracious reader, and she would often hide away somewhere with a book. But generally, she would appear for supper.*

PROSECUTION: *And she did not?*

MN: *No.*

PROSECUTION: *When did you first learn that she was missing?*

MN: *When Mr. Ellingham's men came to the door at dawn and told us to get the children packed and ready to leave.*

"Now," Fenton said, taking the transcript back and turning to a later page, to testimony from July 22, 1938, from Margo Fields, the local telephone operator who connected the ransom calls. Fenton had highlighted more lines:

PROSECUTION: *Miss Fields, you were working at the telephone exchange in Burlington on April 13, 1936. Is this correct?*

MARGO FIELDS: *Yes. I was. Yes. At work. Yes.*

PROSECUTION: *How long have you been a telephone operator, Miss Fields?*

MF: *Six years this June. I started as soon as I left high school. I didn't know what I wanted to do, but there was an opening and I applied for it, and I got it and I've been doing it ever since.*

PROSECUTION: *What can you tell us about the telephone lines going to Ellingham Academy?*

MF: *Oh, there are a lot of them. There are seven lines going into the house, and then a lot of the buildings have their own telephones. There are sixteen lines going to the property in total.*

PROSECUTION: *Seven lines go into the main house?*

MF: *Yes. I didn't know a house could have seven phone lines until Mr. Ellingham came along! Imagine, seven telephones in one house!*

PROSECUTION: *Can you tell us where the lines go?*

MF: *Well, one goes to Mr. Montgomery. He's the butler. There's one to the kitchen. There's one to Mr. Mackenzie—he's Mr. Ellingham's secretary, one to Mrs. Ellingham, there's a guest telephone, and a housekeeper's telephone, and then, of course, there's Mr. Ellingham's telephone. Most of the calls to the house or going out of it go to Mr. Montgomery or Mr. Mackenzie or Mrs. Ellingham, unless there's a party up there, then the calls come and go from all the phones all day. And the calls that go into Mr. Ellingham's telephone—they come and go from all over!*

PROSECUTION: *Let's go to the afternoon of April 13, Miss Fields. When do you get to work?*

MF: *Well, that day I was doing a shift starting at five p.m. I have lunch at Henry's before I do that shift. So I sat down at my station at five p.m. and took over from Helen. Helen Woolman.*

PROSECUTION: *I'm entering into evidence exhibit 56A, Your Honor. Miss Fields, is this the logbook you use to record calls?*

MF: *It is.*

PROSECUTION: *Can you tell us about the telephone call you connected at seven fifteen that evening?*

MF: *Yes, I can. That phone call came from a telephone booth on College and Church Streets. They called Mr. Montgomery's telephone. I don't see many calls coming from telephone booths going to the Ellingham house, but that's right by the market, so I thought it might be a delivery or some such. But I was curious, you know?*

PROSECUTION: *Can you describe the voice on the line?*

MF: *Rough. Very rough. With a strange way of speaking. He sounded like he was speaking through a tube or something. That telephone can have a funny connection, though.*

PROSECUTION: *Was there anything else about the voice? How was it strange?*

MF: *Oh, it had an accent.*

PROSECUTION: *What kind of accent?*

MF: *Not American. European, I think. My neighbor, Mrs. Czarnecki, from down the street, she's from Warsaw,* in Poland, and it sounded a bit like her, but not quite? I stayed on the line just long enough to hear Mr. Montgomery answer. I wish I'd hung on, but we don't do that. Oh, I wish I had. You don't know how I wish I had. I don't know what I would have done.

PROSECUTION: How long did that call last?

MF: Five or six minutes.

PROSECUTION: What happened after that?

MF: The next call was outgoing. This was at seven forty-five. Mr. Mackenzie telephoned out and asked to be connected to . . . that would be George Marsh. That's another common call. After that, Mr. Mackenzie called me back and asked me to make a special note of where all calls coming in and out of the house came from that evening. He sounded a bit funny, but he said something about Mr. Ellingham just needing to know for some business reason. And he asked where the previous call had come from, and I told him. I usually go on a half hour dinner break at seven in the evening, but I ate my sandwich at my station because Mr. Mackenzie had asked me to pay special attention, and we always take care of the Ellingham lines. He's done so much for those children. I remember I had a cheese and tomato jam sandwich, and a call came in as soon as I took a bite.

PROSECUTION: What can you tell us about the other calls?

MF: All right. I've recorded here that at 8:03 p.m., there was an incoming call from New York City that went

to Mrs. Ellingham's personal telephone. That was
unanswered. I didn't know why then, but I do now, of
course. That was from a Manhattan exchange—a line I
saw often. I think it's a friend of hers.

PROSECUTION: That call was identified as being from
Mrs. Rose Peabody, and she was a friend of Mrs.
Ellingham.

MF: Yes, there was nothing really new about that call. Now,
the next call, that was incoming from another telephone
booth, which was odd. This was at 8:47. This was a
telephone by the gasoline station as you go out on Route
Two. Do you know the one? That call was to Mr.
Mackenzie's line. Now, this was the same strange voice
as the first call, I'm sure of it. Very rough. I stayed on
long enough to hear Mr. Mackenzie pick it up. There was
another call at 9:50 to Mrs. Ellingham's line, the same
number from New York City, Mrs. Peabody, and it went
unanswered. I went off duty at midnight and I called Mr.
Mackenzie to tell him so and I read off the information to
him.

PROSECUTION: Those were the only calls?

MF: Yes.

PROSECUTION: Coming in, going out, even between the
buildings?

MF: Some days the Ellingham lines are very busy, but
the evenings are generally quieter, and I think Mr.
Ellingham was in town that day, so his phones were
quieter. So it wasn't that odd.

PROSECUTION: *The voice you heard. Could you identify it if you heard it again?*

MF: *I . . . think I could? I might. It was a strange voice. There was something wrong with it.*

PROSECUTION: *Something wrong?*

MF: *I can't explain it.*

PROSECUTION: *But you think you would know it?*

MF: *I think I might?*

PROSECUTION: *Your Honor, I'd like to ask the defendant, Mr. Anton Vorachek, to read something out loud.*

DEFENSE: *Objection, Your Honor.*

JUDGE LADSKY: *I'll allow it.*

PROSECUTION: *Mr. Vorachek, I've written something on this piece of paper. I'd just like you to read it in your normal speaking voice.*

ANTON VORACHEK: *I am not an actor. I won't be in your play.*

JUDGE LADSKY: *You are out of order, Mr. . . .*

ANTON VORACHEK: *This court is a farce! You are all puppets of the capitalist state!*

JUDGE LADSKY: *Mr. Vorachek! I am on the verge of having you removed from the courtroom.*

PROSECUTION: *Your Honor, that may be enough for my purposes. Miss Fields, you've just heard Mr. Vorachek's voice. Was that the voice you heard?*

MF: *Oh, voices are strange. You hear so many of them down the lines and you pick up little things and you think you*

can pick them apart, but then they all go back together
again. I just got the feeling that this person . . . didn't
want to be understood? It was such a terrible night. I
didn't know that then, of course, but after. But . . . yes.
I think, maybe yes.

PROSECUTION: No further questions, Your Honor.

Stevie knew better than to say, "What about it?" She looked to Fenton for a clue as to where this was going.

"She says that there were no other calls from nine fifty to midnight," Fenton said. "And Miss Nelson says that she found out about the kidnapping in the morning. So, I did a little checking."

There was a pile of yellow legal pads on the corner of the desk. She sorted through the stack until she got the one she wanted.

"I told you I had some new information," Fenton said. "I talked to a lot of people. I got some very interesting, very important information. One of the people I found was Gertie van Coevorden. Gertie van Coevorden was—"

"A student from Minerva," she said.

"Right. A very rich one, one who liked to talk about that night to anyone who would listen. I interviewed her and recorded it and transcribed it. Here's what she said: *'It was a terrible night, so foggy. We were all of us gathered in the common room. We were all such good friends in Minerva, and we cared about each other so much. Dottie hadn't come home and we were all so worried about her. Dottie was one of my dearest friends. Something* was wrong, and I kept saying to Miss Nelson, our housemistress, that someone should be looking for her. I was thinking about doing it myself, but then the phone rang upstairs. Miss Nelson went to answer it. It was right before ten in the evening because there was a radio program we liked to listen to that came on at ten o'clock. But Miss Nelson made us all go to bed, and she started acting very strange.'"

Fenton looked up from the pad.

"There's no mention of connecting a phone call at ten o'clock," Fenton said. "So then I look again at what Margo Fields actually says. Prosecution: Coming in, going out, even between the buildings? And Margo Fields doesn't say, yeah, that's right. She says something totally different. She says, 'Some days the Ellingham lines are very busy, but the evenings are generally quieter, and I think Mr. Ellingham was in town that day, so his phones were quieter. So it wasn't that odd.' Which is not actually an answer. So what do we have?"

"A discrepancy," Stevie said. "Gertie van Coevorden says that there was a call and the records say there wasn't."

"And we have a telephone operator who is being evasive on the stand. She isn't lying if she moves around the topic. So, which story is correct, do you think? Gertie van Coevorden with her phone call, or the evasive phone operator?"

Stevie sat back and spun this around in her mind.

"Why didn't anyone notice what Gertie said about a phone call before?" she asked.

Fenton smiled and tapped a finger alongside her nose.

"Exactly the right question. *Because no one ever asked her.* They seem to have gone to great lengths not to ask anyone in

Minerva House about phone calls. And Gertie van Coevorden did not strike me as being one of the nation's great thinkers. I don't think she noticed that the phone call was missing, from the accounts of things. But I did."

"So what does it mean? Someone called Minerva? That makes sense—they'd be looking for Dottie."

"Right again," Fenton said. "So why does the record of this phone call not exist? The answer is in the building plan of Ellingham Academy."

She went to the wall of black-and-white photos of the house and grounds.

"You know there are tunnels up there, right? You've been in the most famous one. But there are others. Many have been partially earthed in or sealed for safety—but the whole point of secret tunnels was that they were *secret*. Personal use. According to Gertie, there was a tunnel in Minerva."

"In Minerva?" Stevie said. "I live in Minerva."

"Any word of a tunnel there?"

"Nothing that I've heard."

"Gertie was convinced of it. She said another student found it, that she had seen this student disappear and reappear."

"Where does it go?"

"If my guess is right, it goes to somewhere on the other side of the campus, somewhere secluded, sort of over here."

She got up and pointed to the area down near the cafeteria and the gym.

"So, if we find this tunnel," Stevie said, "where does it get us?"

"I have a little theory," Fenton said. "If I can prove the tunnel exists, my theory is more likely."

"What's the theory?" Stevie said.

"For me to know. But if I'm right, and this book turns out the way I think it will, you'll have been a part of it. There's your assignment. See about that tunnel. Scout around."

Stevie decided not to mention that tunneling was kind of frowned upon. Best to leave that alone. She had just been given an official assignment.

Hunter was sitting in the living room as they walked out, petting a big orange cat on his lap.

"All done?" he said. "You need a ride, or . . ."

"Leave her alone," Fenton snapped. "They have a coach."

Fenton sneezed, then yanked a copy of her book off a pile of what looked like old copies.

"Here," she said. "For you."

Stevie had one already, and this one had yellowed edges, but she accepted it. Fenton went off to the kitchen, their exchange finished.

"I just meant if you needed one," Hunter said. "Sorry. She's . . . abrupt."

"No, it's fine," Stevie said. "They don't let people come up to campus, anyway."

"Oh, right." His cheeks flushed a bit. "Yeah. Stupid. Sorry."

"Don't be sorry," she said.

"Look," he said. "Is it weird if I give you my phone number? Just since you're working with my aunt and . . ."

He looked toward the kitchen, where Fenton was humming loudly.

". . . you may, you may want it. Or. You may not."

"Sure," Stevie said, offering her phone.

She wasn't sure why he was giving her his number—whether it was the smile he had given her before, or the erratic nature of Fenton that suggested that something was not quite right with this whole arrangement. It was a phone number in any case, someone else to connect with.

It wasn't the worst feeling.

13

At six that evening, as the day drew to a close and the shadows fell over Ellingham, Stevie Bell stood in her room, tucking herself into the suit that still smelled strongly of mothballs and must from the costume attic. She stood before the mirror and did what the famously fastidious Belgian detective would do—she adjusted her mustache until it was perfect. She tucked a pillow into her front to fill out her belly a bit and take up some of the extra space in the baggy suit. She'd found a walking-stick prop and some white gloves, and the overall effect was pleasing.

This tunnel stuff was stupid. If there was a tunnel under Minerva, someone would have found it by now. David. Ellie. Someone. It would have loomed large in the legend.

Still, a passable effort would need to be made. Hercule would look.

The source of the tunnel would have to be on the first floor. This meant the possible entry points were the kitchen, the common room, the hallway, either one of the two bathrooms, or any of the three bedrooms. She had already crawled all over Ellie's floor. There was no evidence of a tunnel in there. Of course, entrances could be carefully hidden, but still. She got down and examined her floor, crawling, tapping, picking at the boards. Nothing.

She could check Janelle's room later. Janelle was deep into her Wonder Woman transformation and could not be disturbed. But it seemed unlikely that the bedrooms were the source. The entry would have to be through the floor.

She went to the kitchen, poking into the back of the cabinets with her stick. It was possible the refrigerator or the stove or dishwasher could have been covering the opening, but then, surely these spots had been checked. You needed to hook these things up with water and gas. The refrigerator was heavy. A hollow spot under it would likely have been found.

She walked around the common room, looking at the flagstone floor. This was a more promising area, as any one of these stones could be a hatch. But it certainly appeared that the seals were tight. Similarly, the bathrooms showed no sign of having a passage anywhere in the floor.

It was a perfunctory check, and she would look more later, but it really seemed that Fenton had to be wrong. Maybe there was a tunnel somewhere on the campus that had not been found, but it probably wasn't here.

She was crawling down the hallway, examining the boards, when Nate came up behind her.

"What are you doing?" he asked.

Stevie stood up and adjusted her pillow stomach.

"Nothing," she said. "Thought I dropped something. Is that your costume?"

Nate was wearing his normal clothes—his grayed-out cords and a loose T-shirt.

"I don't do costumes," he said.

Janelle's door swung open, and Wonder Janelle stood in the doorway.

"You think you're getting away with that?" she said to Nate. "I guessed this was going to happen."

She reached behind her door and plucked out a long gray cloak made of some coarse material, a wizard hat of a similar color, and a gray beard. She extended the outfit in his direction.

Nate stared and did not move.

"You just . . . had that there?" he asked.

"EBay," she said. "And a little sewing. Take it."

Nate took the costume and put it over his arm.

"And here."

She reached back again and produced a tree branch that had been roughly fashioned into a staff.

"How . . ." he said.

"Listen to me," Janelle said. "A lot of bad things have happened this year. It's been scary and sad and horrible. But we're here, and this is a holiday, which means we are going to celebrate because not everyone from this house can do that. So put on this wizard stuff, let me fix my tiara, and we go."

She shut her door.

"She's had this," Nate said. "All along."

"She's Janelle. She can see around corners. Are you going to wear it?"

Nate felt the material between his fingers, then picked up the staff and examined it.

"It's a pretty good Gandalf outfit," he said. "I guess she made this staff? Like she went out and found a branch?"

"Because she's Janelle," Stevie said.

They went to the common room and Nate started to slip into the robes. There was the creak of footsteps moving overhead. Janelle stepped out of her room, her tiara now perfectly in place, with a round shield on her back and a sword in her hand. She regarded Nate with a satisfied nod.

"Good," she said. "Team Minerva. Where's David?"

There was a patter of steps and the ungodly creak of the stairs, then, out of the dark of the hall, he emerged.

"Oh," Janelle said. "That's . . ."

"You did the . . ." The words were dying in Stevie's mouth. ". . . Sherlock thing."

David had, in fact, done the Sherlock thing that Stevie had dismissed for herself, specifically, the BBC one. He was wearing a sharply cut blue dress shirt, slender, tailored pants, and a long gray-black coat with a red interior. He had teased out his hair a bit and made sure it curled. In many ways, it was a perfect costume while not being a costume at all. And it was obviously intentional, directed at her.

Stevie's legs decided to debone themselves and her body became a hormonal swamp. She clutched her pillow belly for emotional support.

"What are you?" he said to Stevie. "A . . . chef?"

"She's Hercule Poirot," Janelle said, as if it was obvious that the baggy suit and fake mustache also translated.

"And Wonder Woman! And Gandalf! And Sherlock! All together! Just like nature intended. Should we go?"

The four of them headed out into the night. They were met on the path by Vi, who was dressed as a perfect Steve Trevor.

"So," David said as the five of them passed under the dark trees to the Great House. "Is this weird?"

"Which part?" Stevie said.

"Is there fan-fic of this? You know, these two. What does that look like? What do we call it? Porlock? Sheriot?"

Janelle and Vi were arm in arm, Wonder Woman and Steve. Nate was off by himself, his cape brushing the lawn.

"Where did you get the coat?" Stevie said, trying to sound casual.

"What, this old thing?" he said, extending his hands in the pockets and showing it off. "I just charged a two-thousand-dollar coat to my dad's credit card."

"There are two-thousand-dollar coats?" Stevie replied.

"He'd want me to have it. I can't look *shabby*, can I? Not at the White House."

This was the first time David had ever said anything about his father's ambitions, and Stevie glanced around nervously.

"They didn't hear," he said. "And wouldn't understand if they did."

They walked in silence for a moment. The world was spinning gently as she comprehended what was going on—he was doing the sexy dress for *her*. Not the other way around. He was trying so hard, reaching for her.

"No chance you know about any tunnels under Minerva?" she asked, trying to regain some composure.

"There are no tunnels under Minerva."

"Not according to Fenton."

"What is a Fenton?"

"Fenton is the professor I work for in Burlington. The one writing a book about the case."

"There are no tunnels under Minerva," he repeated. "You think I wouldn't notice a tunnel under Minerva?"

"Secret tunnel," she said.

"I repeat."

"She seems pretty sure."

"Well, I'm pretty sure too. You haven't said if you like my coat."

"I like your coat." She meant it to come out dry and unaffected, but instead her bastard throat betrayed her with a tiny croaking sound on the last syllable. The body was the enemy of the mind.

Ellingham had gone all-out for the Halloween party. The Great House was made for occasions such as this, quite literally. All the overhead lights had been turned off and illumination came in the form of hundreds of tiny flickering electric candles. They were on every surface and lined the staircase. The diffused light winked off the crystal. A fire roared in the big fireplace, where a s'mores station had been set up, manned by Kaz, who was dressed as David Bowie, with a lightning bolt across his face. Call Me Charles approached dressed as Charlie Chaplin.

"You guys ready for some fun?" he asked.

"No," David said.

Charles let this slide and pointed toward the door of the ballroom with his costume cane.

This was not a silent party tonight. The ballroom, with its mirrored walls and its carnival mask decorations, flickered with light and was rich with sound. There were orange and white fairy lights draped from the ceiling, and hundreds more tiny electric candles flicking along the walls and floor. A table was set up with drinks and snacks. A few regular suspects were in the middle of the floor, dancing away, including Maris, who was wearing a red flapper outfit, a choice that felt inevitable to Stevie. Dash was there as well, dressed as Han Solo. Vi extended a gallant hand to Janelle, who took it. Wonder Woman and Steve began to dance.

"Hey."

Mudge was standing next to them, dressed as Mickey Mouse. A six-foot-five Mickey Mouse, with big ears coming off his jet-black hair.

"Cool Gandalf," he said to Nate. He looked a bit more confused by Stevie and David, but nodded politely.

"I'm a watch ad," David said. "She's a hipster grandpa. Together, we solve crime."

Mudge cocked his head at this and decided his time

might be better spent elsewhere. Nate also looked around the room from under the massive brim of his wizard hat and immediately decided that he was going to the s'mores station. Stevie and David were left standing on the side.

"You want to dance, Grandpa?" he asked Stevie.

"Her-cule."

"You want to dance, Hercule?"

Hercule was feeling nervous. The fine cloth of David's shirt was soft and fitting. She could sense what it would be like to put her hands against his chest, to work them around to his back, to press against his body.

"Maybe a s'more," she said.

He gestured for her to lead the way.

They stepped back into the main hall, where the less dance-inclined of the Ellingham student body were playing some games. There was another table of snacks out here, and David walked over to it and grabbed a few sticky balls of pretzel and marshmallow.

"A tunnel," he said, taking a bite. "I'd know."

This was safer, steadier ground.

"You don't know everything about the tunnels."

"I would know that if it was in the floor of the building I live in."

He sat down in a crepuscular spot under the shadow of the grand stairs. A person dressed as a skeleton bopped by.

"If they wanted to have a real Halloween party, they'd let us into the basement," she said. "It's nuts down there. It's like a maze."

"Now you interest me," David said, straightening. "How does one get to this basement?"

"No," she said. "I promised Larry."

"A promise is only . . ."

"I promised *Larry*," she said, casting her eye in the direction of the doorway to the kitchen.

"Well, this is fun. Sitting on a bench."

"Then go dance or something," Stevie said.

"You don't want to dance."

"You don't need my permission," she said.

"But maybe I'd rather stay with you," he said.

David stretched out his legs a bit and tapped gently at the inside of her ankle with the toe of his shoe. He turned his eyes up to her. What *was* this? Flirting? Flirting was sending an unexpected text message. This was something else, something that made her feel like she did when Ellie gave her that warm champagne to drink on the first day—bubbles in the bloodstream, an air of unreality. No. This was more than that. This was like she'd gone through a stargate into the life of some parallel universe Stevie. She was used to feelings that butted up against each other, the way that anxiety brought bad excitement. She could handle that now because she knew that feeling. This was something like good nausea, which made no sense, and therefore she was back to anxiety and its bad excitement, except there was a new chemical level.

And in this case, because everything stunk of Edward King, no good move to make. There were no answers here, except to avoid, avoid, avoid.

She tried to look away from his tapping foot and concentrated on the stairs sweeping above them, and the door to the kitchen underneath. The door to the kitchen under the stairs. A lot happened under staircases in old houses. Under the stairs, that's where the servants worked. Harry Potter lived under the stairs. Even Albert Ellingham had written about something being under the stairs. "Where do you look for someone who's never really there? Always on a staircase . . ."

"But never on a stair," she said out loud.

"Come again?"

Stevie was already on her feet, and David followed. As they passed the door, Call Me Charlie Chaplin regarded them with confusion.

"Going so soon?" he said.

"I forgot something," Stevie replied. "My . . . medication. Have to take it. Be right back."

Charlie Chaplin tipped his bowler hat. Stevie and David—or Hercule and Sherlock—walked double-time down the path and under the trees, quickly enough that Stevie worked up a cold sweat.

"So what's happening now?" he said.

"Under the stairs," she said. "Did you ever look under the stairs? In Minerva?"

"Meaning what?"

"The stairs are enclosed, but there has to be space under there. It's the only place you can't see and wouldn't be likely to look."

"Under the stairs," he repeated. "What made you think of that?"

"I just did," she said. As they hurried, she noted that they were passing by one of the cameras, the dark glass and the little blue pinpoint of light recording their movements. Maybe Edward King watched these, maybe he saw this now—Stevie and David together. He would approve. Here Stevie was, doing his bidding. She wasn't even in control of it anymore.

Inside of her jacket pocket, she gave the camera the finger.

Back in Minerva, she and David went right to the stairs, those creaky beasts that would always remind her of Hayes on that first day, when he got her to carry his stuff. On that day, the light poured in through the stained glass. She walked behind him, staring at his muscular calves, covered in light-colored hair, as she hauled a box. He was talking about Hollywood and his show. That was only about two months in the past. Now his death was a memory.

Tonight, the hall was dark. There were lights, but they did little to illuminate the end of the hall. Maybe this was intentional, she thought—keep the attention off the stairs, make details harder to see. The stairs were a tight coil, and underneath was a curved bit of wood that met up with the wall. She felt the wood, running her hands up and down to feel for any openings. David knocked on it.

"Sounds kind of hollow," he said. "I guess I never thought to go and beat on the stairs before."

She knocked as well. There was definitely empty space

behind. It was entirely possible that there would be nothing at all behind this structure, just dust and air, but her heart was thumping and her brain felt clear.

While she had a flashlight on her phone, she needed something more. It was time to employ the tactical flashlights that the school issued to every student in case of power outage. She went to her room and got hers. These were no simple cylindrical flashlights that gave you a gentle beam—these were monsters with handles that blinded and confused the enemy and summoned passing planes. Stevie took hers into the hall and switched it on. Suddenly, the end of the hall was flooded in a white light that exposed detail.

"Hold it," she said, shoving it into David's hands.

Bathed in clinical illumination, the staircase began to offer up its secrets. While the surface appeared smooth, she could just make out the finest trace of a doorway. It had been expertly fitted to be virtually invisible. The 1930s had not anticipated this kind of luminosity.

"Hello," she said.

"Holy shit," David added.

There was no visible way of opening the door, and the opening was no wider than the edge of a piece of paper, possibly even more narrow. There had to be a catch somewhere, something that would pop it. Stevie felt all along the floor, the walls. Nothing.

"In movies you pull down a candlestick on the wall," David said as he set the flashlight on the floor. He took off his two-thousand-dollar coat and bunched it up to make a wedge to prop the light toward the wall.

"This isn't a movie. We don't have a candlestick."

David came over to help her feel the wall. He examined the steps, running his fingers under the lip of each one.

"Why are you fondling the wall?"

They had not heard Nate return and slink up to them in his wizard robes.

"Do you really want to know?" Stevie said.

"Oh God."

"Then I'd turn around," she said. "You won't like it."

"I don't like anything. What are you doing?"

"Looking for a tunnel," she said.

Nate looked at Stevie with an expression that said, *Make this stop happening.*

"It won't be like last time," Stevie said. "This is just for research."

"So was the last time. You guys . . ."

"Wait," David said. "Back up, back up."

He motioned Stevie to clear, then took a step back and threw himself against the wood, hard. Nothing. He backed up a step and rubbed his arm.

"Good one," Nate said. "Keep doing that."

"I thought I felt something," David said. "Let me . . ."

He threw himself up against the wood again, letting out a little groan as he made impact.

"Yeah," Stevie said. "Maybe . . ."

One more time. And this time, there was a pop. Just a small pop.

The panel had shifted, just the tiniest bit, and now there was an opening about a quarter of an inch wide.

"Cool," Nate said. "Just slip on through there."

"Screwdriver," Stevie said.

She did not have one, but Janelle certainly would, and Janelle usually left her door unlocked. It was wrong, of course, to go in, but this was an emergency. Janelle's room was an expression of its inhabitant—perfectly organized, every bit of space cared for and optimized. The air smelled of perfume and honeysuckle from a scented oil diffuser. Her workstation was by the window. She had repurposed her desk and put all her tools there. After a moment of looking through clippers and more confusing devices, Stevie found a small hammer. That would do.

She returned to the back of the stairs and wedged the hammer in, first by the small claw end. The passage gave another inch or two, and she put in the end of the hammer handle and used it as a lever. The door did not want to open. Years of nonuse, or possibly a catch she could not see, made it resistant. It groaned in revolt.

"You're going to break the stairs," Nate said.

"Want me to try?" David asked.

"No." Stevie shook out her hands from the pressure of holding the hammer. She went in one more time, putting all her weight on the handle of the hammer.

Then the back of the stairs swung open, revealing a small dark space.

"This is a good Halloween," David said.

Stevie was able to nudge the doorway open a bit more, shine the light in, and reach around. At first she thought she was touching tar, but then she realized that it was about eight years of dust and dirt that had gone sticky and formed into a new and exciting substance. There was no difficulty finding the hatch. It was right there, in the floor, bolted closed. She tested the bolt, expecting to find that it was stuck in place, but it moved and slid open. She took the handle and pulled, revealing an opening about two feet around.

"This guy really liked crawl spaces," David said, leaning over her shoulder into the space. "What is that?"

"It's a hole," Stevie said, trying to block the view.

"It's got a ladder in it. Is that a tunnel?"

"Here we go," Nate said.

Stevie pushed back and sat on her heels, taking in the view in front of her.

"How does this keep happening to you?" David said.

"Because I look," Stevie replied. "A lot of things happen when you go out and do them on purpose."

"Okay, Stevie." Nate was squatting by her side. "I know this is a thing for you, but for real, Pix will be back and they're kind of . . . Things are kind of sensitive around here, and you just got back. See what I'm saying?"

"*Look at this*," Stevie said.

"Yeah, I know, but remember how these things can be unstable? That, is a hole. A small hole. Anything could be down there. There could be wires or something. There could be water."

David hung down into the opening with the flashlight.

"I don't see any water," he said. "Or wires."

"Seriously," Nate said.

Stevie knew he had a point. Also, she had made one other promise—to Larry. No tunneling.

Still . . .

"Nate's right," she said.

She sprang up from her crouch and went looking for her phone.

"We can't just go in there. Here's what we do," Stevie said. "We call Janelle. For sure she has a little drone with a camera or something and we fly it down there and . . ."

"Time for hole-diving!" David said, turning himself around so that he was feet first. He started lowering himself down.

"David!" she said. "Seriously. We don't . . ."

"But we *will*," he said. "If I don't come back in ten minutes, avenge me. Or are you coming? You know you want to."

Then he started climbing down. Nate shook his head and started to disappear into his robes.

"It's cool down here," David yelled up. "You should come in. There's . . ."

He emitted a scream, which caused both Nate and Stevie to leap. Stevie almost threw herself on top of the hole. David peered up and smiled.

"Kidding. It's fine," he said, looking up at her. "You guys are so jumpy."

"What if it collapses?" Nate said.

"Like, suddenly? Just when we're in it? For no reason?"

"We could wait for Janelle. . . ."

"Come on," David said. "You don't get chances like this all the time. Come on come on come on come on come on. You can't resist."

Was it the smile? Was it the coat and the suit? The glint in his eye? Or was it just the pure tunnelness of it all? Because he was right. She could not resist.

"He can't go alone," she said to Nate.

"He can. We could shut the hatch."

"Just watch for us?" she said. "I promise, promise, promise we'll be careful, but I can't let him go by himself."

Nate yanked his beard down to his chest.

"Why. Do. People. Do. Stupid. Things."

"Because we're stupid," she said. She tested the top rung with her foot. Nate grabbed her arm—not hard, but enough to get her attention.

"Hayes didn't die from the tunnel coming down," he said. "He died from a gas. You have no idea what's down there."

This gave Stevie a moment's pause. He was right.

"But that gas wasn't in the tunnel before," Stevie said. "Someone put that dry ice there. The tunnel was fine before. I went in it. Look, we're just going to . . . go a little bit."

"You make it really hard for me," he said.

"I know," she said. "But, dragons."

"Don't."

"Okay," she said. "I'm sorry. But will you watch anyway?"

Nate rubbed a tired hand across his forehead.

"Do I have any choice?"

"Technically, yes."

"Yeah, but you'd go even if I didn't. *He's* down there."

Stevie wondered what that meant, but there was no time to wonder much. There was a tunnel to explore.

14

STEVIE HAD ENTERED A TUNNEL AT ELLINGHAM ACADEMY BEFORE—
the famous tunnel. That tunnel was wide as a highway in
comparison with this one. This was a crack in the earth, too
tight, too low, and much, much too dark. Stevie turned her
flashlight straight down, forming a pool that splashed up the
walls around her. Unlike the tunnel to the sunken garden,
which was made of even brickwork, this was made of rough
rock, possibly pieces left over from the mountain demolition.
They might not cut you open, Stevie thought, as she tenta-
tively felt along the wall in front of her, but they would rub
you raw if you made contact with your bare skin. She couldn't
extend her elbows more than a few inches in either direction,
so she hesitantly reached overhead into the dark; the ceiling
was only a little more than a hand's length above her head.
And with each step, the walls grew a little closer.

It was, in a word, unwelcoming. In two words, a mistake.

Some part of Stevie possessed enough basic self-
preservation to know that structural integrity and air quality
were important parts of staying alive, and not being in tunnels

was an important part of Larry not busting her ass right off the mountain. But some louder, wilder, definitely stupider part of her kept her moving forward.

And it wasn't just because David had gone down first, no matter what Nate said.

Stevie tucked her hands up into the arms of Poirot's jacket to keep from being cut and numbly felt her way along, taking half-sized steps, and right into David's back.

"That's you, right?" he said. "I'm afraid of monsters. Also, it stinks down here."

This was true. There was a low-lying funk in the air.

"The drone would work better," she said. "You know, if that's a leaking gas line or something."

"Did you just say leaking gas line?" Nate said from above.

"Smells more like ass than gas," David replied. "Tight, dark, smelly. This tunnel has it all! Five out of five stars."

"It's really okay to leave him to die," Nate said. Then, perhaps remembering that someone actually had died the last time they went into the tunnel, he went silent.

The space felt like it was getting smaller, and she wondered if they might get to some point where they actually got stuck, like people who dove into caves and their hoses caught on rock and they never got out, except this wasn't underwater. This was almost worse.

"Now *this* is a Halloween," David said. Stevie could only see a bit of the back of his shirt. She kept one hand in the middle of his back as a way of maintaining pace. Now that they had proven there was a tunnel under Minerva, it was unclear to Stevie how far they had to go in this exercise. But if she knew anything about David, it was that he was going to find the other end of this passage, and if the other end was at the Great House, that was a good distance away.

So they went farther into the dark, step by step.

"So," David said, his voice low, "I've been thinking. Maybe we just need to clean the slate."

Stevie hesitated for a moment, losing contact with the back of his shirt.

"What do you mean?" she said.

"Maybe I should give you everything so there's nothing left for you to snoop for. Do you want to know about me? About my dad? Do you want to know the whole deal?"

Now? Now he was doing this? In some death crack under the ground?

But it made sense, in a way. It was dark. They couldn't see each other. No one could hear them—not even Nate, who was too far away at this point. This was as private as you could get, and they were invisible to each other.

"Okay?" she said.

"I don't tell people my dad is Edward King because he's Edward King. But I also don't tell people because it's pathetic. It's like every other dumb divorce story. But here goes."

Stevie wasn't sure if the sudden airlessness in the tunnel was her imagination. Probably.

"My mom was a concierge at a swanky resort in Marin," David began. "She did things like set up the wine-tasting weekends and the spa experiences and golf trips. Edward

217

King went to some event there, some fundraising thing, and he and Becky locked eyes. This was before he was a big deal. He wasn't a senator yet, just some local politician on the rise. My mom is very pretty. And Edward King is rich. It's not that Becky is just after money, it's more that she doesn't get that money doesn't make you smart. She thinks people who have it are . . . maybe not better, but more complete, or something. I don't think she's worked out that you can be rich and have done nothing to deserve it. Which is weird, because she dealt with rich people for a living and should have known that's not true. She's not stupid, but she has some issues. You don't get together with Edward King if you feel great about yourself. It's not a *solid emotional choice*."

He paused, and Stevie wondered what was happening. She could not see his face, or really even his back. But she could tell that the caustic tone in his voice was forced. He was talking into the dark because it was easier, because he could not be seen while he revealed himself. Even though nothing physical was happening, this was the most intimate they had ever been.

"No," she said into the beating pause.

"No," he agreed. "It's really not. They got married pretty quickly in some shady, private ceremony in a judge's office and I came out seven months later. Eddie put Becky and me in his house in Harrisburg and went off to DC to continue his career. And that was the end of the romance. I was the result of the most consequential bang Eddie ever had. Captain Personal Responsibility paid the bills. I never really remember him being around much. Maybe at Christmas. He pulled us out to use us as props at a few things, but then that stopped. Becky was bitter and had nothing to do, so she started drinking. One time when I was maybe nine I heard water running. I was playing on my Xbox, but I always listened. When you live with an alcoholic, you have to listen a lot. The water was running way too long. I went upstairs and the carpet in the hallway was all wet and there was water coming out from under the bathroom door. Becky went in there with a bottle of Chablis and passed out. She was red all over—the water was turned all the way up on the hot side. I had to pull her out, then shower her in cool water because of the burns. She didn't wake up. So I called Eddie. I got his assistant, who told me to call 911. So the ambulance came. She was okay in the end— just drunk, minor burns. Eddie called me later that night and basically told me off for calling him and letting his assistant know about what was going on with my mom. I should have handled it. That was the night I decided that Edward King could fuck off, forever. That was one of the things I liked about you right away—you also know that Edward King should fuck off, forever. It's a good quality to have."

She noticed that he had slowed his pace. She kept her hand on his back and pressed in a bit, assuring him of her presence.

"When I was ten, Becky got pregnant with a magic baby. It wasn't Eddie's. I mean, I don't want to brag, but I can count to nine. And Eddie was not around nine months before my sister, Allison, was born. Her dad is probably this guy in the state legislature who went to Becky's gym. He came around the house a few times. I never remembered his name, so I just called him Chad. To his face. Right after Allison was born, Chad left the state legislature, and then the state. One does not simply sleep with Edward King's wife. Then Eddie and Becky got a nice quiet divorce."

"How did people not know about this?" Stevie said. "That he was married before?"

"That's the magic of Edward King," David said. "He made sure we were gone before anything big started happening with his campaign. He married Tina, former intern Tina, to use her full title. Tina is a good campaign wife. She has great teeth. Great big white teeth. It looks like she has a mouth full of kitchen cabinets. How am I doing so far with the full-disclosure thing?"

"It's . . . a lot."

"Good thing we're at the end," he said, stopping. "Literally. The end. Of the tunnel."

"Let me see," she said.

"How? I can't move around you."

"Bend down."

David squashed himself down and Stevie shone her light at the wall. There was a short metal ladder, just eight rungs, leading up to a round hatch.

"Keep the light on it," he said, standing again. He set his light down, shook the ladder once, then climbed and reached up his hand, testing the hatch, pushing hard.

"Nope," he said. "That's not opening. A long, dark journey into nothing. But good tunnel."

He climbed back down. Stevie lowered her light so he would not be blinded. For a moment, they were face-to-face in the dark, though they could not really see each other. She turned her flashlight down to the ground.

"Why did you decide to tell me all this?" she said.

"Like I said. Clear the slate."

"But why?"

"Because . . . my dad has messed up everything in my life. Now he's making a career of messing up everyone's lives. But he can't have this. He can't have you. It sounds cheesy, but it's all I've got."

But your dad does have me, she thought. Could she say it? Tell him right now?

He was reaching for her in the dark, his hand searching, landing on her shoulder, finding its way to her neck, to feel along her chin.

Tell him now. Tell him right now. He just told you everything.

He ran his fingers down her jawline gently. Her breath snagged and she leaned her hip up against the wall for support, which was easy because the wall was only an inch away. He kept coming closer, slowly, testing his way, until his chest was against hers and she did not move.

The heavy flashlight was weighing down her left hand. She found herself leaning down to put it on the ground. Then she rose and reached for his head with both hands, intertwining them in his curly hair. When her lips met his, she felt something release inside of her, something she didn't know she had been holding. There was something frantic about the way she kissed him, like being with him was the only way she could breathe. They couldn't move to the left or right, so they stayed locked together. She kissed down his neck and he let out a soft moan, then a little, happy laugh.

"This went better than I hoped," he said. "I thought . . ."

"Shut up," she said, kissing him again.

He reached around, gripping her and lifting her a few inches off the ground. Had there been enough room, she would have put her legs around him. But the tunnel walls did not stretch to accommodate her desires.

"There's something," he mumbled against her lips.

"What?" she mumbled back.

"Light. Nate has to be signaling."

He set her down gently. She wished she could see his expression now, but they were blind to each other. He held her face in his hands for a long moment, saying nothing—not kissing, not moving, not seeing.

"Nate," he said again, after a long pause.

"Nate," she replied.

"Your turn to lead."

She fumbled around, her hands shaking and her legs wobbly, trying to find the flashlight. Then she turned awkwardly. She was very glad that David had taken the lead on the way in, because she had only seen his back. Had she had a good look at the long, tight way forward, she would never have gone on, and what had just happened would never have happened.

They walked back, David at her heels, his hand playing with the tips of her hair, teasingly poking at her ribs, tickling the back of her neck. The world was perfect and hilarious all of a sudden, even if they were busted down here. It would all be all right. Her life had been building to this—this tunnel, this moment. She was warm and giddy. She was a new Stevie.

Her light caught something on the ground. At first glance, it was simply more black in a world of blackness, but this was a different, deeper black against the gray, and it had a bit of shine. She bent down and reached for the thing and David took the opportunity to reach around her waist and hug her.

"What is it?" David said. "*Treasure?*"

She held it under the flashlight beam. It was plastic. A bit of bag, shiny and black.

"Just a piece of bag," she said.

There were no plastic bags in the thirties, probably. Probably? Stevie rubbed the fragment between her fingers. There was something, something that clicked in the back of her mind. Her brain was always doing that—clicking and not talking to her about the clicking.

"You okay?" he asked.

"Yeah," Stevie said absently. The bit of plastic slid coolly between her fingertips. "It's nothing."

The internal clicking got louder. There was a Geiger counter in her brain. Then she saw it. It had been hard to see the way they came in, because it was on an angle—another opening, about two and a half feet wide.

"There's another tunnel," she said. She shone her light down into the space.

"I'm ashamed of myself for saying this," David said, "but we should get back up before Pix comes home or Nate seals us in."

Stevie took just a few steps into the new branch of tunnel. On the ground in front of her was another piece of plastic. She picked it up. It was the same shiny black plastic. Garbage bag plastic, that's what it was.

Click. Click. Click. Her mind was going faster now, showing her picture after picture. Garbage bags in the kitchen at home. Her clothes in garbage bags when she came back to Ellingham. Garbage clothes. Ellie wearing a skirt made of garbage bags at the silent party . . .

Up ahead, there was some trash on the ground. That's what it looked like anyway from a distance. There was a subtle sheen from more garbage bag plastic, then something formless, purple . . .

She didn't have to go any farther to know what she had found.

INTERVIEW WITH MARION NELSON
CONDUCTED IN NEW YORK CITY BY
AGENT HENRY EVANS, NYC OFFICE, AND
AGENT GEORGE MARSH, VERMONT
FIELD OFFICE
APRIL 20, 1936

HE: Thank you for coming in to speak to us, Miss Nelson.

MN: It's no trouble at all. None at all.

HE: You understand what has transpired? I don't need to explain anything to you.

MN: Yes. I know. I know about it.

HE: You are the housemistress of Minerva House at Ellingham Academy, is that correct?

MN: Correct.

HE: How did you get your position?

MN: I knew Mr. Ellingham from here, from New York. I worked as a secretary at his newspaper.

HE: Directly for him?

MN: No, for the editor in chief, Max Campbell. But I got to know Mr. Ellingham from his visits to the office. He was very involved in the day-to-day.

HE: You became friends.

MN: Yes.

HE: Good friends?

MN: I . . . yes. Good friends.

AGENT MARSH: We first met when you worked at the paper.

MN: *Yes, when you saved Mr. Ellingham from that bomb.*

HE: *And he asked you to come and be a housemistress at his new school.*

MN: *Yes. He wanted people at the school he knew and trusted.*

GM: *You're the only person from the newspaper to come and work at the academy, Miss Nelson. Just you.*

MN: *Yes.*

GM: *Why do you think you were the only one he brought from the newspaper?*

MN: *I suppose . . . I was the only one with the right skills. I'm not a reporter. I was a secretary.*

HE: *Did you have any other position at the school? Did you teach?*

MN: *Biology.*

HE: *So you taught biology and lived at Minerva House.*

MN: *Yes.*

HE: *Miss Nelson, we've been going through the files on all the faculty at Ellingham Academy. None of the other faculty members had a direct connection to Albert Ellingham's business life. Not just the newspaper. All the businesses.*

MN: *Yes. What of it?*

HE: *I understand that was not a question. Just an observation. It's just that out of the hundreds and hundreds of people who work for Albert Ellingham, he chose you to come to the academy.*

MN: *And you, Mr. Marsh.*

GM: *I don't work for Mr. Ellingham, Miss Nelson. I work*

*for the Federal Bureau of Investigation. I was posted
locally to Mr. Ellingham. But he picked you, out of
everyone who works for him.*

MN: *Like I said, Albert—Mr. Ellingham wanted people he
knew. . . .*

HE: *You must be close. You call him Albert?*

MN: *I don't know what you're implying.*

HE: *Nothing at all. I am making an observation. But I now
need to ask, Miss Nelson, and I must remind you of the
serious nature of the matter at hand, is your relationship
with Albert Ellingham . . . more than friendly?*

[Subject had no reply.]

HE: *Miss Nelson, I'm not asking this to embarrass you. I'm
asking because we need to understand everything that
happened at the academy that night. We need information.*

MN: *I know you need information.*

HE: *So will you please answer my question?*

[Subject had no reply.]

HE: *Miss Nelson, when you left Ellingham Academy, you
took a train back to New York with several students.
Then you went to an apartment at 1040 Fifth Avenue.*

MN: *Who told you that?*

HE: *It's not important how we know. It's important that
we find out the facts. Is that correct?*

MN: *Yes.*

HE: *Who owns that apartment?*

MN: *The Ellingham Corporation. I don't have an apartment of my own right now. I live at the school. Mr. Ellingham let me stay in one of his properties.*

HE: *And when did he tell you you could stay at one of his properties? When did he convey this to you?*

MN: *When . . . when he told us we had to go.*

HE: *Miss Nelson, do you understand that lying to a federal agent is a serious matter? I need to point out again that we need information if we are to find Iris and Alice Ellingham. Without information, there is nothing we can do. Any delay in getting that information means we are delayed in our search, and if we have false information, we go down false roads. Do you understand what I am saying?*

[Subject is visibly distressed.]

MN: *Oh God. Oh. How did this happen? Can we stop for a moment, please? Just a moment, please?*

HE: *Miss Nelson, I'm going to need you to be honest now. There is nothing to fear in being honest. We are not out to shame you or Mr. Ellingham. We just need to know. This is information that could be used against Mr. Ellingham, or you. We need to have it. Is your relationship with Albert Ellingham purely friendly?*

MN: *You know, you know! Why do you keep asking? Why do you keep asking what you know?*

[*Subject needed some time to regain composure.*]

HE: How long has it been going on?

MN: Seven years.

HE: Does anyone else know? Does Mrs. Ellingham know?

MN: She doesn't know. She's . . . distracted.

HE: What does that mean?

*MN: She's . . . I don't want to speak ill of her. I know
how that looks, especially now. But you have to
understand, she's not like him. She's not serious-minded.
We understand each other. He can talk to me.*

*HE: On the night of the kidnapping, Mr. Ellingham could
not be found for a period of approximately forty-five
minutes, around two in the morning. He was in his
office, and then, he wasn't. Do you know anything about
that missing time?*

[*Subject had no reply.*]

*GM: Take your time, Miss Nelson. We're not looking to
embarrass anyone. We just want to know what happened.*

MN: We met.

GM: Where?

*MN: We have a meeting place, where they're building the
gymnasium.*

*GM: Do you have any sense of how Mr. Ellingham got to
you without being seen leaving his office, or the house?*

MN: We have . . . a way.

[*A photographic copy of the Truly Devious letter was presented.*]

HE: *Have you ever seen this letter?*

MN: *No.*

HE: *Did Albert Ellingham ever mention it to you?*

MN: *No.*

HE: *When you worked at the newspaper, did you get letters like this?*

MN: *We got threatening letters, of course. Someone put a bomb in Albert's car there. We got letters, all sorts.*

HE: *Look at it carefully. Did you ever get anything like this at the newspaper?*

MN: *Nothing exactly like it. Never cut-out letters.*

HE: *Is there anything else that we should know about? Anything at all? Anything related to Iris or Alice?*

MN: *Little Alice. Oh. Albert lives for her. You don't understand. He lives for that little girl. You'd think she was . . .*

HE: *Was what?*

[*Subject had no reply.*]

HE: *Was what, Miss Nelson?*

MN: *You'd think she was the only person in the world. That's all. The only person in the world.*

15

"DAVID," STEVIE SAID QUIETLY. BETWEEN HER HEAVY HEARTBEAT AND the smell, she felt like she might vomit at any moment, but she had to hold it down, had to get some control over this. "Back up."

"What's going on?"

"It's blocked," she said. "Just back up."

No matter how calm she tried to keep her voice, there was a note in it that gave away the fact that something very bad was happening. He stepped around her to look to see what was in the passage.

"What the hell is . . ."

She heard him figure it out.

"Back up," she said gently. "Back up, back up. This is how we help her."

"Stevie . . ." There was a lightness in his voice. It was almost giddy.

"Turn around," Stevie said, moving him back, foot by foot. "I need you to turn around."

Now she was echoing Larry's words to her. Turn around.

Don't look, because if you look it stays with you forever.

"We can't leave her," he said.

"We're getting help. Turn. Come on."

She had to maneuver him back into the main artery of the tunnel. Her adrenaline had taken over. Somehow, she knew how to do this, how to grab David's hand and lead him back to the end.

When they reached the ladder, Nate was hanging over the opening, his wizard hood drooping around his neck.

"Up," Stevie said. "Move, move."

Nate backed up, and she and David scrambled out. When David got up, he staggered into the hallway and bent over, half gagging.

"What's going on?" Nate said. "What's down there?"

Stevie shook her head, partially because she could not find the words and partially to hold down the feeling of sickness.

"*What is happening?*" Nate said again.

"Ellie," Stevie replied. "Ellie is down there."

"Ellie is down there? Hiding? I have to call for help!"

Stevie shook her head, and Nate got the message and fell back against the wall.

Stevie pulled her phone from her pocket. David lurched along the wall and reached for it, pushing it down.

"Don't. No, I have to call," David said, pulling out his phone. "Both of you should go in your rooms. Put some headphones on. That's where you've been. Play something loud. Go."

"What?" Stevie said.

"You can't have been down there, Stevie. You get it? Nate, you get it? She wasn't there. I went down there alone. Just me."

"What, we're lying now?" Nate said. "To cops?"

"You know what it means if Stevie was down there. I'll be okay. She won't be. All we're doing is reporting. That's all."

There was an urgency in David that was entirely unfamiliar, a high flush to his cheeks and a rasp in his voice. Nate turned gray, as gray as the wizard robe he was still wearing.

"Just go in your rooms and shut the door," David said again, his voice pleading. "That's all you have to do."

Nate swore under his breath but pulled himself away from the wall.

"Are you going?" he asked Stevie.

Stevie was not sure where she was. Moments ago, she had been in the tightness of the tunnel, in David's arms, embraced by the earth, alone in the universe. Then, there was Ellie.

Nate shook Stevie's arm.

"I'm not going if you're not," he said. "Tell me what you're doing. I don't understand anything right now."

David looked at her. His hair was still tousled from where her hands had been. She had kissed the fine smoothness of his neck. . . .

The smell of the tunnel poisoned her memory.

David would be safe. Nate didn't know why, of course.

"Yeah," she said. "Go to your room."

This felt entirely wrong, what she was doing for herself,

233

but entirely right for Nate. Nate didn't need this. Nate had been struggling enough with what happened to Hayes.

"Jesus Christ," Nate said as he went past them, tripping on the hem of the robe as he went up the curve of the stairs.

Stevie gulped down some air. She started moving on autopilot, stumbling toward her room.

She heard the first arrivals about five minutes later. She had put in earbuds, but turned nothing on. Her heartbeat echoed back at her in her ears. There was another arrival. More voices in the common room, in the hall.

She turned on some music. Loud. She closed her eyes and put her head back against the wooden bed frame. When the knock came on Stevie's door, she actually didn't hear it at first. She had put the volume up too high. Pix eventually cracked the door.

"Stevie?" she said.

Stevie peeled her eyes open. The effort was tremendous, the light from the ceiling offensively bright.

"Stevie," Pix said again. "Can you . . . stay in here for a few minutes? There's something going on. Nothing to worry about. Security just has to look at something in the hallway."

"Sure," Stevie said. Her voice sounded sleepy.

"Sorry to disturb you. Go back to sleep."

Stevie closed her eyes again and let movies play out on the backs of her eyelids. She summoned the feeling again, of David's kiss and touch. There was so little time to savor it.

The memory would fade, the sensation would be corrupted by whatever was coming.

This had all happened before. The same, but different.

Pix returned and told her to pack some things in a bag. "Take your time," she said, but her face betrayed her shock. "There's an issue in the house and we're sleeping somewhere else tonight."

Stevie got out of bed and began mechanically filling her backpack. Medicine, clothes, her computer and phone, everything shoved into the backpack until it squeaked a bit from the strain. She was about to close it when she had another thought. The tin. It would not fit. She pulled out a shirt that was taking up valuable space and put the tin in its place. Better safe than sorry.

There was a security officer blocking the view to the end of the hall. Nate was sitting at the table in the common room, and Janelle, still dressed as Wonder Woman, was grabbing at things in her room and packing her own bag. Pix stood at the table, her expression grim.

"Where's David?" Stevie asked Pix.

"He's over at the Great House. He found Ellie, Stevie. In a tunnel. She . . . wasn't okay. She died." Pix waited for Stevie to absorb this.

"Where are we going to go?" Nate asked.

"We're setting up for the night in the yurt. They're going to bring in beds, and we'll hang dividers from the ceiling. It'll be nice and cozy. We can talk."

"Oh good," Nate said, picking at the table surface with his fingernail.

"As soon as Janelle is ready, we can go. I'm going to get my things."

"She must be tired of having her students die," Nate said when Pix went upstairs. "Think of the paperwork."

When Stevie did not reply, Nate nudged her hand.

"Are you okay?" he asked.

"I have no idea."

"How the hell is this happening? Didn't we just do this? I thought she ran away, like she went off with circus people or something. Not that she was . . . under us."

"She wasn't really under us," Stevie said. "She was kind of far away."

"Oh, *good*."

"You know what I mean," she said.

"I know what you mean. I know that this place may suck. Two people are *dead*."

"It's not the *school's* fault."

"No, but . . . maybe? Maybe this place . . ."

"Are you saying this place is, like, cursed or something?"

Nate shook his head.

"I'm saying, two people have died, and that's a lot more than the number who died at my last school. I know shit happens. Terrible shit happens. But this is *weird* terrible shit with tunnels and dry ice and people suffocating to death underground . . ."

Stevie pulled her shoulders closer into her body. Her

mind drifted away. It went to David and his story of his mom and his sister, of the promises she had made, of the coldness of the case she wanted to solve and the coldness under the ground.

Janelle emerged in a pair of fleece pajama bottoms and a massive fuzzy sweater, a silver overnight bag on her shoulder. She walked over to Nate and Stevie and dropped an arm around each. There were tears at the edges of her eyes.

"Pix said Vi could come over to the yurt too, if that's all right with you. I'd just really like to see them."

"Sure," Stevie said. "Of course."

Nate nodded absently.

"David found her. They took him over to the Great House."

The blue door creaked open and Larry came inside in his red-and-black fleece coat, his walkie-talkie buzzing on his hip. He surveyed the group at the table.

"We're going to take you over to the yurt now. We haven't told the school at large yet. Some people are still at the party. I'd ask you, if you don't mind, not to spread this. I know Vi Harper-Tomo has permission to come over. But please don't text this to anyone."

"We won't," Janelle said.

Larry's focus landed on Stevie. He was reading her. She tried to shut herself, as loud and cleanly as shutting a book.

But people aren't books, unfortunately.

The group made its way into the night, the two officers flanking them. The night was cold and still as glass, with only a sliver of a moon. Vi met them halfway, with the head of Juno House as an escort.

"What's going on?" they said. "Are you okay?"

They looked at Janelle closely, then thumbed away the tears under her eyes.

"We'll talk over there," Janelle said. "I'm okay. We just have to go."

Nate put on his headphones and lowered his head. He was checking out of the situation. Stevie wasn't sure which one of them led this movement, but it seemed that she and Larry were at a different pace than the others, and a fractionally different trajectory, until they were on their own little path together. Either he wanted to talk to her or she subconsciously had to talk to him. Whatever the case, it was something she could not bear to hold in. As they passed the conference of statue heads, Stevie came to a stop. Larry nodded to the others to keep going. He leaned against one of the plinths and examined her.

"You need to talk?" he said.

"I was down there," she replied.

"I know."

He held up a fake mustache. It must have come off when she was making out with David. She had forgotten she had been wearing it.

"What you need to do, right now, is tell me the truth."

Stevie dug into her pocket and pulled out the fragment of trash bag. She handed it to Larry.

"I found this on the floor down there."

"What were you doing, Stevie?" he said. "I told you. No tunnels."

"Fenton—Dr. Fenton—thought there was a tunnel. I looked. I found it. It was homework, sort of. I didn't know Ellie was there. I had *no idea* she was there. It was just a tunnel. I didn't want to go in. But he went inside."

"David."

Stevie nodded.

"I had to follow him. I thought he might . . . I don't know."

"Did you find anything besides this, aside from . . . ?"

Larry held up the fragment of garbage bag. Stevie shook her head.

"There was . . . a smell."

"The first time you experience that, you never forget it. You can get used to it, to dealing with it, but it's hard."

"Did she just get stuck down there?" Stevie asked. "When she left the Great House that night?"

"That would be my guess," Larry said. "We tracked up to the other end of the passage. We had no idea it was there. Goes to a hatch in the Great House basement floor that blends in with the other stones. She went in, something blocked her way out."

Stevie's mind immediately went to the Edgar Allan Poe story, "The Cask of Amontillado," about a murderer who lures his victim down to a vault, who is then shackled to the wall and bricked in. The horror of it was too much. Stevie inhaled the cool, clean air greedily. The smell was still there, molecules of it, clinging to the inside of her nose, her skin, her mind.

"What do I do?" Stevie said. "Do you have to tell the police I was there?"

Larry put his hand on his leg and tapped one finger. Then he inhaled deeply and let out a long sigh.

"Nate?" he asked.

"Nate didn't go down," Stevie said.

"He's not as stupid as the two of you."

"He told us not to go. He stayed at the top in case something happened."

"Definitely not as stupid," Larry said. "All right. This is about finding and reporting an accident victim. Technically, it sounds like David was the one who found her. You can't report something you didn't see." This was wrong, but Stevie made no correction. "If anything changes, then you step forward. You do it at once. You don't go in any tunnel here ever again, for any reason. You follow every rule down to the letter."

"Thank you," she said quietly.

"Don't thank me. This isn't about thanks. It sounds like you tried to follow someone who was doing something stupid, even if that meant doing something stupid yourself. I know enough about David Eastman to know he would jump in without looking. He'll be all right, no matter what happens. I think you know why."

Out of all the things that had happened, this was the one that made Stevie freeze.

"You've met his father," Larry said. It wasn't a question.

Stevie nodded.

"And his father played a role in you coming back?"

"He told you?" Stevie asked.

"No one needed to tell me," he said. "That wasn't a tough one to work out. The sudden change of heart, your parents work for the man, the sudden flight back, the fact that there are no flights back at that time of night and that you probably wouldn't fly anyway . . ."

Stevie let out a loud exhale.

"What did he give you?" Larry asked.

"A ride."

"What else?"

"Nothing," she said.

"What did he want from you?"

"Just . . . to be here. Because of David. I just wanted to come back."

She wasn't sure if she was saying this to Larry or herself. Larry let out a low noise.

"It's not you," he said. "Edward King is a son of a bitch and his son is a piece of work. . . ."

She got the sense that there was a lot more he could have said, but unlike a suspect who starts talking and can't stop, Larry shut the valve.

"So Edward King gave you a chance to come back if you kept an eye on David. Now things become clearer."

"David doesn't know," she said.

"Well, I'm not going to tell him that. This whole thing . . ."

He shook his head and cut himself off again.

"Could I see him, though?" she said. "He did just find his friend's body."

Larry let out a long sigh.

"He's at the library," he said. "They took him over there because there are too many people in the Great House. I'll take you over, because of what happened tonight. But you need to remember, it's not your job to protect David Eastman. I feel bad for the kid, I do. But it is not your job. Do you understand?"

"I know."

"No," he said, "I don't think you do. Don't follow someone into the dark, Stevie. I've seen it happen too many times."

Stevie wasn't exactly sure what that meant, but the general idea was clear enough.

16

There was a thick, fecund smell of dropping leaves that night as Stevie and Larry made their way over to the library. Why was Ellingham always at its richest at times like this, heavy with the smell of earth and air, extreme in light and shade? Why did the Great House loom higher with its orange lit windows, where the party was wrapping up and the school still unaware that another of its company had been lost?

What was the problem with this place? Maybe Nate had a point, she thought, her footsteps hard and clear on the path. It was called Mount Hatchet. Maybe that was a sign. Don't go there. Don't blow a chunk of the face of this place and build your empire.

And don't come looking for death and murder, Stevie, because you'll find it.

She was definitely not warm enough in her vinyl coat, even with the heavy Ellingham fleece underneath. Her jeans were too thin. She had no scarf, so the cold tickled the back of her neck.

Ellie, wrapped in garbage bags, underground.

She could still smell it.

It. Her. It.

A few people trickled out of the Great House, still in costume.

Of course Ellie was dead.

Of course she'd been found on Halloween. Sealed in a tunnel.

It was distilled Ellingham, pure as one of the streams that ran down the mountain.

It would have been dark for Ellie. Absolutely dark. She wouldn't have known where she was. She would have had to feel along those walls, going back and forth, looking for a way out. How long? For hours? Days? Crying. Probably hyperventilating. Stevie thought of the depths of her own panic—the world-ending feeling of nothing. Ellie would have panicked. She would have gone back and forth and back and forth and screamed. Banged. Scratched and clawed. The thirst and the hunger and the confusion would have set in. . . .

No. She had to keep these thoughts out. Paint over them with gloss and let them harden. She had a job to do now: find David, who had found Ellie.

The Ellingham library was quietly buzzing. Several security officers were there, talking to the local police. There were no police cars parked out on the oval—they must have taken the service road and parked out back to keep people from freaking out. Despite the activity, the library felt like an empty cathedral. It had that strange architectural property of trapping any wind that came in through the door and spinning it up in a soft vortex that had nowhere to go. The higher you went, air whistled through the elaborate wrought iron of the circular steps and balcony guards, and loose pages trembled, as if alive. The noise of the conversations below swirled all the way to the ceiling, smashing against the books. Stevie looked straight up, noticing for the first time the constellations painted on the blue ceiling. The stars were inside, closer.

Larry had a quiet word with one of the security people.

"He's upstairs in one of the reading rooms," he said to Stevie. "With a counselor. Let me see what's going on."

Stevie watched Larry wend his way up to the second floor and disappear into the stacks. He reappeared on the balcony a few minutes later and waved Stevie up. The iron rail of the staircase was cold, and each of her footsteps reverberated as she climbed. It seemed like the library didn't like this interruption of its peaceful routine.

"You can go and talk to him," Larry said in a low voice. "The counselor said that would be helpful for both of you. But you remember what I said."

He guided her to the end of a wide aisle between the geography and geology sections, a row of green-spined books that concluded in one of the library's somber wooden doors with the gold painted lettering. The counselor was waiting by the door. Stevie recognized her from before, when Hayes died and Ellingham deployed therapists in all directions.

The reading room was a small spot, separated from the rest of the second floor by walls that were half-paneled in frosted glass. The original furnishings had been replaced with a gray love seat and four fuzzy beanbags and an equally fuzzy rug, just in case any of the other six hundred cozy reading nooks at Ellingham didn't satisfy.

David had avoided all of these options and was sitting on the floor against the wall, once again wearing the two-thousand-dollar coat. His knees were partially bent and he was staring at his shoes. The counselor was hovering next to him on the arm of the love seat. She got up and came over to speak to Larry and Stevie in the doorway.

"Would you like to come in?" she said to Stevie, in that professionally calm way that therapists have.

Stevie stepped into the room cautiously, and David looked up. He was pale, his face all raw edges.

"Hey," Stevie said.

"Hey."

There was a dry crackle in his voice, but otherwise, nothing gave a hint about what had just happened.

The counselor backed out and shut the door quietly. Stevie found that she did not quite know what to do with herself. Her arms felt gangly and useless at her sides. She wasn't sure if she did want to sit, but standing was getting weird. She considered perching on the arm of the love seat as the counselor had, but that was strange and clinical.

After an awkward moment, she slipped down the wall and sat next to him. There was warmth radiating off his body. The room felt humid. Considering all that had transpired between them that night, there was no reason to be uncomfortable. And yet, Stevie felt twitchy in her skin.

"They're setting up a place for us to stay in the yurt tonight," she said.

"Like camp," he said. "Sadness camp."

He clenched and unclenched his hand several times on his knee, then suddenly reached for Stevie's and held it.

"Okay," he said, coughing out a humorless laugh. "You told me not to go down there. I should have listened to you. If *you* say not to sneak in somewhere . . ."

Stevie could only concentrate on the feeling in her hand, the warmth of his palm against her skin, the message it conveyed. It was a need. A need for her strength. The sensation rippled up her arm and was transmitted to the rest of her body in a wave.

"She knew," David said. "About me. She was the only one before you."

"About your dad?" Stevie asked.

"We were a little drunk. I told her. I didn't think she'd judge me for it. I remember we were sitting in the attic of the art barn. She was making a collage and she had a bottle of some German stuff that tasted like cough syrup and ass. When I told her . . . she laughed. She said it didn't matter. She could have told people. I know she never did."

David's voice was thickening. Stevie stared at the floor, the original tiles, with their scars and dings of decades of students scouring the aisles. There was a storm brewing, something that felt like falling and spinning. She wanted squirrels to come flooding toward them. She was about to ask

David how he had managed to get all those squirrels, when he began to sob.

She had absolutely no idea what to do.

Well, she did. The thing to do was to put an arm around him. Kissing him had been easy. This was pure and intimate and happening not in the dark of the tunnel, but here in the dim light, in full view of the books.

She began to sweat. She felt the swirl in her brain, the speed of life. Her promise to Edward King mocked her now. Befriend him. Take care of him. Make him stay. Make a mockery of every feeling she had about him to get what she wanted and needed so badly. She could no longer figure out if she had done those things with David because she wanted to or because it was all part of the deal, the miserable, evil deal. Edward King had made her into a liar. He had turned her into someone like him and everything that had happened tonight was tainted. If she touched David now, she would be complicit.

But she couldn't leave him like this either. So she took his hand and squeezed it. She tried to make the squeeze speak for everything inside her, everything she couldn't say. He squeezed back, then he fell against her in heaving sobs.

Stevie bolted herself to the wall, unable to move. This outpouring of emotion was making her panic. After a few minutes, he leaned back, wiped his eyes, and caught his breath.

"Fuck," he said. "I'm tired of sitting up here. Let's go to the yurt of sadness."

He was entirely unembarrassed by what had happened. Not that he should have been. It's just that Stevie would have been. David was free with the way he expressed himself. He stood and offered his hand to help her up, then continued holding it. They were simply together now.

Out at the end of the aisle, along the balcony, the counselor was consulting with Call Me Charles, who had been called to the scene. He had stripped the Charlie Chaplin mustache and hat and was wrapped in his normal black coat, but the strange pants and shoes were still visible underneath. Halloween was a weird night.

"How are you both doing?" he said as they emerged. She saw him take note of their clasped hands.

"About how you'd expect," David said.

Charles nodded solemnly.

"Can we go to the yurt now?" David said. "Do they need me for anything else?"

"I think they're done for now," Charles said. "There may be some more questions later, but for now, you should be with your friends and get some rest. I'll get someone to walk you over."

"Can we skip that?" David said. "Can we just go? It's not like you won't know where we are."

"I think that will be fine," Charles said. "The two of you can go together."

David started to go, Stevie trailing along, linked to him.

"Don't worry, Stevie," Charles said quietly as they left. "Everything will be all right. We'll speak to your parents."

David turned at this, taking note, and then the two of them went down the iron staircase and out into the cold night.

The stars were bright overhead. On nights with no clouds, the star fields over Ellingham were like nothing Stevie had ever seen—so many of them, so many more than she knew. There was a half moon, low and buttery yellow, casting a bit of light over the lawn and the Great House.

They were approaching one of the pathway lights, where a security camera perched above them. He stopped and stared at the camera.

"The school seems to be very understanding," David said after a moment.

"About what?"

"About your parents," he replied. "Making sure they don't get freaked out. It must be hard to keep everyone calm when your students keep dying."

"I guess," she said.

"You must have given your parents a really good speech to convince them to let you come back," he said. "What did you say to them?"

There was thunder in her ears.

"I . . . I don't know what motivates my parents."

It was a nonanswer, and it did not work on David the way it had on Nate.

"I was on the roof when you got back," he said. "I saw you come home. It was late. I mean, I was pretty high at the time, but I know it was late on a Friday night."

It wasn't a question, and that was terrifying.

"You guys must have been driving for a long time," he said.

"I flew," she said.

"Oh. Sweet. Didn't you drive up the first time?"

She had to open her mouth and answer, because every passing second told the tale for her. But how? Because the truth now was a confession, not a gift.

The blue eye of the camera observed them coolly.

"The plane is nice," he said. "Did he try to get you to eat the chips?"

Several seconds ticked by. Or was it a minute? Time was starting to stretch and bleed over the landscape. The stars crowded to hear her answer.

"Listen . . ."

Such a terrible word to start with, *listen*. So defensive.

"I'm listening," he said.

She wanted to go back, rewind, back to the tunnel, back to the kissing. Back to the laughing. Back to the dark. She could have told him then. He would have understood. But you can't go back. You can't re-create the conditions.

David sat down on one of the benches along the path and stretched his legs out long in front of him. He crossed his arms over his chest and waited.

"How did I not work this out before?" he said. "It was so obvious." He smirked and shook his head.

"He came to my house," Stevie said. "He was there when I got home from school on Friday. He was talking to my parents. He brought information about all of this security. He convinced them I should be able to come back."

"That was nice of him," David said. "And he said, 'Come on my plane'?"

"I didn't want to talk to him. I didn't want to be with him."

"But you took the ride," he said.

"*Of course* I took the ride," she shot back. "I needed to get back. I knew he doesn't do stuff just to be nice. I asked him what he wanted and he said . . . nothing . . . I just needed to *be* here, because . . ."

Stevie couldn't find her foothold. She'd made her lunge, and now there was nothing—just a smooth, slippery surface. David was doing what good interrogators do: when someone is confessing, you let them talk. And the impulse was there. She had to talk.

"He wanted me to, just, talk to you. Because he said you were freaking out. And that was it, and I . . . Would you say something?"

"Like what?" he said. His voice was cool. There was still a trace of thickness from when he had been crying, but all other emotion was gone.

"I don't know what you want from me," she said, her voice cracking.

"What I *want* from you? Yeah, you've been hanging with my dad. Even you. He even got you."

A few more tears trickled from his eyes, but he laughed, hoarse and miserable, his every last suspicion of the world confirmed.

So Stevie did what guilty people do when confronted. She ran. It was a ridiculous impulse, but it was the only one that made sense at the moment. She took off down the path, her feet thudding against the brick. But it seemed absurd to be running away in full view of David, so she turned to go across the relative dark of the green. Running is one of the most human responses of all. Fight or flight. Like her therapist said, once you start the circuit of response, you have to complete it. If you feel like you have to fly, you fly until your body tells you to stop or until you are stopped by an outside force.

Stevie, not being a regular runner, stopped when she got to the tree cover on the other side and heaved a bit, her throat raw. She slowed just enough to hear if David was following her. Of course, he wasn't. David wouldn't be behind her anymore.

She continued on to the circle of statue heads, the gossipy stone chorus that gathered eternally between Minerva and the yurt. She held on to one of the plinths and caught her breath. She had to get herself together. Think. Her friends would be at the yurt, waiting for her. That was where she was expected. But she couldn't face them, couldn't risk another encounter with David.

She circled a bit under the dark sky and hated it for being so wide.

Maybe she should call her parents and leave.

No. That was fear talking. She had to get a grip. She needed . . .

She spun her bag and opened the front pocket, feeling around until her fingers hit a small metal tumbler, about half the size of her thumb. She twisted it open and dumped the contents into her palm.

One small white pill. The emergency Ativan that she carried "just in case." The one she never really expected to take. It was not a large pill, so she put it on her tongue and tossed her head back and force swallowed a few times until it went down dry. It would take a little while to work, but at least she knew it was heading for her stomach, where it would be picked apart and sent to her bloodstream.

She felt the need to sleep. Just put her head down somewhere, anywhere, and sleep. If not home and not the yurt, then . . .

She pointed herself in the direction of the art barn, taking broad, fast steps. Upon reaching the barn, she tapped herself in and pulled the door closed behind her.

She walked along at a clip to the yoga studio—a high-ceilinged, bare room with a mirrored wall and a bamboo floor. She pulled that door closed tight as well and then, for no reason she could understand, grabbed one of the yoga straps and ran it around the door handle, lashing it to a barre. It wasn't the tightest security, but it was something. Then she switched on the light, assured herself that the room was utterly vacant, then turned it off again.

Once you start doing something weird and you fully embrace it, it's much easier to get on with it. Stevie proceeded to build herself a tiny bunker in the alcove where the yoga supplies were stored. She made herself a thick bed of mats, which she covered in several blankets for padding and for warmth. She folded another blanket as a pillow. Then she stacked the rest of the supplies next to this nest, making a short protective wall around herself so that anyone peering into the room would see nothing but a small pile of yoga blankets and mats. She climbed into the bed she had made for herself, pulling several blankets over her. It was quiet and dark and she was very alone. The wind whistled alongside the building and the trees scraped the art barn roof. The yoga blankets were a little stinky and scratchy, but they were warm and soft enough. She took out her phone and wrote a text to Janelle and Nate.

I am fine. Going to bed.

Nate's reply came quick: Sleeping where?

Janelle's followed a minute later: You okay? Where are you?

She replied to both: Fine going to sleep see you at breakfast

Maybe she would stay here forever.

Ellie . . .

Ellie was a missing person, now found. Someone who had blown into the wind, and now the wind had blown her back.

And David . . .

She had destroyed whatever was there. She had killed it. She had murdered her feelings and his, but now all was exposed. She closed her eyes. She was so tired.

Larry would know where she was—her whole, embarrassing path would have been visible. She would not be lost, like Ellie. It was as if Larry alone was watching over her slumber, and that was the only thought that consoled her.

17

STEVIE WOKE THE NEXT MORNING, WHICH WAS A GOOD START. WHEN things are bad, give yourself a point for everything.

She sat up. (Another point.) She was stiff and sore, her mouth dry, her hair definitely sticking up on one side. She felt a waffle pattern of yoga blanket on the right side of her face and the faint smell of lavender and patchouli permeating her being. It was like she had been run over by a boulder made of hippies.

She reached around, trying to find her phone in her belongings. It was stuck between some of the yoga mats she had been sleeping on. It informed her that it was 9:50 in the morning.

"Crap," she said.

When she took an Ativan, she tended to sleep hard and a lot. People could have been trying to access the yoga studio and she would have had no idea. She peeked over the short wall of blankets and mats to see if there were any angry yoga fiends waiting at the door to get their chakras on. No one in sight. She crawled out of her nest. You were supposed to roll your mat and fold your blanket at the end of class and say namaste and things like that, but this was not class, so Stevie shoved everything back into something resembling the right position and unwound the strap that was holding the door closed. Outside, she saw gray skies and there was slanting rain smacking into the windows.

"That checks out," she mumbled.

She reached up and rubbed her hand roughly over her short hair, taming it as best she could. She rubbed any sleep out of her eyes and away from her mouth. She had slept in her vinyl coat, so now it had a weird flipped-up bend in the bottom. This was not a good look or a good feel, but this was something detectives had to do. She might have to spend the night in a car, or an abandoned building on a stakeout. Detectives were always rough and sleepless. Of course, she thought, as she pushed open the studio door, not all of them slept in yoga studios by choice, but she would build up to it.

Outside, the mountain morning slapped her in the face in the form of the rain and wet wind. It wasn't pouring, but it was steady and cold. The sky was colorless, and even the brightness of the trees was dimmed. The day subtracted from life. The rain helped flatten her sticking-up hair and slicked her coat. Stevie marched on away from the art barn. As she approached the Great House and the green, there were a few police cars and vans, but the presence was subdued.

"Hey," someone said.

Stevie turned to see Maris coming up behind her on the path. She was dressed in a massive shaggy black coat with black tights and red boots, and was huddled under a large umbrella that was black on the top and had a print of a blue sky and clouds underneath. Her red lipstick was the most vivid thing in miles.

Stevie stopped and waited for her, even as the rain intensified. When Maris reached her, she tipped her umbrella at Stevie in an attempt to be helpful, but Stevie only got the edge, which made it worse.

"How are you?" Maris said.

Stevie shrugged.

"Holy shit, this is horrible," Maris said, producing a vape pen from the depths of her shaggy coat. "I can't believe . . . well . . . I guess I can."

That summed up the experience pretty well. You can't believe until you can. Then it just *is*.

Stevie didn't want to walk with Maris, really. They had never exactly bonded. But to be fair, Maris was the only person who seemed genuinely, properly hurt by Hayes's death. They had not been a couple long (not that they had even been much of a couple), but she had cared about Hayes. Maris had been friendly with Ellie as well; they were both art people. Maris deserved some sympathy.

"I haven't talked to you much since you got back," Maris said. "And now . . . I don't know. Maybe the whole place will close down? But they can't let that happen, right? Do you know what happened? How she got down there?"

Stevie shook her head.

"I guess she and Hayes tunneled a lot," Maris went on.

"They seemed to have a lot of secrets together. Do you . . . Did you really think Ellie did it? Killed Hayes? I mean, honestly? I thought you were wrong. But now . . ."

That's how it should have been. Stevie's idea must have looked farfetched at first, until Ellie ran and hid in a tunnel for so long that she ended up dying in it. But as Stevie turned and looked in the direction of the Great House, which was now a looming bulk on a dark day, her conviction was starting to evaporate. Maybe it was David's belief in Ellie. Or maybe it was guilt.

Something was crooked in the landscape. She couldn't see what it was, but the edges did not line up correctly.

Maris was still waiting for an answer.

"I just know about the script," Stevie said. "That she wrote *The End of It All*. That she took his computer."

Maris puffed for a moment and blew out a trail of smoke.

"If she killed Hayes and died down there," she said, "*good*."

That seemed a bit harsh. Actually, that seemed a lot harsh. But there was a solidity to it.

Stevie's phone started ringing. She pulled it out. The number came up as unknown, which was the first bad sign.

"I'll see you later," she said to Maris. Stevie jogged off a few paces toward the portico to answer the call.

"Sorry to call at a time like this," said a familiar voice. "I understand there was some trouble last night."

Senator King sounded like he was in a hallway, with people chattering all around him.

"Element Walker was found," he went on. "By David, if I understand things correctly. Do I?"

"Yes," Stevie said. She was surprised that she did not shake upon hearing his voice.

"Well," he said. "I suppose that answers the question of where she went. Very sad, of course. Terrible. The poor girl."

Edward King sounded about as sad about Ellie being found as someone who had just seen someone else drop half a doughnut on the ground. Stevie waited. David had obviously called his father. Whatever was coming, she could and would deal with it. She could unload all of her anger, all of her confusion, everything. It was time. It would feel good. Everything here would end, but . . .

"How do you think he took this?" Edward King said. "Finding the body. How did he seem? He won't tell me how he is, so I have to ask someone else."

This was not the question she was expecting.

"Upset," she said.

"Well, at least that's normal. That's good. He seems to be doing much better. I think you're having a very good influence on him, whatever you're doing. I'll make sure to put in a call to your parents today, make sure whatever comes of this is smoothed out. Really, when you think about it, it means there's less to be concerned about. All right. We'll talk soon."

With that, he was gone.

Well, Edward King didn't appear to know that Stevie had blurted everything out. Not yet, anyway. Stevie twitched a bit, thought of turning back, and then remembered there was no back to turn to. Home was still a crime scene—or, not a crime scene, but a scene. Off limits. She had promised Janelle and Nate she would meet them, and she needed them right now.

She continued on to the dining hall. The moment she went through the doors, it was clear that everyone knew what had happened the night before. For a start, everyone was there, which was weird on the night after the Halloween party. There was a low, electric chatter. Maris was with a group of people by the fireplace and chairs just inside the door. She wasn't sitting, though—she was standing on one of the chairs. Squatting, actually. Like a chicken. It was a weird move, like something Ellie would do.

Ellie was gone. The new Ellie was taking over.

Janelle stood and waved to Stevie from one of the booth seats. Stevie headed over toward her. Nate was there, and Vi. Stevie slid in.

"Where did you go last night?" Janelle said.

"Camping," Stevie replied.

"Where?"

"In the yoga studio. It was peaceful in there. The rain on the roof was really nice."

"You should have stayed with us. Are you okay? Did you sleep in there?"

A tray lowered itself onto the table. It was attached to David, who sat down with them. He didn't look up at Stevie. He just picked up a piece of bacon and started snapping it into pieces.

The veins in Stevie's forehead began ululating in alarm.

"I'm fine," she said.

"Are *you* okay?" Janelle asked David. "You weren't there either."

"Great," he said. "I'm great."

He snapped his bacon again. He looked right at Stevie, but her image seemed to bounce right off his eyes. Stevie felt herself vanishing, shrinking away. The toxic awkwardness of this conversation was obvious. Nate looked like he was trying to retreat into his sweater. Vi flashed a look of concern at Janelle. Janelle, of course, continued to face it all head-on.

"The yurt is nice," she said. "They moved in some beds, and they made little rooms for us with these tapestries."

"Good to hear," David said. "I've always wanted to live at a renaissance faire."

"I'm going to get some food," Stevie said, pushing back from the table.

Though it had been some time since she had eaten, Stevie found she had no appetite. She walked along the counter, gazing into the amber depths of the warm maple syrup vat with its tiny ladle. Gretchen came up behind her, sliding her tray along delicately, careful not to touch Stevie's, as if whatever Stevie had was catching.

"You guys are having a bad year," Gretchen said quietly. "I liked Ellie."

"Me too," Stevie said. Now that she was saying it out loud, she realized she really had. Ellie was goofy and colorful. Ellie had been friendly from the word *go*. She was ridiculous in her tattered clothes, rolling off the hammock chair in the common room.

"Do you think she did it?" Gretchen said. "Really?"

"I don't know," Stevie said, sliding her tray along.

"Sorry," Gretchen replied.

Stevie shook her head, indicating all was fine, even though all was not fine, and moved quickly along the line. She grabbed a portion of melon as a breakfast gesture so that no one would ask her why she wasn't eating, and started the long walk back to the table.

She had not done anything wrong, she told herself as she looked up at the judgmental faces of the carved pumpkins that sat on the eaves above. She sat with David in his grief. Then she told him the truth. That was all.

Did she do it in a kind of mean way for no reason she could work out after he bared his soul?

Stop, she told herself. *Just . . . stop. It's fine. Just sit. It's fine.*

The space between her and the table loomed—stretching and shrinking. People turned and glanced up at her as she passed, some still with traces of their costumes of the night before present on their skin and hair. Glitter here, smudged eyes there, colors in their hair.

Stevie was about halfway back to the table when the cafeteria doors opened and a small crew of faculty came in, including Call Me Charles, Jenny Quinn, and Larry. There was the school nurse, the counselors, Pix, a few other teachers. They cleared a bit of space. They gave Stevie just enough cover to sit down next to Janelle and start shoving melon into her mouth.

Charles, today dressed in somber gray pants and a black shirt, stood up on one of the chairs. Jenny Quinn stood beside him, quietly surveying the room. She was also wearing gray and black—black crepe pants, low black shoes, and a massive, thick cardigan of gray wool that swept down to her knees. It was the kind of wild, magical thing that looked like it had come from one of Stevie's Nordic Noir shows. She had pulled back her hair into a perfect bun that sat on the crown of her head like a doughnut. Her face was firmly set, and she ticked her gaze back and forth across the room like a scanner. She was looking for something, but what, Stevie had no idea.

"Everyone, everyone," Charles said, holding up his arms. "Could I get some quiet for a minute?"

The cafeteria settled in a moment or so. Stevie turned to listen. She could feel David looking at the back of her head.

"As I think most of you know by now, we suffered a terrible loss. Last night, Element Walker was found. She was not, I hate to have to say, alive."

The air-sucking quiet in the room said that everyone did know this, but hearing it was another thing entirely.

"I want to tell you what we know and what will happen next," Charles went on. "It appears that Ellie suffered an accident and became trapped in a tunnel—a tunnel we did not know about, a tunnel that will immediately be surveyed and sealed. One building, Minerva House, was affected, so we will be working with Minerva residents on accommodations . . ."

He shifted a bit and put his hands in his pockets. Jenny's attention was now pointed in the direction of the Minerva table.

". . . the last few weeks have been a time of such sadness. What you need to know, what you *must* know, is that your safety, your health, your emotional well-being is what matters the most. We are going to be here for you. We're going to have . . ."

"Counselors," Nate mumbled under his breath. "*You* get a counselor and *you* get a counselor, and *you* get . . ."

Janelle reached over and took Nate's hand and he stopped.

". . . every available resource. Some of you may need some time to visit home. We'll work to arrange that, if you need it. You can come and speak to *any* of us, at any time."

Charles continued burbling about procedures and feelings. Stevie shoved another square of melon in her mouth and chewed it slowly. Her mind decided this was nowhere to be and took a little trip back to anatomy class. *Dis* means apart. So many *dis* words. *Discover. Dismember. Distance.*

All of it applied to her life.

Charles relinquished the chair. Order was returned, and the cafeteria began buzzing gently again, everyone conferring about what they had just heard.

"So is the school going to shut down or something?" Nate finally asked.

"We hope not." This was from Jenny Quinn, who had approached their table. Though she had seen Dr. Quinn many times, or overheard her several, Stevie had never really been part of any face-to-face discussion with her. Dr. Quinn was one of Ellingham's most formidable academics. She was on more committees and was a member of more institutes than she had fingers and toes. Think tanks courted her. Harvard still missed her and was waiting for her to call. She was second in command to Charles, which seemed unlikely, until you remembered that Charles was a guy. Even at Ellingham, the patriarchy reared its shaggy head. She was also the first person Stevie had ever seen who was clearly wearing fashion. Not just things that were cool. Things that had been on *runways*.

"Nathaniel," she said. "I wanted to see how you were doing."

Nate visibly gulped.

"Fine?"

Jenny's eyes were still tracking, going from face to face. She glanced at Nate, glided over Janelle and Vi, paused a beat when she caught Stevie's glance, and then landed on David. David got a hard, long look before she looped back around to Nate.

"If this causes problems with your book . . ." she said. "Just come to me."

She did the track of the table again. Whatever Jenny Quinn had come over here for, it was not to see how Nate was doing in the worlds of feelings or dragons. She had some other agenda she had decided not to share, and that agenda had something to do with David, who was now looking down at his plate and stabbing at his food.

"I have a question," Janelle said. "I need a job. I need to do something. What can we *do*?"

A look that could have been approval spread over Jenny's features.

"I think a strong, positive message from the students would go a long way," Jenny said. "If there is press, and there will be, then the students should be part of the message. Ellingham is an institution, and we have been here for many years and we will be here for many years to come, hopefully. In fact, we are likely about to expand, maybe even double in size. So perhaps you want to organize the students? Make yourselves heard. You can work with me to develop a message and work with our media team."

"I can do that," Janelle said. "I can do that."

"Definitely," Vi said. "I've worked on messaging with all kinds of campaigns."

"Good," Jenny said. Then she made her exit. Janelle and Vi huddled at once to start discussing this. David picked up his tray and walked to the door, dumping the tray in the busing bin as he left.

"So," Nate said, turning to Stevie and speaking in a low voice. "Are you going to tell me what the fuck has been going on?"

18

"So wait," Nate said, walking up and down. "David Eastman is Edward King's son."

"Don't tell anyone that," Stevie said.

She was sitting on the stack of yoga mats in the gloom of the rainy midmorning. Nate was one of those people who couldn't quite sit still or look at you if the conversation went on too long, so he had been traversing the room, half lifting himself on the barre, tracing his finger along the edge where the mirrors met on the wall. He was doing everything to keep from standing still.

"You're here because of Edward King. And your job is to make sure David is stable?"

"Basically," Stevie said.

"Is this normal?"

"How am I supposed to know what normal is?" Stevie said, pulling at a loose thread in the cuff of her hoodie.

"But you told David," Nate said. "That his father is why you're here."

Stevie had given Nate the overview on this, but not the

bloody details about the crying and how she ran away.

"Except that Edward King didn't seem to know that when he called me this morning," Stevie said.

"He called you this morning?"

Stevie had not gotten that far in the story. It was a lot of story.

"Jesus Christ," Nate said, banging his head delicately against the mirror wall. "Is this even a school, or are we in some kind of experiment?"

Stevie shook her head.

"So what happens now?" Nate said.

"I don't know."

"If David tells his dad, you could be gone, whenever? How?"

"I guess he talks to my parents or something," she said. "They listen to him. He has influence and . . . planes. He can do pretty much anything."

"Jesus. *Jesus*, Stevie."

"You wanted to know," she said.

"Does Janelle know?"

"No. I couldn't tell anyone."

"Are you going to tell her?"

"Probably. She already hates David." Stevie rubbed her temples. "Look, I have to do something. There's one more thing I have."

She unzipped her bag and removed the tin and set it on the floor.

"What's that?" he said. "Are snakes going to come out of it?"

"It's proof," she said, "that the person who wrote the Truly Devious letter wasn't the person who kidnapped the Ellinghams. I found it in Ellie's room."

Nate tipped back his head and laughed. She had never heard him laugh like this before. It was deep and bounced all around the mirrors and the floor.

"Now you are shitting me," he said. "You're in some secret deal with a senator, who is David's dad, two people are dead, and you have proof about the Ellingham case."

"This is why my anatomy grades are bad," Stevie explained.

"You can't be a real person."

"Whatever happens to me here, this case has to get solved. If they take me away, I need you to help me."

Nate pinched his nose and paced from one side of the room to the other.

"Okay," he finally said. "Okay. Yes. Okay. Sure. Let's solve the crime of the century. Why the fuck not?"

Stevie's phone rang, and she pulled it from her pocket. The number was unknown.

"Oh God," she said. "I think it's him."

"Who?"

"Edward King," she said. The phone continued to ring. Stevie considered throwing it at the wall, then decided that it would be better to answer than be kept wondering forever.

But it was not Edward King. It was Larry.

"There's someone here to see you."

"Someone *here*?" she said.

Nate raised an eyebrow.

The first rule of Ellingham Academy was that no one was allowed at Ellingham Academy except the students and faculty. Even parents could only come at appointed times. The road could not withstand heavy traffic, and the school was big on fostering a creative spirit of learning, which meant no randos. Visitors were rare and had recently been only of the police variety.

So, her parents. They had come. It was over. She felt herself sag into the yoga mats.

"Dr. Fenton," Larry said. "She's waiting at the Great House for you."

When Stevie arrived at the Great House, Fenton was there, leaning on the security desk, deep in conversation with Call Me Charles. And she had not come alone. Hunter sat in a chair by the door, looking like he wished he could sink into the floor. He was wearing some old jeans and a long-sleeved T-shirt, and had the general air of someone who had been dragged along on someone else's date.

". . . it's a real work of scholarship," she was saying. "It far surpasses the original."

"I'll have to be sure to read it," Charles said. For once, Captain Enthusiasm looked like he had been bested by someone much more exhausting than himself. He shifted uncomfortably and looked at his watch.

"Stevie," he said as she approached. "Dr. Fenton has come up to—"

"I just wanted to check on some of these references," Fenton interrupted, holding up the pad. "It looks like I may have come on a bad day."

"Yes . . ." Charles said. "I think what would be best is if you came to my office and we'll look at the schedule. We'll be a few minutes."

"Is there any chance my nephew could have a look around? He's always wanted to see the place."

Hunter continued drilling into the floor with his mind.

"I . . . think that would be all right," Charles said, not sounding at all like this was all right. "Stevie, maybe you could take Hunter on a brief . . ."

He didn't linger on the word, but the point was made.

". . . tour of the campus. Dr. Fenton, if you could come with me . . ."

As they stepped outside, Hunter sighed loudly. The rain had given up a little bit, leaving the day gray and soggy, but good enough to walk in.

"Sorry," he immediately said, "she made me come. I know we're not supposed to be here. She knows it too. I'm really sorry. You don't have to give me a tour. I can wait in the car."

"No," Stevie said. "It's fine. Today is . . ."

"Bad," he said. "I know."

"You know?"

"Word spreads," he said. "Is it true? They found that girl?"

Stevie nodded. She did not add that *she* had found that girl. In the gray of a new day, the knowledge settled on her shoulders. She had found a body, and she was . . . okay with it. Not great. Not happy. But she was holding her own. Some coping mechanism had been triggered.

"How did you get up here?" Stevie asked.

"She told the person at the front gate that she had an appointment with Dr. Scott. He must have said we could come up."

"What do you want to see?" Stevie asked.

Hunter looked across the vista, past the Neptune fountain, at the wide expanse of the green.

"It's really amazing," he said. "I'm sorry to come like this, but it's still cool to see it. I don't know where to start."

"I guess, around?" she said.

Stevie started walking toward the grass.

"Sorry," he said again. "Could we do the path?"

He held up his crutch.

"Oh, God. Sorry. Yeah."

"Don't worry about it. It just sticks in the ground, especially when it's wet."

Stevie decided that of the two possible directions, it was best to head toward the left, to the classroom buildings. It seemed like these would be less populated. David seeing would make this whole weird thing even worse. The library was as good as any place to start, so she took Hunter there.

Hunter was appreciative of everything he saw, his eyes growing wide. She could see longing on his face.

"This place is nuts," he said as they walked between the classroom buildings. "It's better than the pictures."

"It's okay," Stevie said.

"You know it's better than that."

She shrugged.

"So someone gets all of this," he said.

"What?"

"If they find Alice. Someone gets all of this."

"That's an internet rumor," Stevie said.

"Not according to my aunt."

"Bullshit," Stevie said, shaking her head. "She doesn't believe that."

"She does," he said.

Hunter stepped ahead a bit and sat down on the bench between some of the statues nearby.

"She says . . ." Hunter sighed deeply. "That Robert Mackenzie told her that there was something added to Ellingham's will that stated that anyone who located Alice, dead or alive, would get some huge fortune."

"That's bullshit," Stevie said, shaking her head. "That's an old rumor, like that the whole thing was faked or that Alice lives in the attic and she's a hundred years old. I've been in the attic, by the way. She's not there."

"My aunt believes it."

"No, she doesn't," Stevie said. "No one who is serious about this thinks that's real. If it were real, everyone would know. That would be the whole point. Tell everyone so that they would go look for Alice. You don't post a reward without telling people to go look."

"According to my aunt," Hunter said, "Mackenzie disobeyed. He said he never felt right about going along with everything on the night of the kidnapping. He thought if he'd gone against Ellingham's wishes and called the police right away, things might have turned out differently. When Ellingham wrote this codicil, he told Mackenzie to publicize it far and wide. Mackenzie always thought that Alice was dead, and even if she were alive, she would be safer if the stakes were lower, if the publicity had died down. If this challenge went out into the world, every con artist and hustler would land on top of them. And then when Ellingham died, Mackenzie felt he needed to protect his estate. He didn't want the money to be stolen away—he wanted it to be used for good. So he made sure the codicil was locked up."

"So there's this magical piece of paper out there that no one knows about that says 'Find Alice, win a prize!'"

"I'm not saying I believe it. I'm saying it's what my aunt believes, and she *swears* Mackenzie told her about it."

Stevie paused and thought about this for a moment.

"Someone would *have* to know," Stevie said.

"She says people do know. The people on the board, who run Ellingham and the trust. And they can't inherit. They all agree to keep things quiet so that they don't get spammed by treasure hunters all the time. Can you imagine? It's a shit-ton of money."

Stevie could imagine. As it was, people had presented themselves as Alice many times, but all had failed to pass the sniff test. There were things about Alice that were kept secret that they didn't know. The only people who had tried more recently failed DNA tests.

"So are you saying your aunt is doing this for money?" she said.

"I think at first she wanted to write a book, but yeah. Now she's basically a dude with a metal detector looking for a lost city of gold."

The idea of doing this for money left a bitter taste in Stevie's mouth.

"I'm telling you this for a reason," he said. "I don't like how she's using you. I don't like how we're here today. It's why I wanted to give you my number. There's something gross about all of this. She's had contacts at the school before. You're not even the first person she's been talking to up there this *year*."

"Who?" she said.

"I don't know. I heard her talking to someone on the phone, someone who had to be here on the campus. She was being very secretive about it. And she mentioned your name."

"What about me?" Stevie said.

"I couldn't make much out. I caught your name, something about Ellingham, that's it."

"When was this?"

"It was earlier in the year because it was warmer and we had all the windows open. But school was definitely in session. Mid-September?"

"Do you think your aunt was talking to Hayes or Ellie?"

"I don't know. She could have been."

If Fenton had been in communication with Hayes or Ellie . . .

Hayes made more sense. It was Hayes who'd had the idea to make the video. Hayes wanted to go into the tunnel. Hayes and his half-baked ideas. Fenton wanted people who would scout for her. Had she gone to Hayes first, and then when Hayes died, come to Stevie? Was she second fiddle to *Hayes*?

She had to ignore that for a second, because the thought was too irritating. Maybe Fenton had somehow convinced Hayes that he could make a huge fortune if he just went tunneling.

There was a noise behind them, and Germaine Batt appeared, headphones on. From outside appearances, she was just walking by on her way somewhere, but that felt unlikely to Stevie. She had the bad feeling that Germaine had heard every word, and that Stevie had just repaid the favor she owed.

19

"WHAT'S YOUR FAVORITE ATTRACTION AT DISNEY WORLD?" MUDGE asked as he removed the rubbery band of muscle and fat from around a cow eyeball.

"I've never been there," Stevie said.

Stevie was standing a few feet away in her lab apron, gripping her coffee in her nitrile-gloved hands. Mudge worked on the dissection tray. The smell of formaldehyde swelled inside Stevie's nose.

It had been five days since Ellie. That's how Stevie thought of it. This was the post-Ellie period. The police had finished with Minerva House. Ellie's things were no longer there, and the only area of interest was the entrance to the tunnel under the steps. They had put a rough bracket over the panel with a very serious-looking lock—not something that could be picked with a pin. There were also three crisscrossing bits of police tape.

Things had, in that way they do, ground back to normalcy. There had been news stories, of course. But the general conclusion was that the Hayes matter had now reached its natural end. The person responsible, having done a bad thing, had gotten herself killed while making another bad decision. There was press for a day, but then the news cycle snuffed out the story when something else came along a few hours later. Parents had been called and soothed. And Edward King had worked his magic again, assuring Stevie's parents that Ellie had gotten exactly what was coming to her and there was no further need for concern.

And David . . . he was there. He did not do morning screaming meditation or sleep on the roof. He continued going to class, but he never spoke to Stevie, not once. It was like she did not exist.

Sometimes, though, he just *smiled* at her. Smiled like he knew something about what existed inside of her, a great cosmic joke that he would never tell.

Stevie hid in her room a lot, coming out only for food and class and sometimes she wouldn't even bother with the food. She claimed to be studying, and Janelle would bring her containers back from the cafeteria.

"You probably think mine would be the Haunted Mansion," Mudge continued. "It's not. I like the Haunted Mansion, but my favorite is the Country Bear Jamboree."

"Once you remove the external tissue," Pix said from the front of the room, "you can go ahead and make the incision into the cornea."

"The thing about it . . ." Mudge set down the dissection scissors and reached for the scalpel. "Is that it doesn't change.

Ever. It's been there since the opening day and some people think it's boring, but . . ."

He made the incision expertly, cutting across the eye. Liquid seeped out onto the dissection tray.

". . . it's actually completely metal. The one bear sings this song about blood on the saddle. You should go. It's great. But if you're talking rides . . ."

"The aqueous humor is the liquid you see," Pix said. "It helps give shape to the cornea. Now, you're going to want to go through the sclera . . ."

"Ride-wise," Mudge said, "I mean, people talk about Space Mountain a lot, but that's not Disney at its best. That's some midcentury space age bullshit. The best ride is Dumbo."

"And what is the sclera, Stevie?" said Pix, who had come up alongside them.

"The white of the eye?" Stevie replied.

"It's the protective outer coating. Move in a little bit. Dissection is hard at first, but you get used to it. Think of the things you may have to see if you become a detective."

These were perhaps the only words that could move her. Stevie took a single step closer to the tray. It was true that she might have to get used to dissections in her chosen career, but this was different. This was a giant eye, and it was looking at her from Mudge's hand as he sliced it in half in the same way some people might slice an apple.

"How have you been doing?" Mudge asked.

"With . . ."

"Ellie's death. You need to make sure you're practicing good self-care." Mudge set the scalpel down and looked through the dissection kit for a probe. "Just so you know, I'm here if you want to talk to me about anything."

Stevie stared up at her tall, black-clad lab partner in his blue plastic apron and his rubber gloves. It was hard to read the expression in his eyes because of his purple snake-eye pupils.

"Thanks," she said.

"Just offering. It's important to make sure people know that you're open to discussion."

"You're going to want to get the iris from between the cornea and the lens," Pix said, circling the room.

Mudge held out the half an eyeball with a *you want this?* gesture. Stevie shook her head no. He set it down and continued working. The smell of formaldehyde stung the inside of Stevie's nose, and it made her think of the smell in the tunnel.

Don't think about that.

"How did she get down there?" Stevie said, out loud.

"Ellie?" Mudge said. "She was always like that. She liked looking for liminal spaces."

"But I was down in that basement," Stevie said. She didn't really mean to talk to Mudge about this, but now that he had elicited her comment, it was coming out. "I don't see how she could have found that opening. She must have been down there before."

"You know," he said, "there are miles and miles of tunnels under Disney World. They're called utilidors. Walt Disney got upset when he saw a cowboy walking through Tomorrowland to get to Frontierland—this was in the California Disneyland. So in Florida he had all these tunnels built. So it's a little like here. This is sort of like educational Disney World."

Stevie had no idea what to say to that.

"Disney World is on a swamp," Mudge went on. "Everything there has to be built up. So the tunnels are ground level. Disney World is actually built on raised ground, on an incline. People don't even notice because it's so gradual."

Mudge triumphantly pulled a clear, squidgy thing out of the eye, about the size of a quarter. It looked a bit like a jellyfish.

"The lens," he said.

He set it down on the tray.

"The lens," she said.

Her phone buzzed in her pocket, and she surreptitiously pulled it out. She had gotten an email. The name of the sender confused her for a moment—Ann Abbott. But then she remembered. The flour lady. The Jell-O and salad lady. She knocked the probe off the edge of the lab station so she could bend down for a moment to read:

Dear Stevie,

Thank you so much for your note! I'm sorry I took so long to respond. I am terrible with email. I am so pleased that you enjoyed *Better Than Homemade*! I didn't even know copies of it were still around.

To answer your question, there is very little
information I know of on Francis Crane. Most of
the family fortune went to her older brother, who
died sometime in the 1960s. There was some kind
of argument within the family, I believe, which
resulted in Francis largely being taken out of the
will.

I did speak to someone else in the family when
I was writing the book, and I seem to remember
they said that Francis may have gone to France
right before the war, and that she lived in Paris
and had a daughter. I'll see if I can find out more.
You have me curious now.

How wonderful that you are at Ellingham
Academy. It seems like a magical place!

Sincerely,

Ann Abbott

Well, it was something. The Francis trail wasn't completely cold.

"Did you lose something?" Pix asked from the other side
of the lab station. Mudge gave nothing away as he glanced
down at Stevie. She slid the phone under her bag and reappeared with the probe.

"I'll get you a fresh one," Pix said, taking it. "Always use
clean instruments, even in things like this. Work clean."

Mudge continued with the incision.

"This here . . ." Mudge poked into the eye, showing her

a bit of filmy substance. "The retina. Here's where the nerve bundles attach. And anything that hits directly where the nerve bundle attaches is the blind spot. The one place where all the information goes in, you can't actually see anything."

He put his hands on his hips for a moment, then scratched behind his ear with his gloved hand.

"Some people," he said, "want the Country Bear Jamboree to go. It's not a ride. It doesn't have a movie. But that's not the point. I think if you get rid of the Country Bear Jamboree, you get rid of the heart and soul of Disney World. It's not about the money. It's about the bears."

As they walked out of class, Stevie hoped that she might see David sitting there, as he had been that one day in his stupid sunglasses. But the bench was empty except for a bird. Her plan had been to go back to her room and sit in her warren of takeout containers and books until the heat death of the sun, or at least until she had a better idea.

She had a better idea. Or, at least, *an* idea. What had Mudge just said? "It's not about the money?" The money. Fenton believed in the money. No one serious believed in the money. The money was fool's gold, a rumor—the kind of thing flat-Earthers believed, or people who were convinced that the moon landing was fake. There was no Ellingham treasure to be had.

However. Fenton was serious. Maybe Fenton was a little off. Fenton had problems. But Fenton did know the material. She wouldn't fall for that *so* easily.

And . . . Stevie found herself walking toward the Great House . . . something she had heard . . . what was it? Something about money. Somebody had just said something about money. Who was it? She flipped back through her mind, rewinding conversations. Money.

There. She found it. When Jenny Quinn approached their table in the cafeteria. She said the school was about to expand. Expansions cost money. Money could come from anywhere, of course. A donor. Maybe Edward King. But this sounded like a *lot* of money. Like, a major-inheritance-freed-up kind of money.

What if it was real? What if they were counting down to getting the Alice money? What if finding Alice was worth the fortune of a lifetime? Several lifetimes?

As this possibility spun in her brain, she noticed that Larry was coming out of the Great House and approaching in her direction. Then she realized he was walking right toward her, as if this was not an accident. His face was grave.

"I'd like to talk to you," he said to Stevie. "Walk with me a little."

He was wearing his red-and-black-checked flannel coat over his uniform. He motioned for her to walk around the back path, the one that led to the empty playing fields and the trees that blocked the river. They were starting to shed leaves, leaving jagged holes in their curtain. Larry was silent until they were about halfway into the field.

"Today is my last day here," he said.

Stevie stopped cold.

"What?"

"My office is packed. After this, I'm going home. I won't be back on campus. They have someone else coming in."

Stevie felt like she had just taken a blow to the stomach.

"Why?" she said.

"My job is to keep everyone here safe. Two dead. That's not keeping people safe. Which is why I have to go."

"You can't do that," Stevie said. "They can't. This isn't your decision, is it?"

"It's the right one," he said. "No matter who made it."

"But this isn't your fault," she said. "What happened to Hayes, what happened to Ellie . . ."

"Happened on my watch. Now listen . . . don't worry about me."

"We can start a protest!" Stevie said. "We can organize . . ."

"Stevie," he said. "*Listen*. I need you to pay attention."

Stevie gulped and became quiet, huddled in her red vinyl coat.

"I want you to be careful," he said. "Don't go off on your own on any investigations. It's over. Leave it."

"Investigations?" she said.

"Not the Ellingham stuff. I mean with Hayes, Ellie, all of that."

There was a steady, warning look in his eye.

"What do you mean?" she said. "They were . . ."

"Accidents," he said.

The wind snapped around them, coming up into Stevie's coat.

"You're saying they weren't," she said.

"No. I'm just saying that . . ." For the first time, Stevie saw Larry lost for words. He was reaching for a danger Stevie could not precisely see, but the form of it was faintly making itself known in the air, in the shade of the trees, and the changing temperatures. She had felt it several times, and now Larry was feeling it too.

"When you spoke at our orientation," she said, "you said that people got stuck in tunnels before, sometimes for days. . . ."

"That never happened," Larry said. "That's just part of the pattern to get people to stay out of any hidden structures they might find, because we weren't sure if there were any more out there. I want you to put my number into your phone. Now. Get your phone out."

He waited until she produced her phone and added him.

"There's no chance you'd go home, is there?" he said.

"Leave? Why? And no. But why? Tell me *something*."

Larry paused for a moment.

"I don't know," he said. "And that's what bothers me. Let's just say I have a bad feeling and I want you to have that number. I want you to use it anytime you want, no matter what. Doesn't matter when."

He inhaled deeply through his nose. She could see the traces of pain on his face as he looked around, probably for the last time.

"They can't do this to you," she said again.

"This isn't about me. But if you want to do something,

you need to promise me you'll take care of yourself and do as I said. Leave it all alone."

Stevie felt her eyes burning and watering. Sometimes the wind made this happen. This was not one of those times.

"You promise?" he asked.

"Yeah," she said. "I promise."

He nodded, and turned back in the direction of the Great House. Stevie's brain continued ticking. The money issue and this development fused into one idea.

"Wait," she called to him. "Can I ask you one favor? Can I get a ride?"

October 30, 1938, 1:00 p.m.

IT WAS FUNNY, REALLY, THAT THE RIDDLE HAD BEEN THE ANSWER.

Albert Ellingham sat in his office, listening to the ticking of the green marble clock on the mantelpiece. This clock had once belonged to Marie-Thérèse Louise, the princesse de Lamballe, and was said to have been a gift from her dear friend, Queen Marie-Antoinette. It was a fine clock, made of deep green Swedish marble run through with gold. While the woman who had gifted it and the woman who had owned it were both beheaded in the French Revolution, the clock lived on, keeping perfect time. He had purchased it in Switzerland around the time Alice was born. The antique dealer had told Albert Ellingham the clock's history, how some of the princess's belongings were removed from her house before the people raided it, how carriages full of art came over the border into Switzerland as the aristocracy in France were dying. He told tales of blood and heads on spikes and superior workmanship.

Albert Ellingham had paid a small fortune for the clock. It pleased him to look at it, so solid, so storied, the green the color of pine.

The wall of French doors that led out onto the patio and down to the garden was heavily curtained. Albert had been keeping the curtains closed since he had drained the lake. He could not bear to look at the hole in the ground, the one that looked like a grave. Today, though, he opened all of them wide, and the view rewarded his courage. The Vermont sky was a particularly perfect blue, and the trees all around painted in golds and reds. The fine days of the season would soon be over, and the snow would come to the mountain. There would not be many days like this.

Today was the day it had to happen.

There was much to be done. There were several objects on his desk, and they all required his attention: a pile of legal documents, a Western Union telegram slip, a copy of the collected stories of Sherlock Holmes, and a spool of wire.

The documents first.

He picked up one, freshly printed on legal parchment. He scanned it until he found the part that concerned him:

```
In addition to all other bequests, the amount
of ten million dollars shall be held in trust
for my daughter, Alice Madeline Ellingham.
Should my daughter no longer be among the
living, any person, persons, or organization
that locates her earthly remains—provided
it is established that they were in no
way connected to her disappearance—shall
receive this sum. If she is not located by
```

```
her ninetieth birthday, these funds shall be
released to be used for the Ellingham Academy
in any way the board sees fit.
```

This bit had been finalized yesterday, and Robert Mackenzie had not been happy with it. Mackenzie brought it in, fresh from the lawyer, and then sat down opposite Albert and stared.

"What is it, Mackenzie?" he finally had to say. "Out with it."

"I don't like it. And you know why."

"I do."

"They'll come out of the woodwork," Mackenzie went on. "Every kind of two-bit scam artist in the world will descend on this place like a plague of locusts."

"One of those locusts may know where my daughter is," Albert Ellingham said.

"It's unlikely. And how would we ever know which one?"

"Because I know something about my daughter that no one else knows," he said. "I will know the truth."

Mackenzie sank back into his chair and sighed.

"You think I'm an old fool," Albert Ellingham said.

"You are neither old nor a fool. You are a father in grief and a very rich man. People will want to take advantage of you."

"I have handled much more than that, Robert."

"I know . . ."

"You are trying to protect me, because you have always

kept my best interests at heart. But it is my money to do with as I see fit. And this is what is fit. It is your duty to get the statement written up, and I will print it in my paper starting next week."

Albert Ellingham looked at the passage again. Mackenzie had a point, of course. By making this offer, he was opening himself up to every kind of flimflammery the world had on offer. Ten million dollars would have the greatest con artists on the planet beating a path to his door.

But it would also turn the entire world into his private detectives.

It was a risk, and Albert Ellingham was comfortable with risk. He had created himself from nothing, and he would take himself back to nothing quite happily if it meant seeing Alice again.

He put the documents back into the large folder, and placed it in his desk drawer.

Second, the Western Union slip. He had written it out earlier in the morning. The riddle had come to him several days before, but he had not yet been able to bring himself to commit it to paper until now, because that meant confronting the truth. How long had he known? Probably since he'd first read the copy of the book. He stared at the riddle for a moment and shoved it into his pocket. Then he drew *The Adventures of Sherlock Holmes* toward him. This particular copy belonged to the school library, and he had found it in the dome when he came to on that fateful evening of the kidnapping. At first, he thought nothing of it—there were too many other things going on that night. Surely, a guest of his had borrowed the book and read it; all of his guests were invited to use the school library for their pleasure reading. But then, as time went on and his thoughts cleared, he made inquiries into the book. No, no guests of his had taken out the book. Dolores Epstein had had possession of it almost exclusively.

Which is how he came to understand that Dolores had been coming to his little hideaway to read, and she had brought one of her favorite volumes that day.

Albert Ellingham had grown up in one of the poorest neighborhoods of New York City himself; perhaps that was why he felt such affection for little Dolores Epstein. He had worked as a news seller from the age of eight, collecting his pennies and nickels. More than once, he had spent a cold night sleeping in a doorway. He sometimes found shelter in the New York Public Library, where he had read Sherlock Holmes—read all the stories, committed many lines to heart.

He opened the book and searched for one that often figured into his thoughts. It was from a story called "The Boscombe Valley Mystery": "There is nothing more deceptive than an obvious fact."

Indeed. This was so.

He had kept this book in his office, and it was by chance that he noticed the mark on the page. It was quite early in the volume, in *A Study in Scarlet*. This had been the thing that set his thoughts in motion. Dolores Epstein, that marvelous, brilliant girl, thinking until the end. To have her sharpness, her presence of mind . . .

Finally, he reached for the wire. He would need to listen one more time, just to be absolutely sure. He stood and went across the room, to a collection of cabinets. He opened one, which contained a Webster-Chicago wire recorder. This machine had been outfitted with a pair of listening headphones. He inserted the wire on the reel, then sat down, put the headphones over his ears, and played the recording.

After several minutes, he switched the machine off and removed the headphones. Everything was there, all falling perfectly into place. When he added in what Margo Fields had revealed . . .

It was all very complete. It was time.

He pressed the buzzer on his desk that summoned Robert Mackenzie. Mackenzie appeared within a minute, notebook in hand. He saw Mackenzie note the open curtains.

"I am going to the yacht club," he said. "The weather is fine and clear. I've asked Marsh to come with me. We could both use some time in the air. We've been in dark places too long."

Albert was moved by the look of genuine pleasure that passed over his secretary's face. Mackenzie cared for him. He was perhaps the last person who did.

"That's a very good idea," Mackenzie said. "Would you like me to arrange for a picnic basket for the trip?"

Albert Ellingham shook his head.

"No need, no need. Here. I wrote a riddle this morning. What do you think?"

He surprised himself with this action. The riddle was a private one, but he shared all his riddles with Mackenzie. This one, perhaps most of all, deserved his consideration. Mackenzie snatched it up, obviously happy that he was returning to his old ways.

"Where do you look for someone who's never really there?" Mackenzie read. "Always on a staircase, but never on a stair."

Albert watched Mackenzie very closely. Would he know the answer? Was it visible to all?

"It may be the best riddle I've ever written," he said. "It's my Riddle of the Sphinx. Those who solve it pass. Those who don't . . ."

He reached over and took the slip of paper back, setting it neatly on the middle of his desk. Mackenzie was turning the riddle over in his mind, but Albert could see that his attention was not on it. Mackenzie was studying his demeanor for clues. Mackenzie himself was looking much older than his thirty years. He needed to get out in the world and live.

"I have something very important for you to do today, Robert," he said, putting a paperweight over the riddle for protection. "Get out in the air. Enjoy yourself. That's an order."

"I'm going to," Mackenzie said. "I have about ten pounds' worth of correspondence to get through first."

"I mean it, Robert." And he did mean it. Suddenly, telling

Robert Mackenzie to care for himself was the most important thing in the world. "The winter will be here soon and you'll wish you took more advantage of days like this."

Mackenzie shuffled awkwardly.

"You're a good man, Robert," he went on. "I wish you had the happiness in your life that I've had in mine. Remember to play. Remember the game. Always remember the game."

This was all sounding a bit much, so Albert Ellingham put on the broadest smile he could muster.

"I promise I will go outside," Mackenzie said, in a way that indicated the exact opposite.

"There is one other thing," Albert said. "All the paperwork for the codicil and the trust is in my desk. Make sure that you get everything ready for the printer. I want to start running the ads tomorrow."

"You're really going through with it?" Mackenzie said. "And there's nothing that I can say to stop you?"

"Nothing. Big, bold type, above the fold. 'Ellingham offers ten million for daughter.' I want people in passing airplanes to be able to read the headline."

"This is a mistake."

"That is mine to make. When you have ten million dollars, you can do with it what you wish."

This was a bit harsh, but the point had to be made. It was time to go. No more moving commentary about the nature of the day. Now that the moment was upon him, he felt the edge of hesitation. Perhaps he should explain. Robert Mackenzie could be trusted.

"It was on the wire," he added as Mackenzie reached the door.

"What?" Mackenzie turned.

No. Robert could not know.

"Nothing. Nothing. As you were."

Mackenzie returned to his office.

Everything was now in place. The other preparations were already made. The materials were in the trunk of the car. The mechanism was an easy matter that he had constructed by the fire the evening before. Albert Ellingham looked around his office once more, to see if there was anything he had forgotten. He reached down and opened the lowest desk drawer. This drawer contained only a few small personal items—a bottle of aspirin, a spare pair of glasses, a deck of cards. He reached back farther and pulled out a revolver. He held it for a moment, heavy in his palm, considered it fully.

The green marble clock ticked away. When had the murdered princess last looked at it? Did she know it was the last time? The cool glass eye had watched as she had been taken from her house. It had been spared the sight of her death, her head put on a spike and paraded through the streets of Paris. The head had even been displayed at her friend the queen's prison window, a ghastly puppet. A sign of what was to come.

It was just a clock. It did not know or understand. But it did know the time, and it was telling Albert Ellingham that it had come. Choose.

No. It was best to do it without the gun. The plan was well-balanced. He returned it to the drawer and got up for his coat before he could second-guess himself.

It was time to play the game.

20

T HE SCHOOL, HAVING JUST RELEASED LARRY FROM DUTY, WAS NOT
inclined to let him drive Stevie to Burlington. However, in
accordance with the "we will do anything to make you feel
better" initiative, there was no objection to her going to Burlington to work with Dr. Fenton. She was given a ride with
a security officer named Jerry who was going off duty in a
half hour. Someone else would come pick her up. Jerry drove
Stevie to Burlington in his old Acura and didn't care that she
was listening to her earbuds the entire time. She needed to
play some music. Things were thrumming in her head and
she needed them all to get into the same rhythm.

They pulled up at Fenton's door, and Stevie sprang out,
gave a quick thanks, and hurried down the cracked concrete
path. She had not texted Hunter, because what she was about
to do required an element of surprise and a bit of recon. First,
she listened. The house was quiet. There were no lights on
downstairs. She had checked Fenton's schedule, so Stevie
knew she had a class to teach in forty-five minutes. She paced
awhile, keeping out of sight and away from the direction

that Fenton would walk. She waited almost forty minutes, before Fenton blew out of her door and started furiously clog-walking in the direction of her classroom building.

She texted Hunter now:

Are you home?

After a moment, came the reply. Yeah why.

Come downstairs and outside.

Stevie waited on the screened porch, with the piles of garbage and recycling waiting in bins. After a moment, the inner door opened and Hunter poked his head out.

"Can I come in?"

"Sure?" he said, opening the door.

The house had a bad odor that day. Clearly Fenton had made no jokes about not having a sense of smell. Even the cats seemed to have abandoned ship.

"I need you to help me," Stevie said.

"With what?"

Stevie could have lied. She had lied before. But the lies had all backfired. Sneaking into Fenton's house was not like sneaking into someone's room, either. In the real world they called that breaking and entering. This required transparency, and a bit of luck.

"I need to go into her office. I need to look at the manuscript."

Hunter's face sagged.

"I can't . . ."

"I'm not stealing anything," she said. "I just need to see her notes about what Mackenzie said."

"I told you . . ."

"Look," Stevie said, moving around the room to find a spot that didn't smell quite as bad. "I may not have forever to do this. I need to show you something."

She found a somewhat clear space on one of the tables and set her bag down. She unzipped it, reached in, and produced the tin.

"This," she said, "contains proof that the Truly Devious letter was written by two students on campus. It was a joke, a prank. Or something."

"Shut up," he said.

She pulled open the tin and produced the photos.

"These two," she said, holding up a photo, "were two rich students. The guy was a poet. The girl was really into true-crime magazines. They were cosplaying Bonnie and Clyde. Here's a poem they wrote."

She showed him the poem.

"And here," she said, showing Hunter the stuck-together photos with the cut-out letters. "Proof, or close to proof. I have actual evidence about this case. And if your aunt does as well, I need to see it. Because I feel like she is playing some kind of game with me. And something is going on at my school. Two people have died."

"Accidentally," he said.

"Yeah, but *something* is happening. If this money theory is something Mackenzie really said, I need to see the notes."

Hunter inhaled deeply and looked at the office door.

"I'm the real deal," Stevie said. "I'm not here for the

money. I'm here to find the *answers*. Please."

Hunter's gaze drifted along the floor, then up to Stevie's face.

"She'll be back in less than an hour," he said. "She never teaches the full forty-five minutes. Come on."

He went through the French doors, and Stevie followed. Once inside, he walked toward a file cabinet. But instead of opening it, he knocked a stack of magazines on the floor out of the way with the tip of his crutch.

"She's paranoid," he said, leaning the crutch against the cabinet and getting down on the ground. He pushed the magazines off and revealed a pizza box underneath. This, he opened. The pizza box was unused, and inside it contained several manila folders. He thumbed through them, then selected one. He sat back on his heels for a moment.

"I think when she talked to Mackenzie, he was sick," he said. "He was old. They had him on a lot of medication. He told her things that he had always kept quiet, because he was vulnerable. But, I guess, it had to come out."

He considered, and then passed the folder up to Stevie.

The tab read: MACKENZIE. It was a thin folder, with only a few papers inside, handwritten on torn-out pieces of yellow legal paper. A lot of the notes seemed to concern whens and wheres of meeting. Then, there was one page with just two points:

* Ellingham left house on night of kidnapping for approx. 45 minutes around 2 a.m., did not go

*through front door. Seemed to leave from office.
Mackenzie seemed sure that there was a tunnel
leading from the Great House out, and possibly
another that went from Minerva, where Ellingham
would house his mistress, to a location on the
opposite side of the property.*

"Gertie von Coevorden my ass," Stevie said. "So *this* is how she knew there was a tunnel."

There was one other point, and it seemed important.

**** Last thing Albert Ellingham said was "It was
on the wire"****

"On the wire?" Stevie repeated.

"Yeah," Hunter said. "She read that to me. She thinks it means on the wireless? The night Albert Ellingham died, there was a big radio show . . ."

"*The War of the Worlds*," Stevie said.

This was something that came up in every book about the case. On the night Albert Ellingham died, there was a radio broadcast by Orson Welles called *The War of the Worlds*. It was a play about an alien invasion landing in New Jersey, told in the style of a news broadcast. Except people in the 1930s weren't used to that kind of meta story, and thousands of people freaked out thinking there was a real alien invasion going on and the world was ending.

"Seems like a weird thing to mention," Hunter said.

"On the wire," Stevie said again. "These are the big reveals? Something about a tunnel and a wire? What about the stuff about the will?"

"She would *never* write that down. Like I said, she's *really* paranoid. She doesn't even like that I have a phone that can take pictures. But I think that's the . . . well, you probably noticed the bottles. And the smell. And everything."

"Kind of hard to miss."

"I should put this stuff back," he said, reaching for the folder. "You should probably get out of here, or . . . you know, we could . . . If you want to take a walk or something? Get some coffee? Go somewhere that doesn't smell like ass? Before she gets back and sees you?"

They walked down Pearl Street, from the university area, down to Church Street, where the shops and the tourist section took over. This street was blocked off to cars, so they walked down the middle. They said nothing for a bit—just let the silence sit between them.

"She went through treatment once," he finally said, "about ten years ago, because my family staged an intervention. She said she went only because they made her, to keep them happy. She always says she doesn't have a problem. I think she believes that."

"Sorry."

"It's okay," Hunter said. "Not for her, but . . . she's not that hard to deal with. She's fine to live with, basically. The house smells because she smokes inside and has no sense of smell. But my room is . . . it's better. I have a giant air filter and a bunch of Febreze up there. I keep the window open a lot. Gets kind of cold."

"Sounds awesome," Stevie said.

"Sometimes I stay over with other people," Hunter said. "My friends on campus. I just crash on the floor. It's no big deal since I only live a few blocks away anyway."

"Why do you do it?" she said. "Live here?"

"I get discounted tuition, I have a free place to live while I go to school, and I keep an eye on her and report back to everyone. With me around I think she's a little more stable. She eats more regular meals. She maybe doesn't drink *as* much. Every once in a while she gets kind of . . . agitated. She's not dangerous or anything. She yells. But that's it. We have one agreement—she doesn't drive. I drive or she walks or takes a cab."

Stevie wondered if Hunter really was as okay with this as he seemed. Living with an alcoholic aunt in a smoke-filled house in return for free room and board and a tuition discount seemed maybe not the best deal in the world, but on some level, she got it. You do what is necessary.

You make deals.

"You haven't asked me about the crutch," he said.

"I didn't think I was supposed to," she said. "You're not wearing a cast, so I guess you use it permanently."

He nodded.

"Juvenile rheumatoid arthritis. I've had it since I was fifteen. The cold doesn't help. I should really live in Florida or something, but here I am, in warm and sunny Vermont."

"Good pick," Stevie said.

"It's a *big* tuition discount. My friends have futons."

There was a coffee place coming up on the right and Hunter headed for it, but Stevie lingered.

"The tunnel," she said.

Hunter turned back.

"What about it?"

"How Ellie died down there. If we had known sooner . . . I don't know. Maybe we could have gotten to her in time. Your aunt knew it was there. I know it's not her fault. I'm the one who made Ellie run."

"If I understand what happened," Hunter said, "and I'm not saying I do, but, what you said was right. Wasn't it? About what Ellie had done?"

"Yeah, but . . . I don't think it was the whole story."

"What do you mean?"

Stevie shook her head. She didn't even know what she meant. There was too much information.

"You know what?" he said. "There are some cool swings by the water. Bench swings. Bench swings make everything better. Want to go try them out? Better than coffee!"

A bench swing sounded nice. Being with Hunter was . . . she wasn't sure. Not terrible. Maybe odd, because he was so friendly. But was that wrong? Was it wrong just to be nice and well-adjusted?

"Sure," she said. "A swing. I could think of worse things."

They turned back off Church and headed toward the

lake. Stevie pulled out her phone to check the time.

"Wow," Hunter said. "That guy is getting the *shit* kicked out of him."

Stevie looked up. There, down at the end of the street, under the bus shelter by the courthouse, there was a group of skateboarders.

One of them was repeatedly punching David in the face.

21

"OH, HI," DAVID SAID AS STEVIE APPROACHED. HE SMILED. HIS TEETH were red with blood. Specks of it dotted his white collared dress shirt. He had dressed up again, just like he had on the first night they had both taken the coach to Burlington. On that occasion, David was trying to trick Stevie's parents into thinking they were dating as a way of convincing them that she should stay at Ellingham after Hayes's death. This time, there was no such explanation. He was just dressed to the conservative nines, getting his face smashed down the block from the courthouse. He was also wearing the two-thousand-dollar coat, which had grime all over it. There was a gash along his right cheek that was trickling blood. There was another cut above his eye. His shirt had torn down near the hem and some of the buttons were undone, indicating that something had happened in the torso area.

"How's it going?" he said casually. "Who's your friend?"

There was a bit of bloody spittle coming out of the side of his mouth.

"Are you okay?" she said. She tried to take him by the arm, but he shrugged it away.

"Fine," he said. "Just hanging out with some friends."

He walked unsteadily over to another skateboarder who had been watching the whole thing and recording it with a phone. David reached up and the guy gave him the phone, then the attackers rolled off on their skateboards.

"What just happened?" Stevie said. "Come on. I'm taking you to . . . Is there an urgent care or a hospital or . . ."

This was to Hunter, who was still staring at David.

"Yeah," he said. "My car is just a few streets over. I'll get it."

"I'm not going," David said, holding up his hands.

"David, *stop*."

"I'll call 911," Hunter said.

"No, no," David said. "No cops."

He sat down on the curb and examined his phone. Stevie turned to look at Hunter, who was watching all of this in total confusion.

"Hunter," she said. "Can I have a minute?"

"Yeah, yeah," Hunter said, backing away. "I'm going back. I'll . . ."

"Yeah."

He headed off the way they had come, looking back once or twice.

"You work fast," David said, still looking at his phone.

"What?"

"Your new buddy. I'm very happy for you both. When will you be announcing the big day?"

"Would you shut up?" she said. She sat next to him. "Let me see."

This time, he did not move away. He even stuck out his head to let her get a better look at his cheek.

"How is it?" he said.

"It looks deep. You need to go to the hospital, and then we need to get the police."

"Why?" David said, rubbing at the blood with his sleeve. "It's not illegal to get your ass kicked in Vermont, is it?"

"It's illegal for them to hit you."

"Not if you pay them. I mean, maybe it is. I'm not a lawyer."

"What do you mean if you *pay* them? You paid some-one—"

"Hang on," he said. He did something with his phone, then nodded in satisfaction. "There," he said, pocketing it. "Uploaded."

"To what?"

"YouTube. To Hayes's old channel."

"What?"

"See, I'm not completely useless," he said. "I can hack a YouTube channel. Now, this has been fun, but you have somewhere to be, right?"

"I don't understand," Stevie said, shaking her head. "Are you doing this because of what I did?"

"You?" He laughed, and a little blood trickled from his mouth. "*You?* Not everything is about you."

He spit some blood into the street, which caused a woman nearby to move away with her small child. David smiled his bloody smile at them.

"I'm not leaving you," she said. "I don't care if you want me to go. You need to go to the doctor."

"If you won't go, I will."

"I'll follow you."

"I know what you're thinking," he said. "You're worried that your deal with my dad is off and he's going to come down in his helicopter and whisk you away."

"I'm worried that you just got your face beaten in and you seem to *like* it."

"I'm touched. Why don't you go back to whoever your new friend is."

"Why are you such a dickhead?" she yelled.

"I think you know the answer to that. I think I told you everything. That was a good move on my part. I think I've finally learned the benefit of confiding in others. I've *grown*."

"Am I supposed to say I'm sorry?" she said. As the words came out, she realized she had no idea what the answer was to that question. David cocked his head in interest. Something curious passed over his expression—something Stevie could not make out.

"Probably," he said. "But we're past that now." He spit some more blood onto the street. "Don't worry about me," he said. "I think you have bigger problems than I do. At least I know I'm messed up."

He pushed himself up from the curb and started walking in the direction of the lakefront, dabbing at his face with his scarf. Stevie paced in a circle, unsure of what to do, then bolted to follow him.

"Why did you upload it?" she said. "Why did you pay to get yourself beat up?"

"I have my own plans," he said. "They don't involve you."

"David." Stevie skipped a step and got in front of him to block him. He walked around her. He moved around again. At this point, blocking him would look like a ridiculous dance, so she continued alongside, keeping up with his brisk stride.

"You want the story?" she said. "Your dad showed up at my house, out of the blue. He had folders full of information about security systems. He talked my parents into letting me back. He took me right to the airport. On the plane, I asked him what he wanted, because I don't think your dad does this kind of stuff because he's a nice guy."

"Good call," David said, tucking his hands into his pockets. People were looking at him as they passed; it was impossible not to.

"That's when he said he was sending me back because he thought you would chill the fuck out if I was there. I didn't tell you because . . ."

"Because . . ."

"Because how do I tell you that?"

"You use your words," he said.

"And you would have done what?"

David stopped.

"If you told me?" he said. "I would have understood. I know my dad. But you didn't tell me. You waited until I found my friend dead and decaying on the floor in a tunnel and then you unloaded on me."

"Because I felt bad," she said. "I don't know how to do these things. I'm not . . . I'm not good. With people."

"No," he said. "You're not."

"And neither are you. You told me your parents were *dead*."

"So I guess we're even," he said simply. "You'll be fine. Until my dad sees the video, I guess. Oh, and the fact that I'm not going back to Ellingham. That could be a problem. But you'll work it out."

"Wait, what?"

"I'm not going back to Ellingham," he said.

"So you just got your face beat in and now you're leaving school?"

"You got it! Well done."

"Why?" she said.

"Again, that's for me to know. You can work out some new deal with Eddie. Why don't you tell him you'll find me and bring me back. That might work. You're good at finding people."

"David . . ."

She reached for his arm, but he roughly shrugged it away.

"This is where we leave each other," he said.

"I'm not leaving you."

"Fine. I'll jump in the lake. Want to swim? It's a little cold and rough, but swimming is the best exercise."

It was impossible to tell with David if this was a joke, and the lake was just at the end of the street.

"Turn around," he said. "I'm serious about the lake."

Tears were streaming down Stevie's face now. It was odd. Stevie did not cry often, and never in public. David watched this with a clinical interest for a moment, then turned and continued in the direction of the waterfront.

Stevie did not follow. Too many bad things had happened in that lake. She was not going to be part of another.

She had to let him go.

By the time Stevie returned to campus, the video of David getting his face beaten in had ten thousand views. Stevie refreshed the page and watched the number go up. Most of the comments were confused, understandably. People came to this channel to watch a show about zombies. And now the zombie guy was dead and in his place was this rando getting punched.

She obsessively checked her phone for texts from him and wondered if she should send something, but there was silence on both ends. Hunter, however, had been in touch several times. Stevie was cagey with her answers. This was hard to explain.

On her return to Minerva, the house was quiet. There was no fire in the fireplace, but things were warm.

Now there were three. Hayes, dead. Ellie, dead. David . . .

How had she lived before this madness? How did she cope? Coping just . . . happened. Reality continued to unwind its sinuous path, and she walked it.

She texted Nate to come downstairs, then went to Janelle's door. It was cracked open a few inches. She was sitting on the floor on a fuzzy cushion, a video about SpaceX playing on her computer, bits of Arduino scattered around her. She was leaning over, looking into her wall mirror, a small pile of eye shadow palettes next to her, delicately applying color with a brush.

"What do you think," she said, turning to reveal one eye stunningly made up in a range of oranges, reds, and yellows. "It's a sunset eye. Does it look like a sunset? I think it may be too orange."

"I need to talk to you," Stevie said.

Janelle spun in her direction and paused the video. Stevie shut the door and sat on the floor.

"There's some stuff I need to tell you about," she said.

"With David?"

"Yeah. You noticed?"

"You want to be a detective, but you're the least subtle person I've ever met," Janelle said. "You need to work on that. What's going on?"

"This is a secret," Stevie said. "A serious one."

Janelle's forehead wrinkled in worry. Her one sunset eye cast an uneasy glance at Stevie. There was a knock, and Nate poked his head in when Janelle called.

"What?" he said. "This is a meeting or something?"

"I need you guys," Stevie said. "You need to hear this."

Nate's eyes had faintly blue shadows under them, matching his faded T-shirt.

"Yeah," he said, sitting down on the floor and tucking up his knees. "Maybe it's time we all compared some notes."

"What have you two not been telling me?" Janelle said, flicking her gaze between them.

"You go," Nate said. "I can't start this."

Stevie took a deep breath and ruffled her hair. It was getting too long. Everything was messy.

"David is Edward King's son," she said.

This took Janelle a moment to process, her sunset eye winking and widening.

"David?" she said. "Is the son of . . . the politician? The guy running for president? The one your parents work for? *That guy?*"

"Yup," Stevie said. "They don't get along. I found out the morning after Ellie disappeared. He came on campus."

"You don't look surprised," Janelle said to Nate.

"I found out the other night."

"It's not something I could tell people," Stevie said. "I wanted to. But no one is supposed to know. I guess it could be a security problem."

"So Edward King really did pay for that security system?" Janelle asked. "That's not a rumor? I thought Vi was wrong."

"There's more," Stevie said. "He brought me back here. That's how I got back to school. He convinced my parents.

317

He did it because he thought if I came back David would calm down. Now, there's this."

She pulled over Janelle's computer and opened up Hayes's channel to play them the video of David's beating. She had seen it with the sound off. It was worse with the soundtrack, with David goading them on. It was painful to see the blows landing on him, the way he smiled up and said something else that begged for more.

There were sixty thousand views now.

"What in the hell is he doing?" Janelle said. "That boy is *not okay*."

Nate turned to Stevie slowly.

"What she said," he added.

"He paid someone to do that," Stevie said. "And then he told me he wasn't coming back."

"Okay." Janelle's tone suggested that she didn't need to see any more. She pushed herself up from the floor and addressed them both from a standing position. "You know I don't love him, but you need to tell someone what's going on. Now."

"Unless he's bluffing?" Nate said. "Do you think he's bluffing? Maybe he's messing with you?"

"I didn't get the feeling he was," Stevie said. "He *paid* someone to beat him up. He put the video up on Hayes's page, which he hacked into. That's deliberate, and weird. He's doing something, but I can't figure out what."

"Destroying our lives," Nate said.

"It *does not matter*," Janelle said. "He paid someone to beat him up. That's not good. Hayes is dead. Ellie is dead. No one else in this house gets hurt. You tell someone. Tell Pix. Do it now."

Janelle was right, of course. Telling someone was the right thing to do. What David had just done was deeply disturbing. But in his eye there was something solid. He was doing this to an end. He had been hurt, but not *so* hurt. And putting it on Hayes's channel was sending some kind of message, if only she could read it.

Janelle was still right.

"I'll tell Pix," Stevie said. "About the punching and that he's not coming back. Not about his dad. But the next thing that happens is that I'm going to get pulled out of school."

"You don't know that," Janelle said.

"I do," Stevie replied. "David's not okay, so the deal is off."

"We'll fix that," Janelle said. "That's not Edward King's call. We'll help you. But now, we tell Pix. And the three of us? No secrets anymore."

"No secrets," Stevie said.

"One exciting thing," Nate said. "This is definitely all worse than writing my book."

22

Stevie was dreaming. The content of her dream was jumbled. She was walking the streets of Burlington, down the same path she had been walking with David, and someone was yelling, "They're pulling people out of the lake!" So Dream Stevie ran down to the waterfront, to where she first met Fenton, and saw dozens of bodies being pulled from the lake. But they weren't dead. They flopped like fish on the waterside. All of these flopping human bodies. Someone came up behind Stevie, but she did not turn. She heard a voice whispering to her, a girl's voice, but she could not make out the words. Something in her told her it was Dottie Epstein, and if she turned, Dottie would disappear. So she kept her eyes on the flopping-fish people on the dock, trying to make out Dottie's words.

Then, the phone.

"Did I wake you?" Edward King said.

Stevie pushed herself up in bed and rubbed at her eyes furiously. Her computer was open on her lap, still on the Websleuths forum page she had been reading when she fell asleep. That was something she did to relax when things got too much. She squinted at it through the sleep in her eyes. It was seven minutes after seven.

"No," she lied.

"I did. My apologies for calling so early. We have a vote on the floor in two hours and I have several meetings before that."

The call was destined to come, of course. She had expected it soon after she told Pix, who took the news of David's beating and escape with a grim resolution. She had lost two students; that another was gone was more weight on an already crushing load. Stevie delivered the news and got into bed with her computer and stayed there.

The strange thing was, she had gotten such a good night's sleep. For the first time in longer than she could remember, there was no worry of anxiety coming for her in the night.

"Are you there?" he asked.

"Yes," she said, trying to keep the morning croak out of her voice.

"Good. Now, there was a video that posted yesterday evening. I assume you saw it?"

"Yes."

"It's not my favorite video, Stevie. We had an agreement. I can't help but think you aren't keeping up your end of it."

"What do you want me to *do*, exactly?" she said.

"That's up to you. You were a possible solution to the issue. If this solution isn't working, I will find another. I suggest you talk to him."

There was no point in arguing, as much as she wanted to.

"Anything else?" she said.

"No. I will be checking in this time tomorrow. Good-bye."

"He's fine, by the way," she said.

Edward King hung up.

She felt an odd sense of clarity. The clock would strike. Every day counted, and every hour of every day. This time, right now, in the cool of an Ellingham morning, was the most precious thing she had.

She ejected herself from bed (points for effort), yanked off her fuzzy pajama bottoms, and replaced them with a nearly identical pair of gray sweatpants. No shower. The old T-shirt she was wearing (one of her favorites—something she dug out of a box of old crap in the attic) would do. Yes, she still smelled a bit of night funk, but that was fine.

Sometimes detectives smell like night funk.

She snatched up her backpack and put in all she could anticipate needing: phone, charger, computer, tablet, a flashlight. One of her favorite true-crime authors who was trying to solve a murder case from the seventies would do everything she could to immerse herself in the time and the place. Stevie had read that she would make playlists of all the songs that would have been on the radio at the time of the murders, and then she would drive around those neighborhoods listening to those songs to finely tune her mind to the atmosphere. Because it all mattered, she said. You had to feel it, to understand it in every way you could, to get inside of it—and the thing might take over, it might try to rule your life, but it was *your case* to solve.

She found a 1930s online station and shoved in her ear-buds.

The morning was apple-crisp. The air cleaned the body from the inside, scraping out the lungs, pumping cold life into the arteries. (Not veins. Veins return deoxygenated blood to the heart. The arteries were carrying this, swinging up the arch of the aorta, shooting up the carotid, giving her brain all the delicious oxygen candy it wanted.) She turned on the music, and a low swinging sound pumped into her ears. She walked in time with it, letting her foot hit the stones of the path with each beat. Become it. Tune into it. Go back in time through the air, the rhythm.

She would walk the campus once. She would start by going between the houses, wandering through the streets and the snaking pathways. She found herself moving gracefully, straightening her back. If she saw anyone in the distance, she changed her path, moving gently around a tree, turning a corner. The rumor was that Albert Ellingham had designed his pathways by following a cat that was walking the grounds because "Cats know best." It probably wasn't true, but you never knew with Albert Ellingham. As she walked her new, musical path, Stevie suddenly had the realization of how right this statement could be. Cats do know best, in many ways. They are hunters, good at tracking, remaining unseen. They can move from the slinking shadows up to the heights and down again. Cats see all the levels, where people generally look straight in front of them.

Who was here? Edward and Frankie, with their gangster cosplay. They had become Truly Devious. But why? Just to play a game back at the game master?

They looked rich. Two rich, bored kids, wanting to be bad. Sort of like a rich boy she knew who had gone and gotten his face punched to gravy last night for no reason she could fathom except making his father notice him. Today wasn't about David, but the connection made sense. She would use it. Edward and Frankie were acting something out that only they understood. So they sent a letter. But they didn't get a car and take Iris and Alice, did they? They would have been noticed, surely. And where would they have put Alice? They weren't the large man out on the dome that night. They didn't beat up George Marsh, or get a boat to collect a ransom on Lake Champlain. There was no internet then, and barely any phones. You don't coordinate something like that when you have basically nothing to work with.

So it was a coincidence, maybe. Or someone used that letter, folded it into the plot.

And what about Dottie? Stevie was walking across the base of the green now, past the statues of the Sphinx. Dottie understood myth. She would have known all about the riddle of the Sphinx. She read constantly.

Stevie stopped and looked at the Great House from this, the farthest point you could survey it on the campus. The music had changed to an up-tempo jazz song. This is the kind of music that would have played that weekend before the kidnapping, when the party was going on in the house. The house, the heart of this place, beating with life and song . . .

What had Fenton told her, about the last thing Albert Ellingham said to Mackenzie? "It was on the wire." Wire? Wireless? Had he heard something on the radio? Was it meaningless? He was just going out for a boat ride. He had no idea he was going to die. He could have been talking about anything.

But . . .

He had been updating his will. The codicil that had long been rumored, what if that was real? What if he had put together a fortune for anyone who could produce his daughter, dead or alive? What if he knew something was about to happen to him? He wrote a riddle. He finalized his business. And he told Mackenzie it was on the wire.

Stevie once went to one of those sushi places where the food comes by on a little conveyor belt. That's what her mind felt like sometimes—facts floating by on a little track. Sometimes she'd have the urge to reach for one, pick it up, feast on it. The wire.

"The wire," she said out loud.

She walked toward the house. It seemed to swell as she approached it. The Neptune fountain was switched off for the season, leaving the god of the sea to regard her from his dry perch.

There was someone in Larry's place by the front door— a younger guy with a uniform from a security company, the same one Edward King had hired to install the cameras. He stopped her as she tried to walk in, but Call Me Charles called out from the balcony above.

"Stevie! Could you come up a second?"

Stevie continued up the steps, passing the Ellingham family portrait. Charles was standing on the landing with Jenny Quinn.

"Have you seen David Eastman, by any chance?"

"Yesterday," she said. "In Burlington."

"Since then?"

She shook her head. Jenny looked to Charles as if to say, *See?*

"Has he called you, or . . ."

"No," she said. "Sorry."

There was no point in telling him that David said he wasn't coming back. This was not her circus, and he was not her clown on the loose. All of that business would come crashing down on its own. No need to rush it.

"All right," he said. "Thanks. You going up to the attic?"

Stevie nodded.

"If he happens to call you, would you tell us?"

"You saw the video," Jenny said. It wasn't a question.

"I'll let you know if I hear from him," Stevie said, continuing up, and then heading to the back staircase that led to the attic.

Stevie usually noodled around when she first got up here, letting herself have a look around, peering into boxes, pulling things from shelves. Not today. There was one thing she had come here for, and she had to find it. It was in the boxes that contained objects from Albert Ellingham's office. The dust and smell of old paper itched the inside of her nose. So many things from Albert Ellingham's office—thumbtacks, petrified rolls of tape that had turned amber with age, yellowed unused notepads with his name embossed on them, scissors, paperweights, letter openers, dried up pots of ink . . .

And a bunch of spools in maroon and white with the words *Webster-Chicago* written on them. Next to that, on a scrap of paper taped down with yellowed tape were the letters: *DE*. She dug down farther, pulling something from the bottom of the box that had been meaningless. It was a cardboard box, the packaging for the spools. She could tell because there was a picture of one drawn on the package. It read: WEBSTER-CHICAGO RECORDING WIRE.

"Recording wire," she said out loud. "*Recording wire.*"

If this was a recording, the question was, what the hell would play it? If you had tapes, clearly something *made* them. Stevie spun around in the tight confines of the aisle. The music changed again, and so did Stevie's thinking. Albert Ellingham had handily made her a guide of things in his house and where they were, and he did it in the form of a giant dollhouse. Stevie hurried to the other end of the attic, pulled off the cover, and carefully opened the dollhouse. She squatted down in front of Albert Ellingham's tiny office, feeling like a giant looking down on this great man's life. There were so many recognizable things in there—some had moved around a bit, but surprisingly little had changed in terms of placement and decor. There were the leather chairs, the trophy rugs, the two desks covered in tiny papers and telephones no bigger than Stevie's thumbnail. The bookshelves were full of impossibly small volumes. There was the globe, the green marble clock on the mantel, and . . .

A cabinet with a weird little object on it, about the size of a computer printer. (Well, this thing was about the size of a matchbox. But it represented something the size of a printer.) She reached down and pinched the thing up. It could have been a radio, but it had words painted on it with what must have been a fine brush: WEBSTER-CHICAGO.

The device.

She had the little thing for reference, and now she had to find the big one. The Ellinghams had so much stuff—hundreds and thousands of things, but nothing mattered right now except *this* thing. She worked methodically, starting on the first shelf that contained office materials. She pulled down one after another, sneezing into documents, hauling down old phone directories, staining her fingertips with dust and muck. She climbed the metal shelving when it was high, not really testing to see if it could hold her. The thing had to be found.

It took almost two hours. It was in a large cardboard box under a box heavy with records. The machine weighed perhaps thirty pounds. It was silver and maroon, very sleek and art deco, the words WEBSTER-CHICAGO still with a bit of a gleam. She looked at the thick old cords, the spools, the dials. She wasn't even sure if it was safe to plug in or how to make it work.

Luckily, she knew a genius.

23

"OKAY," JANELLE SAID, FASTENING HER TOOL BELT. "LET'S HAVE A look at this thing."

The ancient recorder sat on a cart in the middle of the maintenance shed. Janelle had a look of pure happiness on her face, and a pair of goggles resting on her head.

The one nice thing about the new security setup was that Larry was not there to question the fact that Stevie needed this dusty hunk of garbage from the attic. She said she had been told to bring it over to the maintenance shed to be cleaned up, and the person at the desk nodded. She lugged it over, where Janelle, Nate, and Vi were waiting. There was nothing like a text that said I NEED YOU TO FIX A MACHINE to get Janelle's attention.

Janelle began by wiping the outside of the machine down delicately with a cloth, then she undid the latch, revealing the four spools of the old mechanism. She got down low to examine the machine, walking around it, peering into the top. Then she closed the box and turned it over.

"This casing has to come off," she said, going over to a wall of tools and picking up a cordless drill that sat in a charger.

Nate was cross-legged on the floor, looking at his phone. Vi was sitting on a pile of wood, gazing at their girlfriend with an undisguised *You look hot with your tools* look. Stevie fidgeted, sometimes leaning against the wall or sitting next to Nate or walking to the door. More than once she crossed the room to where the dry ice container had been, the one that had contained the substance that caused Hayes's death. It had been taken away, possibly for good or maybe stashed somewhere else. A few loose rakes and shovels leaned against the wall in the spot.

There was the quick *bzzzzzzzt* of the drill as Janelle took out the screws that held the casing.

"It's going to snow in a few days," Nate said, looking up from his phone. "A lot. Some kind of monster blizzard is coming."

"Oh, good!" Janelle said, setting the drill down on the floor. "I love snow. Bet it's amazing up here."

"Do you like a lot of snow?" Nate asked.

"Yes, but define 'a lot.' I'm from Chicago. It snows there."

"Three feet. Possibly more with drifts."

"That . . . is a lot of snow," Janelle said approvingly. "You probably don't like snow, right?"

"Oh, I like it," Nate said. "Snow makes it socially acceptable to stay in."

Janelle's laugh rang from one end of the workshop to the other as she carefully turned the machine over and lifted off the casing, revealing the naked mechanism underneath. It was a gray-and-brown mess of spools and wires and grungy metal places.

"Pretty girl," Janelle said. "Dirty girl. First thing, she needs a cleaning."

"You think you can get it to work?"

"You gotta have a little patience," Janelle said, lowering the goggles over her eyes. "I have to do my thing. I'm going to blast it with some air and clean it out."

She retrieved something that looked like a clunky toy gun with a slender, hummingbird beak of a barrel. She poked it into the machine and began shooting air into it, releasing little puffs of dust and debris.

"Okay," Janelle said, pushing the goggles back and stuffing the air gun into her belt. "This looks like it's been preserved pretty well. I think what I need to do is switch out these capacitors and maybe wire on a new power cord. I have capacitors in my supply box, and I'll find a cord and strip it down, wire it in."

This was all having an effect on Vi, whose eyes had almost turned to heart shapes.

"Love is in the air," Nate said quietly. "Love may be on top of your machine in a minute."

After about an hour of work, Janelle replaced the casing on the machine.

"Okay," she said. "Let's see how this goes."

She turned one of the dials and the reels began to spin. Stevie and Nate jumped from their places on the floor.

"You did it?" Stevie said. "Seriously?"

"Of course I did it," Janelle said, reaching into her bra and producing a lip gloss, which she applied without looking. "I'm the queen of the machine."

Vi wrapped themselves around Janelle.

"Okay," Stevie said, handing over the wire. "How does this work?"

"Yeah, I was looking that up," Vi said, detaching themselves from Janelle. "People collect these. Lots of tutorials. This is the best one I could find."

They passed their phone over to Janelle, who watched a video. She picked up the wire and spooled it, consulting with the video a few times.

"I think that's it," she said. "I don't want to record over it. I think that's it. Want to try it?"

Stevie nodded and Janelle flipped the switch. The wire turned on the spools. For a moment, there was only a crackling and hissing noise, then a few muffled booms, as if something was hitting a microphone. And then . . . a voice. Deep, male. Albert Ellingham, unmistakably.

"Dolores, sit there."

"Sit here?" A girl's voice. Dolores Epstein, speaking. Stevie reeled in shock. Dolores was a character, a person from the past, lost. Here she was now, among them, her voice high and clear, with a very thick New York accent.

"Just there. And lean into the microphone a bit," Albert Ellingham said.

Janelle looked to Stevie with wide, excited eyes.

"Good," he said. "Now all you have to do is speak normally. I want to ask you a bit about your experiences at Ellingham. I'm making some recordings about the school so people know what kind of work we do up here. Now, Dolores, before I met you you got into all sorts of scrapes, didn't you?"

"Is this for the radio?" Dottie asked.

"No, no. You can speak freely."

"I like to look around, that's all," she said.

"And that's a good thing! I was exactly the same way."

"My uncle is a cop in New York. He says I'm like a second-story man."

"A second-story man?" Albert Ellingham asked.

"A second-story man is a thief, who, as the name suggests, enters through a second-story window. Slightly more sophisticated than a snatch-and-grabber. But to be honest, it's my uncle who taught me how to get into places. Police officers know all the tricks. And I've always been interested in locks and things like that."

"What did you think when you first came here? It must be very different from New York."

"Well, I was frightened, honestly."

"Of what?"

"I'm used to the city. Not the woods. The woods are scary."

"The woods are lovely!"

"And dark and deep, as the poet Robert Frost says. When I told my uncle I was coming here, he said it was all right because you have an attic man here."

"An attic man?" he asked.

"Another colloquialism. What's above the second story? The attic. My uncle always said cops who could get the drop on the second-story men—that means catch them in the act—needed to be right above them. You have a policeman here from New York. Mr. Marsh. I felt better after that. I like it up here now."

Albert Ellingham chuckled.

"I'm glad to hear it. And what would you tell the world about Ellingham Academy?"

"Well, I'd say it was the best place I've ever been. It takes elements of the system developed by Maria Montessori, though I see elements of the work of John Dewey, who is from here in Burlington, actually, did you know that?"

"I did not. I learn something new every day here at the school. We learn from each other. Like I've also just learned about second-story men. Now, let's talk about what you do every day here. Tell me about your studies. . . ."

Mudge's voice was suddenly in Stevie's head. They were looking at the cow's eye. *The one place where all the information goes in, you can't actually see anything.*

There was a kind of flash behind Stevie's eyes. All the pieces that she had collected and seen over years of reading about this lined up in place. She wanted to move around a little, so she had to keep grabbing them, making sure they didn't move. She walked quickly to the door. She couldn't hear anything more, couldn't talk to anyone or she would lose her grip on it.

"Hey," Janelle said, stopping the machine. "Where are you . . ."

Stevie waved a hand. The sky had turned a candy-colored pink and the air had a wet, frozen note to it. Good, clear air for thinking. That's the reason Albert Ellingham had bought this place to begin with—he thought the air was conducive to learning and thinking. Maybe he was right. Once you got used to having a little less oxygen, everything seemed to move a bit faster.

Think, Stevie. What was the thing she was missing? What had she seen?

The Ellingham library stood in stark relief against the pink sky, its spires dark. The library. Dottie left her mark in the library.

Stevie broke out into a run. She blew through the door as Kyoko looked like she was ending her shift for the night. Stevie almost skidded up to her desk.

"Kyoko . . . I need one thing."

"Can it wait until tomorrow?"

Stevie shook her head.

"The book. Dottie's book. The Sherlock Holmes."

"*That* can't wait?"

"Please," she said. "I'll be so quick. Five minutes. Two minutes."

Kyoko rolled her eyes a bit, but she reached down and got the keys and opened the back office. Stevie followed her along, past the metal shelving and the boxes, back down to the row where the treasures of 1936 were kept. She removed the sepia-and-white book from the box.

"Be quick, but be careful," she said, passing it over.

Stevie accepted it like it was a holy object, carrying it over to one of the worktables.

"What do you need this for in such a hurry?" she said.

But Stevie could not hear her. She was busy looking for something she knew she had seen, something so small, a blip . . .

There it was, in *A Study in Scarlet*. The mark in the book, one rough pencil line: *Sherlock said, "I consider that a man's brain originally is like a little empty attic, and you have to stock it with such furniture as you choose."*

In *A Study in Scarlet* a body is found with the word RACHE written over it in blood. Rache, German for *revenge*. A victim-left sign of what had transpired.

"Did you find what you were looking for?" Kyoko said, leaning over the table.

"Yeah," she said, getting up. She was almost stumbling now, catching her foot on the table leg in her haste.

"Are you okay?"

"Yeah . . . fine. Definitely fine."

She hurriedly closed the book and passed it back to Kyoko, who placed it gently in a carrying crate.

"Thanks," she said. "I have to . . . Thanks."

Stevie hurried through the library, past people working at tables with their headphones on. Once outside, she gulped in air that was full of gentle flurries. They floated into her nose and melted on the back of her throat. She yanked her phone out of her pocket and called Fenton.

Fenton's phone rang five times.

"Come on," Stevie said, bouncing on her heels. "Come on. . . ."

She paced along the path in front of the library.

"Hello?" Fenton's voice was slurred, and loud.

"Hey," she said. "I need to talk to you. I've—"

"Can't right now, Stevie," she said.

"No, you don't get it," Stevie replied, trying not to yell. "I—"

"Not now . . . " she said, her voice lowering to a hiss. "I will call you back in a bit. The kid is there. *The kid is there!*"

"What?" she said.

And with that, she was gone.

Stevie stood with the phone still pressed to her ear, the glass surface getting cold and fogging with her breath. She stepped along the stone path. Sounds echoed louder in the cold. Each footfall was crisp and distinct.

How could Fenton just hang up on her? How was she alone in the dark of this mountain, with no one to share these little threads of her thoughts that were being woven together by the little mice in her brain?

How did she explain that she knew who kidnapped Alice and Iris Ellingham?

October 30, 1938, 5:00 p.m.

IT WAS AN IDYLLIC SCENE: ALBERT ELLINGHAM'S SPORTY LITTLE SPARK-
man & Stephens daysailer, *Wonderland*, idling on the waters of
Lake Champlain. It had one red sail and one white, both stiffly
at attention, though the boat was drifting ever so gently. The
fine October afternoon in Vermont was oversaturated with
color, like a paint box turned over on the landscape. Albert
Ellingham kept one slack hand on the wheel. George Marsh
sat on the padded seats that lined the boat, comfortably leaning back, his arms spread wide, enjoying the afternoon.

"Do you read much, George?" Albert asked.

"No," George replied.

"You should, you should. Reading is one of the great pleasures of life—maybe the greatest."

"You must never have had a Cuban cigar."

Albert Ellingham laughed.

"It's true. All the money, all the power—none of it com-
pares to a good book. A book gives you everything. It gives
you a window into other souls, other worlds. The world is a
door. Books are the key."

"You've lost me," George said.

"What about Sherlock Holmes? Ever read *A Study in Scarlet*? Surely you've read that one?"

"Afraid not," George said.

"You should, you really should. It introduces Sherlock Holmes. It's a marvelous story, very instructive. You learn about how Sherlock Holmes sees the world and approaches his work. As someone in law enforcement, it would interest you. As a matter of fact, that story made me who I am. When I was a boy, growing up in the boys' home, we had only a few books. A collection of Sherlock Holmes was among them. I opened that book and read it, oh, perhaps a hundred times or more. It taught me to look—to see the world around me. It's one of the most instructive things ever written."

"All right." George Marsh laughed and pulled out a cigarette. "You've convinced me. I'll get a library card."

"I've done my good deed for the day, then. Oh, and apologies, George. No smoking on the boat, if you don't mind. Fire and boats don't mix well."

George Marsh nodded and tucked the cigarette behind his ear.

"I'm going to drop anchor here. We'll sit for a bit. I like it up here by Maquam Bay."

Albert Ellingham idly unwound a line from the rope spool and spun it around his hand, lowering the anchor into the water.

"You know," he said as he worked. "When they found Dottie Epstein, she was reading Sherlock Holmes. She's so often forgotten in all this. That's my fault. I focus on Iris, on Alice . . . Little Dottie Epstein from the Lower East Side gets swept aside in the shuffle. It's not right. She deserved better."

"That poor kid," George Marsh said, shaking his head.

"Dolores Epstein," Albert Ellingham said. "Dottie, that's what she went by. Exceptional girl, truly exceptional. She was the first student I picked for the school. Did I ever tell you that?"

George Marsh shook his head.

"No?" Albert Ellingham said. "No. I suppose it never came up. I heard about her from one of the top librarians at the public library, this girl from Avenue A who read Greek and slipped into one of the rare books rooms three times. They said she was trouble, but good trouble. Good trouble. You understand me, George?"

"I do," George Marsh said. "There's some good trouble in you, if you don't mind my saying so."

"Not at all, not at all. I appreciate it. I went to her school, spoke with her principal. I could tell he was both happy to be rid of her and heartbroken at the same time. You don't get students like that every day. I remember the joy on her face when she arrived at the academy—when she went to my library and found out she could have any book she wanted. . . . George, I'm a rich man. I own a lot. But I'll tell you something—the best money I ever spent was on Dottie Epstein's books. I was feeding a mind. She was a tremendous kid."

"What happened to her was terrible," George Marsh said, nodding solemnly.

"Beyond terrible. Beyond terrible. So much was lost that day. That mind of hers. And you know, in the dome, when they found her, there was a copy of *The Adventures of Sherlock Holmes*. She had been reading it when it happened. So strange . . ."

Albert Ellingham paused, pulling the rope tight around his fingers for a moment before tying it off. The boat spun gently and rocked in position.

"You know," Albert Ellingham said after a moment, "in that copy I saw she made a mark under a famous quote: 'I consider that a man's brain originally is like a little empty attic.' I got to thinking about this line she underlined. It wasn't neat—it was scratched in, in pencil. Rough. Uneven. No other marks in the book. But who thinks about a mark in a student's book? And I was so caught up with Iris and Alice. I was looking, like Watson, but I failed to observe. But something must have lodged in my mind. You know how your mind works on a problem? It ticks away in the background. That mark under that line. It *bothered* me."

Albert Ellingham squinted a bit as the boat turned toward the setting sun.

"I went over to the library and I had a look through the books Dottie Epstein had checked out. Not a mark on them, George. I confirmed this with the librarian. She checked for things like that. You don't get things past librarians. It could have been another student, of course, but as it turns out, Dottie liked that book so much that no one took it out but her. She had it constantly. I think many of the other students were used to having their own books and didn't use the library quite like Dottie did. I went a bit further. I looked at the police report about what was found in the dome and basement. A pencil was found on the floor of the liquor room—it had rolled off to the side of the room. It was dull. One of the student pencils. They're blue and have 'Ellingham Academy' written on the side. So, it's reasonable to conclude that Dottie made that mark, and made it that day, in the dome. But why?"

"It could have been an accident," George Marsh said. "She gets startled, or someone grabs her. She accidentally slashes the page with a pencil. . . ."

"No, I understand why you might think that, but no. An accidental mark wouldn't have been so precise. This was deliberately underlined. I think Dottie Epstein was making an effort to send a message she was hoping I would understand. She was counting on me, and I let her down."

"Albert," George said, "you can't do this to yourse—"

Albert Ellingham waved down this injunction.

"I appreciate what you're trying to do, George, but it's true. I understood Dottie. She was someone who played the game. Her uncle was with the New York City police, actually, like you. She claimed that she learned many of the techniques for breaking into places from *him*."

Albert Ellingham chuckled a bit, and George Marsh smiled.

"Yes," Albert Ellingham said, "she was a very clever girl, Dottie, and she didn't go down without a fight. Oh, do me a favor. There's a panel under your seat. Reach down between your legs and slide it to the left. Have a look inside."

George Marsh bent down as instructed and slid the panel. Under his seat were tight bundles of dark sticks of explosive, firmly fastened to the body of the boat.

Albert Ellingham looked right at the sun.

"This boat is rigged," he said calmly. "There's four more like that one. I've just set the trip wire and it is connected to the rope around my hand. If I release it, we will both go up. I could have used a gun, but it's too easy to get a gun away from someone, and I don't like guns. Frankly, I couldn't trust myself. My desire to shoot you is too strong. This requires me to have some self-control if I want to find out all I need to know. Your only option right now is to sit very still and tell me how it all happened."

24

Stevie sat on the concrete floor of the cupola, the cold seeping through the fabric of her jeans. Around her was a scatter of dried, dead flower petals. Many of the tributes were gone, but a stray card had escaped maintenance and their brooms and bags. It was a small piece of blue paper, the edges covered in a hand-glued rim of black glitter. The message on it was written in one of those fancy lettering styles that people who were really serious about their bullet journaling used. It read: NEVER SAY DEAD, NEVER STAY DEAD. LOVE FOREVER, MELODY.

Stevie set the paper down.

She had no proof, of course. She couldn't take it to court. She could not immediately write a book—not that she knew how to write a book. She had seen Nate trying to write a book, and the process looked terrible. She had never actually worked out what she would do once she solved the case. Who did she tell? Did she shout it at the moon? Tweet it? Update her Facebook status to "crime solver"?

Which is why she needed to talk to Fenton. She stared at her phone.

"Why aren't you ringing?" she said to it.

The phone sat there, blank and unknowing. She picked it up and texted Hunter.

What is your aunt doing? I need to talk to her right now. Can you tell her she needs to call me?

She stared, waiting to see the message go from delivered to read. Nothing.

Breathe.

She got up and walked around in a circle, running her hands through her short hair, feeling the sides of her fingers slide up and lose the strands. What could she do with this thought she was having? How could she check her work?

There was only one thing, of course. Do it like they did in the stories. Gather the suspects, run through the theory of the crime. Not physically, of course. In her mind. She would call down the dead. Line them up. Go point by point.

Around the cupola, she set a ring of imaginary chairs. In two of them, she placed Edward Pierce Davenport and Francis Josephine Crane. Edward had his flashing, poetic good looks. Francis her blunt, raven-colored bob. Francis was dressed in a chevroned twinset, a sweater and skirt. Tight. Wool. Brown and cream. And she wore a beret tilted sharply to the right. Edward was wearing a white shirt, a tie loose at his neck, and an open black vest. He leaned over his knees to look at Stevie, his eyes flashing, while Francis sat back, cool and considered.

"You," Stevie said to them in a low voice. There was no

one in sight, and talking out loud helped. "You wanted to be outlaws."

"We were outlaws," said Francis.

"We wrote the poem," said Edward.

"It's a stupid poem," Stevie replied. "I've *read* your poems. You're a bad poet."

Edward drew back in offense.

"Your stupid poem messed up the case for years," Stevie went on, circling the space. "Everybody thought this was about Truly Devious. But there *is* no Truly Devious."

"We were playing the game," Francis said. "Like in the poem. '*The king was a joker who lived on a hill and he wanted to rule the game. So Frankie and Edward played a hand and things were never the same.*'"

"But you wrote that before you left school," Stevie said, "before it all went wrong. You had no idea what was coming. You had something else in mind."

Francis smiled quietly.

"So you're in this," Stevie said. "But you're not responsible. No. You weren't the person who was never there, the one on a staircase but never on a stair. You *take the stair away*—that's what he was saying. Take the stair away and you have . . ."

The figure of George Marsh materialized in the seat next to Francis. He was wearing a pinstriped suit and a fedora. He was a large man, strongly built, with a square jaw. He folded his arms and stared at Stevie, challenging her.

"You've got nothing," he said. "I'm in the FBI. I know when you have no case."

"You're wrong," she said to him. "You made a mistake. You were seen by someone *who loves mysteries.*"

One more ghostly figure appeared in the circle—a girl, with curled hair and a gap between her teeth. She wore a plain brown wool dress and slightly crooked glasses. She clutched a book to her chest. She looked at George Marsh for a long moment, then turned to Stevie and nodded. Stevie nodded back.

The dark forms of trees, the pillars of the cupola, the statues all stood in witness.

"Gotcha," she said to him.

Her phone rang. The phantom circle vaporized into the night, leaving Stevie alone with the flower petals.

"Are you coming back?" Nate said. "What are you doing?"

"You wouldn't believe me."

"Try me."

"I solved it."

A pause.

"Where are you?"

"The cupola."

"I'm coming over," he said.

Stevie lowered the phone from her ear and checked her messages again. Hunter had still not read the text. What the hell was Fenton doing? *Not now. . . . The kid is there. The kid is there!* Sure, people said stuff when they were drunk, but that was so specific, so insistent.

Suddenly her brain was itching.

Of course, people sometimes don't answer their phones.

Sometimes people say strange things. But these were discordant notes. She looked at the cement she was standing on. The remains of Hayes's tribute crunched under her shoes. Ellie had been under them all along, all that time. They had walked over her. Had she heard them above, heard her friends passing overhead as the air grew stale, as she shivered, as she starved and dehydrated? The fear must have been extreme, beyond anything Stevie would ever know. Did she realize she was dying, down there in the dark? Did she make friends with that dark, with the thing that came for her in it? That insidious friend in the shadows who came to take her pain and fear away . . .

Why was the phone so quiet?

He said to do it. He said whenever. She clenched and unclenched her fists several times, then made the call. Larry answered on the second ring. Stevie could hear the television in the background and a barking dog.

"What's wrong?" he said.

"I don't know," she said.

"All right. Talk me through it."

"I know who kidnapped Alice and Iris," she said. "I know who killed Dottie."

"What?"

"But that's not it," she said, her breath coming fast. "That's not what's wrong. I think . . . I'm worried? About the professor I work with in Burlington. And I don't know why. Something's wrong. I feel it in my gut."

"Give me her address," Larry said.

October 30, 1938, 6:00 p.m.

IT HAD BEEN QUIET ON THE SAILBOAT FOR SOME TIME. GEORGE Marsh and Albert Ellingham sat looking at each other as the sky turned a volcanic red and orange. A sensational Vermont autumn sunset was beginning.

"Be dark soon," Albert Ellingham said, breaking the silence. "Very peaceful out here at night."

The water lapped gently against the sailboat.

"Albert . . ."

"No, no," Albert Ellingham said. "It's too late for that, George. Carrying secrets is exhausting work. I know this from experience. The burden seems bearable at first, but as time goes on, it increases in weight. It pulls on you. Now it is time to put that burden down."

"Albert . . ."

"You see," Albert Ellingham said, ignoring the interruption, "I picked the right girl in Dottie Epstein. She was one in a million. I'm not sure anyone else could have gotten the answer to me. I'm only sorry it took me so long, Dottie. I was slow. I let you down. But I finally got there."

He addressed this remark to the setting sun.

"I think perhaps I figured it out on a subconscious level, George. You must know that feeling as a police officer. You know on a level you can't reach. It was clear someone inside the house had to be involved in the kidnapping. I had everyone investigated to within an inch of their lives. I found out about the cocaine that Leo had, that Iris was taking. I found out so many things about so many people that I didn't want to know, but I didn't find anything that explained what happened to Iris or Alice. The most obvious thing is the thing I missed. You really never do see the thing that's right in front of you. I wrote a little riddle to myself the other day. It went like this: Where do you look for someone who's never really there? Always on a staircase but never on a stair? I sometimes come up with my riddles automatically. My mind generates them and I have to solve them for myself. There are many things to try when solving riddles. Always on a staircase but never on a stair. In this case, the riddle is telling you to remove the word 'stair' from staircase. What word do you get? Tell me."

"Case?" George Marsh said reluctantly.

"*Exactly*. Who is always on a case? An investigator. Who is someone who is never really there? The guest who isn't a guest? The police officer, there to protect, never part of the crime. You were the person standing on that vanishing stair. Dottie told me. She told me in her own words. You see, when the students first arrived, I did some recordings of them talking about their experiences at the school. I was thinking of putting together a little reel to show before films. Dottie said something very amusing. She said she had been frightened to come to the woods because she was from the city. Imagine that! For Dottie, the city was the safe space, and nature was wild and frightening. But her uncle the police officer told her not to worry. He said there was an 'attic man' at the school. I had no idea what she was talking about, so she explained that thieves are often called second-story men, and that the police were attic men, who were on the floor above—they'd jump down and catch the second-story men. Her uncle knew who you were—George Marsh, the famous cop who saved Albert Ellingham. And so did Dottie."

Another boat came by at a distance, heading in for the night. Albert Ellingham raised his hand in greeting as if nothing was wrong.

"I don't know it all," Albert Ellingham said as he waved. "That's why we're here. I'm going to tell you what I've worked out and then you'll fill in the rest. I know that on the afternoon of the kidnapping you were in Burlington. You were seen at the post office, at the police station—you were all over Burlington when Iris took the car out. So you probably were not involved in the physical act of kidnapping, though I could be wrong. You must have come up to the house in the late afternoon. I imagine the fog helped—not a lot of cars out, hard to see. There were no unusual tire patterns, so I suspect you parked where you always park. You didn't play around with anything silly, like wearing shoes that were too large and trying to leave fake prints. If any traces of you were around—well, so what? You were at my house all the time. You are the person who is always and never there. You went into the tunnel. You went up into the dome, and there you were, face-to-face with one of the brightest girls in New York City. You had some kind of weapon, I'm sure, but she had something greater. She had her book. She looked at you and she recognized the attic man. Maybe she knew her time was limited. She wasn't going to let you get away with it. Like the dying person in *A Study in Scarlet*, she left a message—a message for me. This is where I need you to take over, George. Explain it to me."

"There is nothing to explain," George Marsh said.

"Then we have nothing to talk about, and if we have nothing to talk about, then I suppose I'll . . ."

He reached for the rope, and George Marsh leaned forward, his hand outstretched.

"That can't be real," George said. "The bomb."

"Oh, it's real. As is my promise to set it off if you don't tell me what I want to know."

"Why would you . . ."

"Because I have nothing left," Albert Ellingham said quietly. "The only thing I need is the answer. I know you have it. If you do not give it to me, then I will end us both. Think very carefully about what you will do next, George. Realize I did not get where I am in life by making idle threats."

Quiet can be deafening. The lapping of the water, the sound of a bird in the distance. Every flutter and every ripple boomed. George Marsh remained where he was, half-lurching forward, sweat appearing on his forehead. He licked his lips and blinked several times. Then the air seemed to go out of him and he slowly fell back against his seat.

"That's right," Albert said, his voice gentle. "You see now. Set it down, George. Talk. Talk and feel the relief. Go ahead, son. We have all the time in the world."

It was the softness of tone that made George Marsh's eyes go red.

"It was never supposed to happen the way it did," he finally said. "That's what you need to understand. There was never supposed to be any violence. Never. It just went wrong."

"Why did you do it, George?"

George Marsh knotted his hands together.

"When I started running with you and your friends . . . I got in a little over my head. I played some cards. I'm good at cards. I was winning. And then, one day, I wound up in the hole for about twenty grand with some guys in New York, real heavies. They knew I was connected with you, so they let me keep betting. I thought I was going to win. . . ."

"Money?" Albert Ellingham said. "George, if you needed money, why didn't you come to me?"

"To pay *gambling debts*?" George Marsh said.

"If you needed help, I would have helped you."

"And then never worked with me again," George Marsh said. "I needed to get myself out of this jam and never get back into it."

"And so you took my wife and child?" Albert Ellingham's

voice was rising a bit. He cleared his throat and composed himself. "Go on," he said.

"One day," George Marsh said, his head down, "I saw one of the kids from the school out reading one of those crime-story magazines. I asked her about it, and she said she was reading one about a kidnapping. She wanted to know if I had ever worked on one. I said I had. She asked me if there were notes, trails of clues. The more she asked me, the more I realized that the kidnappings I had seen were simple. You take someone, you get paid, and you give them right back. As long as no one sees your face, the matter is largely settled. Then I thought about the money in the safe in your office. It all came to me. I'd ask for that money. Honestly, I thought Iris would . . ."

"Would what?"

George Marsh looked up from wringing his hands.

"Enjoy it," he said.

"Enjoy it?"

"She was looking for thrills, Albert. She was using cocaine. You know that. You know what kind of company she kept. She wanted fun and adventure. She was bored up here. All that was supposed to happen was that she would be grabbed and put in a barn for a few hours. You could see Iris telling that story over dinner."

If Albert Ellingham could picture this, he did not say so.

"I got two guys I knew—real two-bit hoodlums, no real brains. They'd steal anything but they never hurt anybody. I offered them two grand apiece to help me out for a few hours. Their job was to block the road with their car, and when Iris went out driving, they were supposed to grab her, blindfold her, tie her up, and put her in a barn a few miles away. I would get the money. Then she would be freed. Maybe she'd have a scratch or two, but she'd be home, laughing. Home and laughing."

"But she is not home," Albert said. "She is not laughing."

"No. No she isn't." George Marsh pulled the cigarette from behind his ear. "Alice was in the car. I think that . . . complicated things."

He faltered, but Ellingham waved him on.

"I was in Burlington that day, like you said. We had a signal set up. I would have lunch at Henry's diner and when the thing was done—when Iris was, you know, with them—they would call the diner and ask for Paul Grady. The waitress yelled out for Paul Grady at five after one. I paid my check and left, but I stayed in town for a while and kept an eye on where you and Mackenzie were working. Then I drove down Route Two toward the house and parked by a phone booth. One of the guys was on lookout for when you left Burlington, and called me. That was when I had to get into place. It was foggy, so no one was really around. I parked in the back and let myself into the tunnel. I was wrapped up in a scarf and coat and hat. All I had to do was wait in the dome, get the money from you, tie you up, and then drive back to the phone booth. I know someone at the telephone exchange. . . ."

"Margo," Albert Ellingham said. "Margo Fields. This was

the one element that always bothered me—we reached you at home that night, and you couldn't have gotten home in time if you were the person Dottie saw. I realized quickly just how simple it would be to have your call connected somewhere else. But Margo had spoken to the police. She said she put the call through to your house. I had to go back and ask her again, and finally she admitted that she put the call through to the phone booth. She said you told her not to say—it was part of FBI business, and that certain things had to be kept from both the public and me. So you go to the dome, and instead of finding it empty, you find Dottie Epstein. What happened to Dottie?"

"You've got to understand," George Marsh said, "the thing had already *started*. We had to go through with it. I didn't want to hurt her. I didn't know *what* to do. She's just standing there, holding her book like a shield or something, telling me she won't say anything. And I'm standing there thinking, 'What do I do with this kid?' I think I said, 'I can't let you leave' or something, and before I knew it, she jumped right into the open hole in the floor. I swear to you, she *jumped*. She jumped right down into that hole trying to get away."

His voice splintered and it took him several minutes to recover.

"God, she must have hit her head so hard on the ground. That fall is what, ten, twelve feet? I climbed down after her. There was so much blood. She was groaning and trying to crawl, but she couldn't make it. She was . . . sliding. Her skull musta been cracked wide open. If I left her, it would have been worse. I swear, it would have been worse. I watched her sliding on that floor, and it was so horrible that . . . I had my piece on me, but if I shot her, that would trace back to my gun. So I grabbed a pipe that was leaning against the wall—some stick or something, you must use it to prop open the hatch—and I just hit her the once and she stopped moving. . . ."

The sky began to properly darken.

"I don't even know what my mind was doing at this point. It had all happened in seconds. I never wanted anything to happen to that kid. You were going to be coming soon. My only thought was—clear the scene. I put her in one of the liquor crates that was down there. It was full of wood chips for the bottles, so it soaked up some blood. I cleaned the floor with booze. I scrubbed my shoes with booze. I put the crate on one of the wheeled dollies and I rolled her up, I got her into my car."

"Why didn't you leave her?" Albert Ellingham asked.

"If there was no body, there'd be nothing to see. No crime scene. I could come back, clean it right later on. I had to clean it up. Then I went back up and took my place to meet you. I didn't mean to hit you like I did—I was so jazzed up because of the kid. I took the money, I went back out of the tunnel, and I got in my car and left. I went to a roadside diner. I'd started having dinner there for a few weeks so they'd expect me. It was closer to your place than my house. I'd always tell everyone I ate before I got to your place because of all that

French stuff you eat—crème de ooh-la-la when a guy just wants a burger. Everyone got a kick out of that. So I had a Salisbury steak and a coffee and waited for the call to come. I knew it would. That's what everything was banked on. If calls came in in the evening and there was no answer at my house, Margo at the exchange would route my call there so I would seem to be at home. From there, I would wait for your call, which came. I would come to the house. I would be the one to go out and get Iris. When I got there, I'd give my guys their cut and I'd bring Iris home. That was the plan. But that's not what happened."

"No," Albert Ellingham said. "It was not."

"When I got there, I gave them the money. I was holding it together, but they were rattled too. Iris fought because of Alice. She struggled. And they weren't as stupid as I thought they were, or as harmless. They said that Ellinghams were worth a lot more than two grand each. I offered them five. They both jumped me. I could have taken them under better circumstances, but one of them got me with a wrench. They said they were in charge now. They had moved Iris and Alice to another location and said they had another guy with them, and that guy was ready to shoot and kill them if things didn't go as they said. They gave me the drop-off instructions. The situation was out of control."

"So you came to the drop-off the next night," Ellingham said.

"By that point, I'd had a chance to think," George Marsh

replied. "I had no idea what had happened to Iris and Alice, but I had to try to get them out of it. I would have done anything."

"But you still took some of the marked bills from the pile," Albert Ellingham said. "To cover yourself. To frame someone else."

"I had to show the guys I had something I could use to get them out of trouble, something to make the whole thing go away. I always had a mark in mind—Vorachek. He was trouble. We would all be glad to see him busted. He'd threatened you before. All I had to do was plant some of the money on him. I was going to tell the guys that, that they'd walk away with no problems. I waited for them to contact me. They never did. So I threw myself into the case. I looked into everything I knew about those guys. I shook every contact I had, but that kind of money can put you into the wind. Then Iris turned up in the lake. . . ."

He looked off the side of the boat at the very waters Iris had been floating in.

"Who killed Vorachek?" Albert Ellingham said.

"I don't know. Honestly, I don't. I wouldn't be surprised if one of his own popped him. Or it could have been someone in the crowd who was just angry."

"Iris," Albert Ellingham said. "Dottie. Anton Vorachek. Three people dead. And then there is my Alice. *That* is why we are here. That is what I must know. Where is Alice?"

George Marsh finally gathered himself enough to lift his chin and look Albert Ellingham in the eye.

"What good is it," he asked, "us dying out here?"

"It is a price I am willing to pay."

"I know where Alice is," George Marsh said.

The reserve that Albert Ellingham had possessed up to this point left him. He half stood, his fist tight around the rope, his face purpling and the capillaries in his eyes marbling. When he spoke, his voice was a low rumble.

"You just claimed," Albert said, "that you knew nothing of what happened to Alice. That you were not involved in her direct kidnapping. That you looked for her."

"And I eventually found her," Marsh said.

"*Is my daughter alive?*"

For the first time in this conversation, George Marsh sat back. He loosened his tie and stretched out his legs as if this was again the relaxing afternoon sail he had been promised.

"I have to ask myself," he said, "is this one of your games? You love games, Albert."

"This is no game. You tell me where my daughter is or—"

"Or you let go of that rope and we'll be blown to bits? Is that it? And if I tell you, you're just going to let me go? Is that what happens? I tell you, and you wind that rope back up and we sail back to shore and then everything is fine and ginger-peachy?"

"We sail back. You get to live."

"Where?" George Marsh put out his hands and shrugged. "In jail? You know what they would do to me in jail, Albert? A cop who kidnapped a kid? *Your* kid? I'd be beaten every day until I was made of pulp—probably by the other cops. If I even made it that far. There is no future for me on the shore."

"If you tell me where Alice is, we could come to an understanding. I don't care what happens to you if I get my daughter."

"We'd have to come to one hell of an understanding. How would it work? You'd let me go free, promise me some money, maybe, and then I'd give you her location. No." Marsh shook his head. "You could never risk it. You can't let me go. As long as I know what happened to Alice, you need to keep control of me. And if you kill me, then you'll never know."

He leaned forward enough to slip out of his jacket. Albert Ellingham watched him, speechless, his face mottled in rage.

"To tell you the truth," Marsh said, standing now, and rolling his sleeves, "I'm amazed it took you this long. I guess I've been waiting for the day when it all dropped, and the day is here. You're right. It does feel better to tell you. I'm tired of it. And you must be too—all your dirty little secrets. I bet Mackenzie doesn't even know them all. You, with your newspapers—all those payments you made, the stories you buried, the politicians you kept on a leash. The great Albert Ellingham . . ."

"I did no such—"

"And Alice. I know about Alice too. Is she the biggest secret of all?"

Marsh stood and finished pulling off his jacket, which he sat on the seat behind him. He reached into his trouser pocket and pulled out a lighter.

"There's no going back for either of us," he said as he put his cigarette between his lips.

Less than a minute later, people nearby saw a bright flash and heard a boom that scattered birds into the night. The explosion tore the *Wonderland* and its occupants into pieces and flung them into the air. Bits and pieces of boat and human would be found for weeks to come, washed up on the shore all along Lake Champlain.

25

"WHY DO YOU WRITE BOOKS?"

Nate was sitting on the ground across from Stevie in the dark of the cupola. Both of them had tucked their knees into their chests and were huddled inside their coats. Quiet places, Stevie noted, were very noisy once you got used to them. The ear settles, and then every sound comes out. Every leaf that falls has a tender impact. Every surface the wind brushes has its own percussion. Everything that lives in the dark—and many things live in the dark—makes a tiny footfall. Owls call. Wood creaks. It's a real racket.

"I don't know," Nate said. "I don't know how to do anything else?"

"That's not a reason."

"I don't know. I just do. Do I need a reason?"

"There are reasons for everything, even if we don't know them," Stevie said. "Motive."

"Okay," Nate said. "My motive is that I prefer dragons."

"To what?"

"To the absence of dragons."

Stevie looked at the Great House at the opposite end of the green. The windows glowed in the darkness, distorted rectangles like stretched-out eyes. The moon outlined the husk of the house; the portico shadowed the door completely, so it was a hulking creature that could see you, but did not allow you access. Outside, the spotlight on the Neptune statue landed on the points of his trident. Now, when it was shrouded and nearly invisible, Stevie saw the Great House for the first time. She saw what it was—a demented place, unwanted by the mountain. Mount Hatchet, that's what they called it, because it was shaped like an ax. Mount Hatchet had not wanted to have its face blasted and its trees cut. It wanted nothing to do with this school, so it had eaten the family that made it. Eaten them in slow, careful bites until there was nothing left.

Her brain was going weird on her.

"What does the Pulsating Norb do?" she asked, trying to push down her thoughts.

"Nothing. It's like a Jell-O wall. Well . . . you can put stuff in it and no one can see it."

"It's a wall that hides things? You didn't tell me that before."

"Mainly it pulsates," Nate said. "It looks like it's breathing. I'm not putting the Pulsating Norb in."

Stevie did not like the sound of this pulsating, breathing wall, not with this diseased house menacing her at the end of the lawn. Why had she come here? Why had she passed through the Sphinxes? Why had she come back after Hayes died? How much warning did you need?

Oh, it was coming. The rising beast in her chest, the thing with the fingers inside that squeezed her heart in broken rhythms, the thing that whispered troubles in her ear until everything fell apart. It was coming now, just as everything built to a head.

"I like it," she lied.

"You don't understand the Pulsating Norb. No one understands the Pulsating Norb."

"I ship it."

"Nobody ships the Pulsating Norb," Nate said. "Do you want to wait inside?"

"No," she said.

"Why?"

"Because I can't move."

That was true at least. If she turned to stone, gripped her phone tight, held on to the reality of Nate and Larry and Fenton and Hunter, she could ride the beast. She had to. She *had the answer*.

"Why did you call it a Norb?" she said, trying to keep herself talking.

"It was a typo when I was typing the word 'orb' and I kept it. Seriously, Stevie, it's cold. Janelle and Vi . . ."

"What if I solved it?" she said. "What if I really did it?"

Nate paused for a moment.

"Then it would be a big deal," he said.

"I'm scared."

To Nate's credit, he did not ask why she was scared, and

he did not tell her not to be scared. Maybe he understood how terrifying it is to do the thing you meant to do. Maybe he could see the monsters in the night. "So why do *you* do it?" he asked. "Why mysteries?"

This, Stevie had thought about.

"With mysteries," she said, "with crime, you get all this information—everything matters. The location. The time. The weather. The building. The ground. Every single thing that floats by. Every object in the room. Everything everyone says. It's a lot of stuff. And you have to look at it all and find the pattern, find the thing that stands out, figure out the thing that means something. Is there a piece of thread stuck in the fence? Did someone hear a noise? Is there a fingerprint under the table? And there could be thousands of fingerprints—so which one means something? You take everything in the world and you figure out what matters. That's what it is. And then you make things right."

"So you want to find out the answers and I want to make up the answers," he said. "I think we just saved a ton of money on therapy."

"Also I want to wear the exam gloves," Stevie said.

"We all want that." Nate smiled a bit.

"It's funny when you smile," she said. "It's like a rainbow on a cloudy day."

"Don't ever say that to me again."

Stevie's phone clattered on the cement. The sound was so shocking that she recoiled for a second. Larry's name came up, and she snatched it.

"Hey," she said.

"Stevie," Larry said with a strangely level voice. "What made you call me?"

"A bad feeling," she said. "I'm sorry. I didn't want to . . ."

Larry went quiet.

"Hello?" Stevie said. "What's happening?"

"Stevie . . . the house was on fire. It was a bad one, Stevie. They think she left the gas on and lit a cigarette. They found a body on the first floor. It was your professor, Dr. Fenton."

Stevie felt herself on the verge of a laugh. It wasn't funny, but the laugh wanted to burble up.

"They found someone else on the stairs. She has a nephew . . ."

The laugh was maybe the urge to vomit.

"Is he . . ."

"I don't know his condition. Stevie, you knew something was wrong. . . ."

Nate was leaning forward. He could tell that something was not right.

"She was being weird on the phone."

"Was there someone else there? What did she sound like?"

Not now . . . The kid is there. The kid is there!

"Stevie?"

Things were getting dark. It was night, of course, but now more night was coming and Stevie felt that it was time to lean back and lay flat on the ground. Nate slid over, and he was asking if she was okay, but she couldn't hear him properly.

She noticed, now that she was on her back and the other lights in the world were dimming, just one point of light above her head. A pinpoint, blue, shining down. It was encased in a shiny black eye that reminded her of the cow eye she had dissected with Mudge. What was that point where it all connects and you just can't see . . . ?

She could have sworn the little blue eye of Edward King's security camera in the cupola ceiling winked at her.

It saw all.

Acknowledgments

WHEN I WRITE A BOOK, I OFTEN FEEL LIKE A LONE WEIRDO, MAKING things up and chattering away to herself. I feel this way because it is a fairly accurate representation of what is going on. BUT! We are never really alone! Books happen because of friends and family, because of publishers, editors, agents, publicists, marketing folks, booksellers, librarians . . . so many people help make and shape a book, and then get that book to readers.

Thank you to Katherine Tegen for your guidance and your support. Thank you to Mabel Hsu, who shepherded this book through the editorial process. Thank you to my incredible editor Beth Dunfey for your incredibly insightful notes and endless positivity. And to everyone at HarperCollins who took care of this book during every step of the process. (And there are a lot of steps.)

Thank you to my agent and partner in crime, Kate Schafer Testerman. She's the best. No one else can have her. Back away. She is mine. Thank you to my assistant, Kate Welsh, and her glorious spreadsheets. Thank you to the Crime Lady,

Sarah Weinman, for her support and for all the crimey stories.

Thank you to my friends, my wonderful friends. I am very lucky to have friends who are brilliant and share their deep knowledge of story and structure. Thank you to Cassie Clare, Holly Black, Sarah Rees Brennan, Kelly Link, and Robin Wasserman. I cannot overstate how much my life and craft are enriched by their wisdom. Thank you to my pal Dan Sinker, who insisted that I make something I love, and got me into podcasting with him. Not sure where I would be without that outlet. And to Jason Keeley, Paula Gross, Alexander Newman, John Green, Kirsten Rambo, Peggy Banaszek, Shannon Skalski, Alexis Fisher, Crista Kazmiroski, and Julie Polk, for everything, generally, all the time. And so many others. You are all great. (Except for you, Keeley. You're *okay*.)

Thank you to my parents for all their love and bottomless support.

Thank you to my beautiful girl Zelda. She is my stinky angel and entirely perfect, even when she is barking for three hours straight when I am writing. Someone has to guard the house from marauders.

I got married in the middle of writing this book! So thank you to my amazing English family, who have taken me on as the newest member. It is wonderful to have in-laws and a new brother and sister and two amazing nephews. It is unclear what I bring to the table here, but I thank you for having me.

Thank you to my husband, who shall remain nameless.

We will call him Truly Lovely. (Gross! So gross! Lolololol so gross.) (But he is. Lovely, I mean.) (Lololol gross.)

And thank you. I mean YOU. Thank you for reading this book. YOU are the reason for the book!

Read on for a sneak peek of *THE HAND ON THE WALL*
Book Three of the *TRULY DEVIOUS* trilogy

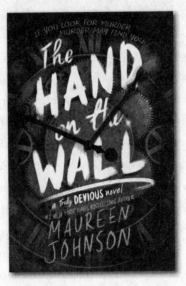

EXCERPT FROM *TRULY DEVIOUS: THE
ELLINGHAM MURDERS* BY DR. IRENE FENTON

*Since his wife and daughter's kidnapping, since the
murder of Dolores Epstein, all during the trial of Anton
Vorachek—Albert Ellingham kept the search going.
Vorachek's murder on the courtroom steps didn't slow
Albert Ellingham down, even if it appeared that the one
person who may have known Alice's whereabouts was
dead and gone. Someone knew something. No expense was
ever spared. He appeared on every radio show. He spoke
to every politician. Albert Ellingham would go anywhere*

and meet anyone who might know where his daughter could be found.

But on November 1, 1938, the police and the FBI were dragging Lake Champlain, looking for Albert Ellingham and George Marsh. The pair had gone out for an afternoon sail on Albert's boat, Wonderland. Just before sunset, a massive explosion ripped through the peaceful Vermont evening. Local fishermen scrambled into their boats to get to the spot. When they arrived, they found fragments of the doomed vessel—pieces of charred wood, singed cushions that had been blown into the air, small brass fittings, bits of rope. They also found something much more disturbing: human remains, in the same state as the boat itself. Neither Albert Ellingham's nor George Marsh's body would be recovered in their entirety; enough pieces were found to establish that both men had died.

There was an immediate investigation. Everyone had a theory about the death of one of America's richest and greatest men, but in the end, no one was ever charged. No case could ever be made. That Albert Ellingham had been killed by a group of anarchists seemed the most likely answer; indeed, three separate groups claimed responsibility. With the death of Albert Ellingham, Alice's case began to go cold. There was no father's voice saying her name, no tycoon handing out cash and making calls. A year later, the war started in Europe, and the sad saga of the family on the mountain paled in the face of a much greater tragedy.

Over the years, dozens of women would come forward claiming to be Alice Ellingham. Some could be dismissed right from the start—they were the wrong age, had the wrong physical attributes. Those who passed the basic tests would be seen by Robert Mackenzie, Albert's personal secretary. Mackenzie conducted a thorough investigation into each claim. All were proven to be false.

Passing years have revived interest in the case—not just about Alice but also about the kidnapping and what happened on that terrible day on Lake Champlain. With advances in DNA analysis and modern investigative techniques, the answers may still be within our grasp.

Alice Ellingham may yet be found.

LOCAL PROFESSOR DIES IN TRAGIC HOUSE FIRE
Burlington News Online
November 4

Local professor Dr. Irene Fenton from the University of Vermont's history department died in a house fire yesterday evening. Dr. Fenton, who lived on Pearl Street, was a twenty-two-year member of the faculty and the author of several books, including *Truly Devious: The Ellingham Murders*. The blaze began around 9 p.m. and was believed to have originated in the kitchen.

Dr. Fenton's nephew, who lived with her, sustained minor injuries in the blaze. . . .

THE BONES WERE ON THE TABLE, NAKED AND CHALKY. THE EYE SOCK-ets hollow, the mouth in a loose grimace, as if to say, *"Yep, it's me. Bet you're wondering how I ended up here. It's a funny story, actually...."*

"As you'll see, Mr. Nelson is missing the first metacarpal on the right hand, which has been replaced with a model. In life, of course, he had ..."

"Question," Mudge said, raising his hand partway. "How did this dude get to be a skeleton? I mean, here? Did he know he'd end up in a classroom?"

Pix, Dr. Nell Pixwell, teacher of anatomy, forensic anthropologist, and housemistress of Minerva House, paused, her hand and Mr. Nelson's lightly intertwined, as if they were considering the delicate proposition of dancing together at the ball.

"Well," she said, "Mr. Nelson was donated to Ellingham when it opened. I believe he came via a friend of Albert Ellingham's who was connected to Harvard. There are a number of ways that bodies come to be used for demonstration purposes. People donate their bodies to science, of course. That may have been what happened, but I suspect it's not the case here. Based on some of the materials and techniques used to articulate him, I think Mr. Nelson is probably from the mid to late 1800s. Back then, things were a bit looser in terms of getting bodies for science. Prisoners' bodies were routinely used. Mr. Nelson here was likely well nourished. He was tall. He had all his teeth, which was exceptional for the time. He had no broken bones. My guess—and it's only a guess—"

"You mean grave robbing?" Mudge asked with interest. "He was stolen?"

Mudge was Stevie Bell's lab partner—a six-foot-something death-metalhead who wore purple-colored contacts with snake pupils and a black hoodie weighed down with fifty Disney pins, including some very rare ones that he would show off and explain to Stevie as they dissected cows' eyes and other terrible things for the purposes of education. Mudge loved Disney more than anyone Stevie had ever met and had dreams of being an animatronics imaginer. Ellingham Academy was the kind of place where Mudges were welcomed and understood.

"It was common," Pix said. "Medical students needed cadavers. People called resurrection men—get it, rise from the dead?—used to steal bodies to sell to student doctors. If he was an old Harvard model skeleton, I think it's likely that he was a victim of grave robbing. This reminds me, I need to send him out to get him rearticulated. I need to get a new metacarpal, and the wire needs repairing here, between the hamate, the triquetral, and the capitate bones. It's tough being a skeleton."

She smiled for a moment but then twitched it away and rubbed her peach-fuzz head.

"So much for metacarpals," she said again. "Let's talk about the other bones in the hand and the arm. . . ."

Stevie knew exactly why Pix had stopped herself. Ellingham Academy was no longer the kind of place where you could make casual jokes about being a skeleton.

As Stevie stepped outside, the cold air slapped her in the face. The magnificent cloak of reds and golds that hung from the Vermont woodland had dropped suddenly, like a massive act of arboreal striptease.

Striptease. Strip trees. Striptrees? God, she was tired.

Nate Fisher was waiting for Stevie outside the classroom building. He sat on one of the benches, with slumped shoulders, staring at his phone. Now that the weather had turned more chill, he could cheerfully—or what passed as cheerfully in Nate-adjusted terms—pile on oversized sweaters and baggy cords and scarves until he was a moving pile of natural and synthetic fibers.

"Where have you been?" he asked as a greeting.

He put a cup of coffee in her hand, as well as a maple doughnut. Stevie assumed it was maple. Things in Vermont often were. She took a long drink of the coffee and a bite of the doughnut before replying.

"I needed to think," she said. "I walked around before class."

"Those are the same clothes you had on yesterday."

Stevie looked down at herself in confusion, at her baggy sweatpants and black Converse sneakers. She was wearing a stretched-out sweater and her thin red vinyl coat.

"Slept in these," she said, as a small rain of crumbs fell from the doughnut.

"You haven't eaten a meal with us in two days. I can never find you."

This was true. She had not gone to the dining hall for a proper meal in two days, and instead subsisted on handfuls of dry cereal from the kitchen dispensers, usually eaten in the middle of the night. She would stand at the counter in the dark, her hand under the little cereal chute, pulling the lever to get another Froot Loops fix. She had a vague memory of acquiring and consuming a banana yesterday while sitting on the floor of the library, way up in the stacks. She had avoided people, avoided conversations, avoided messages to live entirely in her own thoughts, because they were many and they needed ordering.

Three major events had occurred to bring on this monastic, peripatetic activity.

One, David Eastman, perhaps boyfriend, had gotten his face punched in in Burlington. He had done this on purpose and paid the assailant. He uploaded video of the beatdown to the internet and vanished without a trace. David was the son of Senator Edward King. Senator King had helped Stevie return to school, with the proviso that she would help keep David under control.

Well, that had failed. Neither Edward King nor David had contacted her.

That alone would have occupied her mind entirely, except that on the same night, Stevie's adviser, Dr. Irene Fenton, had died in a house fire. Stevie had not been close to Dr. Fenton, or Fenton, as she preferred to be called. The event was still incredibly jarring. There was only one upside—the fire was in Burlington. Burlington wasn't *here*, at Ellingham, and Fenton was identified as a professor at the University of Vermont. This meant that the death wasn't attributed to Ellingham, marking it as Death Academy. The school probably couldn't survive if there was another death. In a world where everything went wrong all the time always, having your adviser die in a fire off campus was one of the few "but on the bright side . . ." elements of her confusing new life. It was a terrible and selfish way of thinking about things, but at this point, Stevie had to be practical. If you wanted to solve crime, you needed to detach.

All of that would have been plenty to deal with. But the crowning item, the one that spun through her mind like a mobile, was . . .

"Don't you think we should talk?" Nate said. "About what's going on? About what happens now?"

It was quite a loaded question. What happens now?

"Walk with me," she said.

She turned and headed away from the classroom buildings,

away from people, away from cameras posted on poles and trees. This was to keep their conversation private and also so no one could see the devastation she was going to wreck on this doughnut. She was hungry.

"Ish olfed decaf," she said, shoving a bite of doughnut in her mouth.

"You want decaf?"

She took a moment to swallow.

"I solved it," she said. "The Ellingham case."

New York Times bestselling author
MAUREEN JOHNSON returns
with the thrilling Truly Devious series!

A riddle. A disappearance. A murder.
Can you solve the mystery?